CONVICTED 25 to LIFE

Convicted: 25 to Life

Chandler R. Williamson

For Jessica.

You've waited a long time for this.

Convicted: 25 to Life

Chandler R. Williamson

CONVICTED to LIFE

a novel by...

Chandler R. Williamson

Convicted: 25 to Life

Chandler R. Williamson

Convicted: 25 to Life

ISBN-13: 978-1-950582-04-4

Timeless Words Publishing
www.timelesswordspublishing.company

Printed in the United States of America

Contents

Chandler R. Williamson

PRELUDE
William Markus

She said *yes*. Now, the most beautiful woman I'd ever known leaned against my shoulder, her grandmother's wedding ring on her finger. Though it'd been almost two hours since I'd pulled off the proposal I'd planned for months, my palms still felt like they were melting with nervous sweat. How was it possible for them to feel both dry and moist at the same time?

Plates of mostly-eaten food sat on the table in front of us, leaving my bloated stomach screaming at me to stop eating the delicious buffet meal. Bea's stomach always amazed me. Whenever we went to The Grand Buffet, she ate more than I did. Yet, she still had the figure of a goddess.

Every once in awhile, Bea nibbled casually on the oysters straggling onto a plate. A brief memory of the night I convinced her to eat one came to me, lifting a low laugh into my throat. She looked back at me and licked her fingers, her smile so bright it lit up her entire face. I'd never seen her so euphoric before. She was generally a happy person, but she had a glow surrounding her tonight even I didn't recognize. It mesmerized me. I never wanted to look away.

My eyes wandered over her appearance again, breathing in every detail as a calm smile relaxed my face. She wore a T-shirt with cats on it, denim vest, and ripped jeans, her signature fedora casting a shadow over her head. Fingerless Christmas gloves warmed her hands as they held securely to my forearm. She nestled her head into the curve of my neck so I couldn't look at her anymore.

She let go of me again, extending her hand to admire the ring. The ruby center glittered in the light above us. When I asked permission to marry her daughter, Emily told me how many times Bea admired that ring since she was little. I could see why. It looked expensive. I found myself grateful I hadn't paid for it.

"Isn't it beautiful?" she asked, her voice content.

Nodding, I pressed a kiss to her forehead. "Almost as beautiful as the girl wearing it."

The gleam in her eyes teased at annoyance, though she giggled happily, her cheeks reddening as she elbowed me.

"You know it's true, Bea," I said, lifting a hand to caress the small cleft in her chin. "You're the most beautiful girl in the whole city."

"I know," she said with a knowing lift of her brow as she sipped her strawberry lemonade. The feigned arrogance in her sideways glance made me pull her in closer and kiss the side of her head. She made loving her so easy.

I chuckled, shaking my head as I draped my arm around her shoulders. "That's why I love you."

She laughed, taking a bite of a lingering chicken leg. "How long were you planning on proposing to me?"

"About two months. Isaac's been nagging me about it practically since we started dating though. He was more anxious for us to get hitched than I was."

"Yeah? That surprises me. How so?" she pressed, turning in her seat to face me.

I shrugged. "He told me that if I didn't do it soon, he'd beat me to it. He probably would've, too."

Bea's adorable, bellowing laugh erupted from her as she bent forward. Nothing made me happier than seeing her happy.

"Originally, I planned on proposing here and he was supposed to be behind the scenes taking pictures, but I couldn't wait," I said, grabbing my champagne glass and gulping down the last of it. It tickled as it squeezed through my throat, still tight with the after-effect of nerves. "I'm sure he'll forgive me though."

She nuzzled her nose against mine. I loved when she did that. "I wouldn't have had it any other way."

I couldn't help myself. I kissed her, cupping her face in my hand as I relished in her presence. Her cheeks felt warm and her lips tasted sweeter than anything I'd ever experienced before. No matter how many times I did it, her kisses brought new excitement with each one.

"I love you so much, Bea," I muttered, brushing the back of my fingers over her smooth cheek.

She sighed a small laugh and rested her forehead against mine. "I love you too, Will."

A silence came after that, filling the air with serenity and the din of a crowded restaurant as I pulled back and just admired her. Every detail of her features beamed with light and bliss. She flipped her hair from her eyes with another sigh as she pulled away, leaning against the back of the booth again.

"Did you ask Daddy?" She cringed with that question.

I moaned, remembering how angry he'd been. If I could've forgotten the man existed, I'd be better off.

"Yes," I breathed, adjusting my position uncomfortably. Suddenly, the seat felt like sitting on a bed of needles.

Her happiness diminished some and she watched me cautiously. "And . . . ?"

Tom's booming voice had a tendency to carry through my thoughts long after he finished yelling at me. Over and over again. The man had two moods. Soft-spoken, loving father and supreme dictator. His demeanor usually sided on the supreme dictator whenever I was involved. He put on a different façade around Bea, however. The most devoted father I'd ever seen. That was the only time I'd ever seen his good side.

Shaking my head, I bit my lower lip. "Why does he hate me so much?"

Her smile disappeared. "Are you serious?"

I shrugged. "I hardly even got to ask before he bit my head off. Luckily, your mom intervened again. *She* was overjoyed. I don't get it."

She stared at me, the disappointment in her eyes palpable. "Daddy doesn't even know you asked me to marry you?"

"I wasn't even really asking him because I knew he'd say no. It was more like telling him I was proposing to you."

"Will," she groaned, hiding her face in her palms. "Why even bother then?"

"Hey, hey," I muttered, uncovering her face. The pout on her face was so adorable it cracked my expression into a smile. "It's okay. He did give me his blessing, though reluctantly and after a few hours of convincing from your mom. Don't worry. It'll be fine."

She frowned. "But he knows we'll never get married in the temple. He'll never forgive you for that."

I sighed. She was probably right. It meant everything to her to get married in her religion's holy ground. She thought it'd mean we'd be together forever. The concept never made sense to me, though I tried to understand for her sake. I knew how important it was to her and I knew it wasn't something I could ever provide. The thought crushed me to think about too hard. I hated disappointing her.

I brushed her hair off her face and kissed her forehead. "I know. I'm sorry."

Her smile was saddened for a moment before she sighed and perked up again. "It's fine. I'm disappointed, but I'll be okay. Daddy, on the other hand. . ."

I refrained from rolling my eyes. "I really don't get it, Bea. "I've done nothing but try to befriend the man, yet he just . . . What'd I do?"

With slumped shoulders, she shook her head. "It's nothing you've done."

"Well, what can I do to get him to like me? He hasn't approved of us dating since before he even met me."

"Be a returned missionary," she said, rolling her eyes.

I moaned. The toxic side of Mormonism that plagued Tom Wixom's mind had been the downfall of our relationship since the beginning. He expected his daughter to marry a man who'd been a member of the Church at least five years, served the full two years in some foreign country, and attended every meeting faithfully each Sunday.

I wasn't that.

I'd never heard of the Church until Isaac invited me to an activity that changed my life. I didn't mind her religion. In fact, I liked attending the meetings when I felt like it. It gave me an excuse to see Bea if nothing else. Religion had never been extremely important in my life until I met her, but the passion she exhibited for it rubbed off on me some. Not enough to ever justify leaving the country to preach for two years, but enough to get me interested.

Tom sure expected me to though if he'd ever see me as worthy of his daughter. I didn't quite understand the appeal.

Bea smiled, nudging her shoulder into my chest in an attempt to lighten the mood and pull me from my momentary daze. "Be a returned missionary and get a haircut. That's what you'd have to do to get him to approve of you."

I narrowed my eyes at her, squeezing her shoulder. "Well, that's not happening. I like my haircut." I ran my fingers through my hair. "Unless it really bothers *you*."

She laughed, twirling a strand of my dark hair between her fingers. "Nah. You're perfectly handsome just the way you are."

Relief swept through me hearing that. I hated changing my appearance. It hadn't changed much since high school.

She smiled, the small dimple in her right cheek appearing. "And I love you. With or without a missionary badge."

Her nose crinkled a little when she rubbed the tip of it against mine again with an adorable giggle.

If only she knew how much it drove me crazy when she did that. It made me want to kiss her every time.

Mischief clouded my judgment of the crowded environment.

Why not?

I kissed her again, all-too-willing to forget any audience surrounding us in the buffet. I didn't care about them. All I wanted to think about was her smooth lips and the fruity aftertaste of strawberry lemonade on her breath. The surprised noise that squeaked from her excited me as she relaxed into kissing me back.

"Are you done?" she teased, smiling under my kiss.

"No." I shook my head, kissing her again. She giggled, her fingers tickling my cheek as she held my face. All at once, I wanted nothing more than to be alone with her. She was so beautiful. I pulled away, standing from the booth. "Let's go."

A scolding twinkle in her narrowed eyes played with me, tempting me to keep kissing her pursed lips as she fought a smile.

"You're not going to try anything, are you?" she asked, a serious edge in her tone as she grabbed her purse from the seat and tossed a tip on the table. She always paid for half when we went there, since the buffet—and everything else—was so expensive at the Grand Sierra Resort.

I tilted my head at her innocently. "I just want to kiss my fiancée without an audience, that's all." I reached for her, wrapping my arm around her thin waist and tugging her close. "Besides, I wouldn't dream of trying anything. I know how you feel about that. Your dad would shoot me in the head then bury my remains somewhere in the Nevada wilderness if I ever did."

Her stunning, brown eyes glistened in the light of the chandelier above our heads when she laughed.

Wow. She's so out of my league.

"What? He would." I laughed with an underlying tone of seriousness. The man terrified me.

"He doesn't hate you, Will," she said, grasping my hand from her back and squeezing tightly as we walked. "He's scared of you and he just wants me to be happy. Which, I am. That's all that matters."

Those eyes . . . She didn't know what it did to me when she batted her thick eyelashes at me like that. I'd never tell her either.

My eyes scanned the casino as we left, though I couldn't really focus on anything specific through the overwhelming number of lights beaming through a haze of cigarette smoke. The bustle of people chatting and slot machines chiming drowned out the light music playing in the background. When it was that busy, why'd they even bother with the music? It just added to the chaos.

Every elaborate detail of the resort casino brought together a sort of Victorian art and design with modern architecture. Picturesque statues and designs adorned the entirety of the building. It must've taken months or even years to create just a fraction of that artwork. I hadn't ever sculpted anything that elaborate, yet I often spent hours getting my artwork to look right

The place really was beautiful to look at. If only the beauty of the building leaked into the environment. The drunken men dangling over slot machines as they hit on cocktail waitresses passing by made the casino a bit less appealing. I knew what those wasted men would most likely do to their loved ones while intoxicated.

The memory that flashed across my mind constricted in my stomach. I didn't want to remember what that was like.

✳✳✳✳

I slid my hand into Bea's as we walked toward the back of the Grand Sierra's parking lot. Her gloved hands were warm against the cold bite of winter air. I looked down at her as she held onto my elbow with her free hand.

She looked so cute. Her fur coat bunched up around her dimpled chin and rounded jaw. Her hair, highlighted in different shades of brown and auburn, tumbled onto her shoulders in loose curls that bounced like springs.

Squeezing her hand, I pressed a kiss to the side of her head. She sighed and nuzzled against my shoulder.

She stopped, letting out a long sigh when we reached my piece-of-crap, vintage Mustang at the back of the parking lot. Though the busy hours were over and the area was void of people outside, the lot was somehow always filled nearly to the brim with cars. Internally, I cursed Bea for always wanting to get in a little extra exercise everywhere we went. That parking lot was almost as massive as the building itself. That said something about its size, considering the GSR had practically everything, including a hotel, casino, underground bar, shopping mall, bowling alley, wedding chapels—

"You know," Bea said, breaking me from my stupor. I leaned in closer to her, ready to listen to what she had to say and following her gaze toward the building towering into the sky. "I've lived in Reno for years now and I don't think I've taken the time to really enjoy the beauty this place has to offer. I mean, look at those lights."

Gesturing to the layered diamond-shaped lights crossing over each other on the side of the building leading to the big *GSR* on top. Their colors, which usually glowed various shades, shifted between the generic reds and greens of Christmas.

"They're so beautiful," she sighed, her breath puffing from her in a cloud.

Gentle snow drifted to the ground, hardly noticeable except through the streetlights. The parking lot echoed with an almost eerie silence. I'd never seen it so abandoned. Then again, the place wasn't quite so lively at that hour, since most people were either busy gambling or hungover in their hotel rooms.

A chill touched the skin on the back of my neck, warning me to move faster. Get somewhere safer. Subconsciously, I rubbed the spot where it like icy breath tickled my spine.

I looked at her once again in the dim light. She looked so beautiful. I just wanted to stare at her as she smiled up at the GSR. There was always an eerie feeling around the back of that parking lot. We'd be fine. Why rush away from such a moment?

The street light closest to us flickered. I could almost hear its dangerously cautious whisper. With a wary sigh, I placed a hand on her back to lead her to the car.

Something was off. I couldn't tell what, but something kept urging me to get her inside. This time, I felt like a hand pushed gently on my shoulder. A strange chill curled my spine.

"Let's go, Bea," I said, opening her door.

A twig cracked and bushes rustled in the breeze. In just one place? I squinted, trying to get a better view of the little island separating the parking lot from the main road. Something was definitely over there but I couldn't tell what.

Get in the car.

I heard that as clearly as if someone said it aloud, though no one else was around. I shuddered, glancing over my shoulder to see if someone was there. No one. But it was as real and clear as it was ominous.

"Wait." She turned toward the Sierra Bay glittering with life. "I want to enjoy this."

Her hair lifted with a breeze that carried whispered warnings, repeating that same phrase.

Urgency suddenly pulsed through my veins. An overwhelming urge to protect her took over as I circled around the open door to approach her. "Bianca, please get in the car before—"

The loud *bang* sprang up from the night, shattering the silence into a sudden whirlwind of noise in my head.

Bea lurched forward, a hand pressed against her chest. Her expression went from contentment to shock, her mouth gaped open, spurts of blood splattered on her cheek.

The world moved in slow motion. A dull ringing clogged my ears. She stumbled clumsily to her knees and I caught her before she fell forward. My head spun. My focus faded in and out as I looked down at the wet spot on her chest right above her heart, clothes blackened around her left shoulder.

I couldn't breathe and yet it was all I could hear. My senses somehow deadened and intensified at the same time. My hands on her back felt warm and wet. I pulled one away to see what it was, confused and dazed with panic. I heard my breath quicken as I stared at her blood dousing my fingers. Turning her limp body around in my arms, I tried to comprehend what'd happened.

The sound of a gun still echoed in my subconscious, taunting me as I held Bea through the pain, trying to understand my own.

ONE

Bianca Wixom

Six Months Before.

I watched him walk into the church gymnasium with Isaac and Matt. His stoic expression was timid and almost lost as he stood aside, hands in his ripped jeans pockets. His hazel eyes scanned the room as his thumbs patted his hip nervously. He was taller than both of them by about a foot.

I'd never seen him before, but new faces were pretty normal in a Reno Young Adult Ward. If there wasn't a confirmation of new members joining our church every other week during Sunday meetings, it was a surprise. Sometimes, however, I wondered how many of those converts were in church because they enjoyed the religion or because they enjoyed the company.

He sighed, a smile breaking the frown on his face when Isaac said something to him, showing off just how nice his teeth were. It created creases around his eyes. Isaac playfully punched his arm and I heard his laugh faintly over the sound of socializing as he wrapped his arm securely around Isaac's neck, biting his lower lip and digging his knuckles into his scalp.

Watching them made me laugh and shake my head. "Male bonding is so weird," I noted to no one in particular. Natalie answered.

"You think that's weird, you should've seen Isaac standing outside the girls' bathroom at Family Home Evening last week in hopes of asking out Marnie Collins," she said, nudging me and sipping her fruit punch.

"What the heck, Isaac?" I muttered under my breath. Isaac was usually a lady's man, though quirky. I'd never heard of him doing something like that. "You're losing your edge, man."

"Yeah, one of my counselors in Relief Society told me about it yesterday at church." Natalie flipped her platinum blonde hair that swayed gracefully around her rounded jaw just above her shoulders.

Leave it up to a large group of girls to have rumors spread about the guys in the ward. Isaac was a lightning rod for the attention and loved every second of it since he was almost considered a superstar among them.

I leaned an elbow against the stage, my eyes scanning the new guy's appearance again as he laughed at Isaac's feeble attempts to push him away. He had the nicest smile I'd ever seen.

I could nearly feel Dad's overprotective warnings being shoved down my throat as I watched him, intrigued by the way he moved in spite of myself.

"Who are you staring at, Bea?" Natalie asked, mirroring my position and letting her focus wander to the group of guys.

"Hmm?" I hummed casually, turning to her with raised eyebrows. She flashed a playful smile at me.

"Checkin' out Isaac?" she teased.

I blinked. Though he'd asked me out before, he was like a brother to me. The image of holding hands with him made me laugh aloud. He wasn't bad looking, though not my type. The mustache-goatee combo was never my thing.

"He'd like that, wouldn't he?" I raked my fingers through the side bangs that hung into my eyes and tilted my head, my focus wandering back to the group of boys. "I *am*, however, wondering if you know who his friend is. I haven't seen him before."

Isaac finally broke free, shoving the new guy back and into Matt.

The mischievous smile in Natalie's tone darkened. "Oh," she started, lowering her voice to a whisper, leaning in close like a gossipy old woman spreading her juicy poison. "That's William Markus. I'm surprised you've never met him. He's been living with Isaac and Matt in that three-bedroom for the past couple of months."

His eyes hit me like a zap of lightning. An unexpected spark fired inside me at the sight of them and my heart leaped into my throat. He looked twice, his expression as astonished as a deer in headlights.

"I heard that William stole his dad's mechanic's shop from him five years ago then got arrested. Wouldn't surprise me, look at him."

I tore my focus away from his to shoot a glare at Natalie. "Excuse you," I snapped.

"Well—okay, that was mean. I know we're supposed to love everyone, but, seriously." She gestured subtly in his direction before folding her arms uncomfortably. "Doesn't he just *look* like he's surrounded by darkness?"

I rolled my eyes, ignoring her blatant disregard for empathy like I would a bug squished beneath my shoe. *Choose your battles wisely, Bea. This one's not worth the fight.*

He did seem a little on the edgy side, but the look in his eyes, to me, seemed like someone who could really use the principles taught to us Latter-Day Saints. It brought joy into our lives to know its teachings. Who's to say it wouldn't benefit him too?

I tilted my head, allowing a relaxed smile to tease the corners of my lips. His cheeks flushed and his smile disappeared. He lifted a gloved hand, fingers exposed, to rub the back of his neck and coyly look away. My smile only deepened at that display of vulnerability as I set my glass of fruit punch on the stage behind me, pushing myself away from it.

"Bianca," Natalie called out to me. I ignored her but kept walking, head high.

Daddy never approved of me spending any time with anyone but friends from church. But he also expected me to be kind to others and invite everyone into my social circle. It was something he and Mom taught me from a young age.

"Hi, Isaac," I cried, tickling his sides as I approached him from behind. He jumped and whirled around, eyes broad with terror before lighting up with excitement.

"Bea," he shouted enthusiastically, the scruff on his black facial hair scratching my cheek when he wrapped his arms tightly around my waist and hoisted me into the air. I squealed, giggling until he set me down again. His eyes squeezed shut tightly every time he blinked, something quirky, yet endearing about him. I laughed.

"So, you and Marnie, huh?" I teased with an elbow in his ribs. I tried my hardest not to stare at William Markus who watched me carefully, his entire body seeming tense and relaxed at the same time.

Matt laughed a hearty belly laugh that bent him forward as he wrapped an arm around my shoulders.

"You know he messes up everything, Bea," Matt said with a firm slap on Isaac's back. "It was only a matter of time until he got rejected by someone other than you."

"Okay, okay, so I messed up one time. That doesn't mean I can't get any girl I want," Isaac said, trying to act cooler by popping his shirt collar.

"Well, ya never got Bea, so that's saying something," Matt retorted.

I noticed Isaac flinch at that and sighed.

"Aw, come on, Matt. Don't be mean. After all, he does still have me and Natalie around, so that's saying something too."

My eyes flashed toward William as he tried really hard *not* to stare at me. I smiled. He was obviously nervous. Something about that made me want to get closer, even if I still heard Daddy's voice in my mind telling me how dangerous 'guys like him' were.

"That's right, Bea's still here and that's all that matters," Isaac said, tugging me out of Matt's grasp and pulling me into a tight hug as he glared playfully at Matt. I chuckled, hugging him back.

"When are you going to introduce me to your friend, guys?" I asked, shaking him slightly and gesturing to William whose complexion paled slightly. He took a tentative step back with a coy smirk that made my heart leap into my throat again.

"Oh, I wasn't planning on it, but if you insist . . . Bianca," Isaac said, running his fingers through his cropped, black hair as he pulled away and gestured to William. "This is my good friend, Will."

I fluttered my eyelashes at Will, who swiped his hand across his denim jacket before reaching out for me. I stepped away from Isaac and took Will's hand. The instant our hands touched, something sparked inside me I'd never felt before. Inhaling sharply, I gave his hand a firm shake and tried to let it slide out of his. His grip tightened slightly before he let go too quickly.

His mouth opened, but he didn't speak more than a feeble, "It's nice to meet you, Bianca."

He had a pleasant voice, deep and classy in its own way. Though he released his grip, his gaze didn't loosen at all. The world seemed to move slower, blurring together like one of the abstract paintings in the art gallery.

"He's our roomie as of a few weeks ago," Isaac continued.

I narrowed my eyes at him suspiciously. "Really? Nat said a couple of months. You say a couple of weeks. Which is it?"

Isaac hesitated, scrunching up his face and pulling out his phone to check the date. I smiled at his inability to keep track of dates and time. He stood in silence for a minute until his eyes glazed over as if thinking incredibly hard.

"Isaac," Matt said, pushing two fingers against Isaac's temple to wake him up from his sudden trance.

He flinched and his eyes darted to Matt. "What?"

Matt turned to me, rolling his eyes. "Listen to Natalie. She knows more about our lives than we do."

"Ain't *that* the truth," Isaac retorted, turning back to his phone. "Anyway, Bea, I didn't introduce you because I knew he'd be up to a little competition."

Will shot a startled look at Isaac, folding his arms skeptically though I noticed his cheeks flush a bit. "Competition?"

Isaac ignored him, wrapping his arm around my shoulders again.

TWO
William Markus

"No."

Did the word escape as a whisper or a scream?

I couldn't tell through the high-pitched, annoying sensation of imbalance as it swayed me back and forth, holding her limp body. Her eyes stared blankly ahead, mouth slightly agape as she convulsed, blood pooling over her lips. "Bea, please—"

Every part of my body trembled. My breath grew quicker and quicker the more I watched her slowly slip away from me into the unknown abyss that sucked her in way too fast.

"W—Will," she muttered. I pulled her closer, intending to savor the faint sound of her voice.

"Bea, I'm here. I'll protect you. You'll be okay."

What good would words do at that point?

"I won't let you go," I continued, my voice shaking violently. I held her face in my hand, red and wet with her innocent blood. "Hold on, Bea."

She coughed, blood spitting from her mouth as she took in a struggled breath.

"Will—It . . . It's not your f—fault."

What was she talking about? Of course, it was my fault. I wasn't there to protect her. I should've taken the bullet for her. She was too good to leave the world like this. Why hadn't I saved her?

She breathed in but coughed before she could get more than a small gasp into her lungs. Her eyes glazed over.

"You d—didn't know," she whispered, her voice barely audible. "It wasn't you . . ." Her voice drifted as her body sunk into my arms. The life left in her eyes dimmed as she stared blankly forward.

"Bea," I muttered. "It's gonna be okay, baby. Hold onto me."

Everything in the universe stood still, me being the only thing allowed to move in the darkness. My limbs tensed. I couldn't tell whether the deep, agonizing ache in my chest really existed or if the whole thing had only been sick imagination. It felt so real. So tangible. How could it not be real?

No.

Bea wasn't going to die.

"Bianca!"

The sound of my own voice felt foreign to my ears. Strange. Unrecognizable. Ugly.

My body felt heavy everywhere. I was drained and exhausted like all feeling had been beaten from my senses.

The world around me shattered. Nothing but a bunch of mosaic pieces that made no sense together. I kissed her forehead.

Frantically, I looked up, my eyes still unable to focus on anything clearly. Nausea swept over me from the scent of gore that permeated the air. Only a few minutes earlier, it'd been crisp, fresh, and full of promise once we'd escaped the smoke-infested casino. Now, it reeked of pain and death. I licked my lips hoping it'd only been imagined. It didn't go away but grew more potent.

I cringed, cradling Bea's lifeless body against me as I rocked back and forth, my clothes wet with a mixture of rain, snow, and her blood.

"Help," I said weakly. I felt as lifeless as the girl cradled in my arms. "*Help,*" I cried louder into the night, hoping with everything in me that someone out there would hear.

I looked back to Bea, her head dangled over the side of my arm. Adjusting my position, I rested her head against my chest. I looked out into the darkness, my vision blurring in and out. My head pounded like a drum against my sweaty temples. Shaking away the wave of dizziness, I noticed a figure standing in the distance. I couldn't tell whether it was a man or a woman.

A sliver of hope sparked inside me as I called to them with all the power my shaky voice could muster. "Help me, please."

Something fell from the figure's hand before they bolted. The sliver of hope pulled away from me as I watched them run from me. Couldn't they tell that I needed help? I froze, dumbfounded.

Something in the puddle where the person had been caught my attention.

A handgun.

I couldn't explain what overcame me in the instant I saw it. My breath quickened, growing thicker and more dominant in my own hearing as it cleared. I glared toward the murderer, setting aside Bea to bold toward the fading figure. Before I knew it, I'd grabbed the gun.

"Coward!"

I shot recklessly into the air above me, knocking out a streetlight. The sound was sickeningly satisfying as the bullet shot from the pistol's barrel.

I couldn't focus enough to see where the figure disappeared to, but I didn't care. At the moment, I didn't care about *anything* except justice and vengeance.

"I'll kill you myself," I screeched, my voice bellowing through the atmosphere as my eyes scanned the hazy environment through blurry vision. My hands shook as I lowered the gun, hopelessness sinking in. The killer was gone.

"Nevada Police," an unfamiliar voice snapped at me. The sound felt like a flick on the back of my neck, annoying and painful. "Drop the weapon and put your hands where I can see them."

Something rustled in the bushes. I flipped my attention toward the sound.

Before I could think twice, I bolted.

I couldn't seem to stop once I'd started. My legs carried me down 2nd Street as fast as they could. The lights of Reno taunted me, hazy in a blur of confusion and shock. I'd dropped the gun back in the parking lot where Bea's bloody body lie on the pavement. As I ran, that sank in.

They'd arrest me for this.

There hadn't been anyone else around when Bea was shot and she was sprawled across the ground. I'd shot the gun and vowed to kill.

What would that mean for me?

Panic kept my legs moving. Sirens rang out behind me, but by then, I'd nearly reached Mill Street. Flashing blue and red lights followed me, hunting me down like a buck. Running out of breath, I pushed myself forward. If I was caught, I'd be booked for sure.

Finally, my legs gave out by the bay. My heart throbbed, screaming at me to stop as I collapsed to the ground, coughing through the thickness congesting my chest. I leaned on my shaking hands and knees, looking up at the cop cars as they gathered on the side of the street, sirens blaring. Five cops blocked off Mill Street with their cars and bodies. My vision dimmed before coming back into focus so many times. It was dizzying.

I groaned, trying to stand again. My knees were too weak. All I could manage was sitting back on my ankles as I tried to catch an even breath.

Something shoved my hands behind my back. My head felt like dead weight as it dangled on my neck. In a panic and unexpected rush of pure adrenaline, I spun around, throwing a clenched fist straight into the man's face. I blinked hard, my body quivering uncontrollably. Eventually, I realized it was a police officer in the process of cuffing me. My wild eyes widened with horror at the potential of what I'd just done.

Forcefully, he stood me up, cuffing me like an angry parent throwing their kid around after a tantrum.

"You're under arrest for the murder of . . . You have the right to remain . . ." The man's gruff voice faded into my haze. "You say . . . held against you."

I couldn't resist anymore. That burst of adrenaline took the last of my strength. He tucked me into his car. The cold air chilled me to the bone. He shut the door, getting into the driver's side, and driving away.

All I could understand was how much I wanted to wake up.

I squeezed my eyes shut for a solid minute before opening them again, hoping to find Bianca smiling at me back at the buffet. Instead, my view was still from the back of a police car.

THREE
Bianca Wixom

"Alright, guys," Dave, the Elder's Quorum president shouted. "The volleyball net is all set up, so choose teams and have fun with it."

I groaned. I hated playing volleyball with the Young Adults because of how competitive they could be. I mean, it's just a game, for Heaven's sake.

Isaac and Matt shouted their elation as they both scrambled toward the net, wrestling over who got to serve the ball. I shook my head, laughing as I watched them tackle each other to the ground. I turned back to Will who stiffened his spine when our eyes met again.

"Are you gonna play?" I asked, walking to the kitchen window by the gymnasium door.

Will sighed, nonchalantly following me as he pushed his hands back into his pockets and shrugged. "I've never been a huge fan of sports."

Surprised, I raised my eyebrows, ladling punch into a clear, plastic cup and turning to him with my backside leaned against the counter.

"Really? Most guys I know were born with a ball pasted to their foreheads," I joked, sipping the fruit punch.

He chuckled, his smile broader than his laugh implied. "You're not wrong," he said with a snarky tone. "When I was a kid, my dad was always *really* into watching sports on TV. Especially hockey. I don't know if he lived a double life as a Canadian or something, but that was his favorite."

I laughed heartily and probably more than necessary, snorting a bit before covering my mouth like it would pull it back in. Will looked at me with a surprised but amused and almost proud gleam in his eyes as he chuckled with me.

"Sounds like it to me," I remarked. "How do you know he wasn't?"

Will casually meandered my way, leaning against the counter beside me. Our shoulders brushed and a wave of heat beat on my face like sunrays.

"Well," he began, leaning in closer and lowering his voice to a whisper. "Between you and me, he wasn't much of a hockey player."

I could hear the teasing in his voice as I looked back at him, confused.

"Oh?" I urged.

He screwed up his face and pursed his lips, shaking his head. "Fell flat on his face the second he hit the ice. The Canadians were so ashamed; they banned him from their country. That's probably why he got hate mail every day with their flag plastered all over the front."

Another laugh burst from me and Will's expression beamed with pride again.

"So why aren't you playing?" he asked, crossing one ankle over the other.

I sighed, directing my attention back to the volleyball game. Natalie joined the group of people diving for a ball and shouting at those who missed. She'd always been sportier than I ever was. Or, at least she pretended to be. Isaac spiked the ball, slamming it against the ground on the opposite side of the net. It ricocheted off the wall and bounced all the way back to his side in one smooth instant. If I'd blinked, I would've missed it.

The move created an uproar in the gym and I laughed at the silliness of my peers.

"Good one, Isaac," I called, cupping my hands around my mouth so I could be heard over the screams of excitement.

He flipped around, frantic before he caught my eye, bowing and blowing a kiss.

"I do it for you, BB."

He grunted as he and Matt bumped chests. I shook my head, turning back to Will whose expression had fallen into a sullen frown.

"I prefer artistic things over active pass-times, though I can't draw worth squat," I said to him, looking at my dark red fingernails, subconsciously picking at the polish. "My passion is music, though I appreciate any art form."

"H—how do you know Isaac?" His tone shifted to a more serious, wary one.

I spat a sound that could've qualified as a laugh but came out more like an exasperated groan.

"We've been friends for about five years since I started coming to the Young Adult Ward. He included me in his group of friends as soon as I came into the ward. He's a flirt, as you probably already know. But don't worry," I said, resting my hand on his bicep. "We're not together, by any means."

A relieved sigh softened his features as his muscle tensed beneath my touch. I inhaled sharply, noticing the subtle flex in his arm.

"Good," he muttered, his eyes meeting mine.

My heart thrashed against my chest as those hazel eyes drug me in. Something was hidden behind them. Something dangerous and exciting.

I'd been teasing, but part of me wanted to assure him that I was available and open to dating. He was attractive in a rugged sort of way. Definitely different than the cookie-cutter, returned missionary Daddy usually urged me to date. But that was partly why I was intrigued by him. I yearned for something different. I'd always wanted to date a returned missionary, but that didn't mean I wouldn't give someone like Will a chance.

Daddy wouldn't like it though.

I cleared my throat, lifting my hand from Will's arm and trying to act calm, though my heart screamed at me. His attention didn't stray from me for a long moment, though I shifted my eyes back toward my friends on the volleyball court.

"So how do you know Isaac?" I asked, wanting to relax into playful banter again. "Did he wait for you outside the bathroom too?"

Will laughed, seeming more confident than before. "Speaking of my hatred of sports . . . I became friends with him through a stupid basketball team my parents forced me into as a kid. They always tried thrusting things like that on me like that would somehow fix my creative mind. We've been pretty close ever since, but more recently he and Matt have been the only ones . . . there for . . ." He trailed off, cringing and bowing his head, rubbing the back of his neck. "S—so, you like art?"

He spoke hastily. The vulnerability and sweetness in his seemingly coy nature was perhaps the most adorable reaction I'd ever seen.

"Yeah, I volunteer down at a local art studio by the Truckee River on Tuesdays when Daddy doesn't pay me to babysit my six younger siblings."

Will's eyes widened and his jaw dropped. "You have nine people in your family?"

I nodded. "I know."

"Where do you fit in?"

"I'm the oldest. I have a brother and little sister serving missions right now and the rest are still living at home. So, technically, I only watch four of them, most of the time."

He tilted his head, adjusting his position with an expression of piqued interest and rapt attention. "Missions? Like Impossible?"

I laughed at the image that popped into my head of Laura and Mitchel wearing their best-dressed, missionary clothes in Argentina and Canada while sneaking around as spies.

"No, silly," I said, pushing on his arm playfully. "Missions as in full-time, proselyting."

I could see he still didn't quite understand what that meant. I frowned. He definitely wouldn't be someone Daddy would approve of.

"What's that?"

Sighing, I thought of a way to explain it to someone who'd never heard of the concept before. It wasn't uncommon for investigators of our church to ask questions like this, but for some reason, I wasn't exactly in the 'member missionary' mood.

"I'm sure you've seen them around. They wander through the city doing what we call proselyting, or teaching people about our religion. My brother just turned twenty, but he's been out for nearly a year and a half while my sister just left the Missionary Training Center last week. She's barely nineteen."

"They're only a year apart?" he asked, seeming baffled and confused.

"My parents adopted Mitchel as a baby when I was three. He's from Africa. We're technically the same age, but I didn't jump on the missionary bandwagon as he and Laura did."

Explaining all of this to a practically complete stranger came with surprising ease. I'd never had a more willing audience before. Will seemed to hang on every word I said with genuine interest.

"Why not?" he asked, nonchalantly hopping onto the kitchen counter, getting comfortable to continue listening. His combat boots tapped together as he clasped his fingers together on his lap.

For the first time, I really noticed his appearance. He looked very rough around the edges. His dark, denim jacket was uncuffed and dangled over his lower arms. I noticed a tattoo of the French word for *Love* and a rose beside it on his wrist. His thin, black gloves exposed his fingers, callouses on his knuckles and graphite and pastel stains between his index and middle fingers. The loose, black tank top he wore under his jacket hung loosely on his torso, draping to expose a bit of his broad chest.

His dark hair lay messily on his head in a quiff style. Most of it was pushed back, but it was much longer than Daddy would've approved of. He looked a bit unkempt as far as *my* dad's standards were concerned. A bit of facial hair lined his jaw, growing thicker on his chin than anywhere else. It wasn't as dominant as Isaac's mustache-goatee combo, but still enough to be noticeable.

He definitely stood out amongst the guys in the ward. But I kind of liked that.

"My decision to stay home from a mission isn't really something I talk about openly," I answered, bringing my attention back to Will's question. I wasn't sure how much of my personal life I wanted to open up about so soon in an acquaintance.

He frowned and his brow creased. "Well, now I'm even more curious. That's not fair."

I didn't answer, picking at my fingernails again and trying to avoid the flashbacks trying to pry their way into my subconscious. I could still hear Jace's voice in the back of my head and I shuddered, rubbing the goosebumps rising to the surface of my skin.

With a hefty sigh, Will mirrored me by picking at his own fingernails. "Okay, different direction. What do you do when you're not volunteering or babysitting?"

I felt as scrutinized as a bug under a microscope.

The memory of Natalie's warning came burning into my conscience. Daddy would be furious if he knew I was talking to someone like Will like this. If I disappointed him, I'd never forgive myself.

He wanted me to set an example for my younger siblings by dating a nice, cookie-cutter guy.

What would he do if I ever dated Will?
He'd kill me.

FOUR
<u>William Markus</u>

I felt like I was about to board a rollercoaster. My fingers, still sticky with her drying blood, curled in and out of fists as I tried regaining feeling in them through the pins and needles. Adrenaline pumped through my veins, making me hot and uncomfortable. Metal handcuffs locked my arms behind my back. The pungent odor of blood and gun powder still stung in my nose like the lingering cloud of casino smoke.

As the cop with the bushy eyebrows drove quietly into the Nevada wilderness, I wondered just how far he'd go before dumping me onto the side of the road. My whole body trembled with fear. How had I gotten into this mess?

Only an hour before, I thought my life was as perfect as it ever could've been. Now, I was in the back of a police car, driving Lord knows where.

"Please, sir," I begged, my breath quick. My hands twitched inside the handcuffs digging into my bare skin. I couldn't feel my fingers or toes. My body still trembled violently. My vision was blurry. I couldn't sit still. "Tell me she's gonna be okay, please."

"You have the right to remain silent," the cop spat angrily without looking behind his shoulder at me.

I bit my lip, rocking back and forth as my eyes darted frantically out the window.

I gasped through the adrenaline at the vague memories flashing rapidly across my thoughts. I had to know if she was okay. *Where's Bea now? How is she?*

Nothing made sense through my hazy consciousness that faded in and out of focus like a bad camera lens. All around me, I heard gunshots. So many gunshots. I was still winded from running so fast. My legs ached to move, though frozen from exhaustion. My lungs hot as blue fire, yet cold as ice. My palms sweat profusely, crammed together behind me.

"I'm innocent," I said before I could shut up.

"Innocent until proven guilty, son," the cop answered lazily, smacking his lips together with a disgusting sound that made my mouth water with nausea just hearing it. "Now, I'm gonna tell you again. You have the right to remain silent. Everything you say can, and will, be held against you. Now, *shut up*."

I flinched, gasping for air through my constricted lungs. If I could've caught an even breath for just a second, I would've relished in it.

He drove and drove until I wondered if he'd take me into the middle of the wilderness to shoot me too. Terror widened my eyes when we approached the sheriff's office. I flew forward in my seat, panicking as it sunk in. Cop cars surrounded the building, some with lights blasting into the air like beacons of fear.

What's the sheriff's station doing in the middle of nowhere?

Why am I here?

"There's been a mistake, I'm innocent—"

The cop pulled into the station with an exasperated sigh.

"Criminals always think they're innocent, kid. Blah, blah, blah, I've heard it all before. Just save your breath for when it matters," he grumbled.

For the first time, I noticed the bruise forming over his bushy eyebrow.

Did I do that?

My heart stopped momentarily as the realization settled in. That was the cop I'd punched. No wonder he hated me.

He parked and got out of the car, grabbing my arm and guiding me with an iron fist through the blaring lights and into the Washoe County Sheriff's Office.

Tall, red pillars held up the gray roof, resembling prison bars. I felt two inches tall walking in. The procedures they drug me through blurred together. They searched my person for any weapons, confiscating the ring box and my keys which happened to have a pocket knife attached to the keyring. I cringed.

What a time to have that on you, Will.

I was drug through the booking process. Question after question. Medical records, full name, date of birth, address, phone number, emergency contact. I answered everything on autopilot. Nothing really made sense through my spinning head.

"Sorry, why am I here again?" I asked. Part of me wondered if some liquor was snuck into that Mountain Dew I'd drunk at the ski lodge earlier and I dreamed the whole thing. Either that or the champagne was more spiked than I'd realized. Maybe I was really passed out somewhere.

The woman interrogating me stared at me a minute before rolling her eyes. She leaned into her hip, hand subtly resting on a gun attached to her belt, a clipboard tucked between her elbow.

"Assault on a police officer and alleged murder," she said flatly like it was something she dealt with on a daily basis. "Who can we contact in case of emergencies?"

I inhaled slowly. My head felt like a balloon floating off my shoulders. I squeezed my eyes shut and tried to make sense of those words.

No matter how hard I tried, it didn't connect in my brain.

Murder?

She wasn't referring to . . .

"We can do this the easy way or we can do this the hard way. Answer the question, sir," she snapped, impatience leaking into her tone as her jaw chomped on a piece of gum between her sharp teeth.

I looked back at her, blinking and trying to remember the question in my cluster of unsettling thoughts.

Was Bea dead?

No, she couldn't be. She's too stubborn to die like that. She'd fight it. She'd win. She'd—

The image of her face flashed across my mind, detailed beyond necessity in my subconscious. It made me want to puke. The lifeless expression in her eyes sent a chilling shudder up my spine.

She was already gone when I shot that gun.

I shot the gun.

I was being blamed for this?

It wasn't me.

"Do you have an emergency contact, William?" she urged again, irritation now coating her tone. She wasn't trying to hide it anymore.

My brain scrambled to think of someone. The only person to come to mind was . . .

"Bianca. . ." I muttered, confused by the name of a dead person's name on my tongue. It tasted stale and unforgiving.

The cop scoffed. The gum snapped between her left incisors with an annoying *smack* that made me want to clamp her square jaw shut.

"You're kidding, right?" she asked, raising her pencil eyebrows with a cocky smirk.

I pulled my eyebrows together. "Wh— why would I kid about—"

"You can't use a murder victim as an emergency contact, genius. Especially when you're the one who did it."

My knees felt like they would collapse. Bea? A murder victim?

She was . . .

"If you don't provide me that information, I'll have no choice but to leave that section blank and hope you don't do anything more stupid than you already have. I don't have all day."

I stared at a spot on the tile floor. Bea's mom, Emily, had taken me in as her son. My own mother disowned me after my father died. She wouldn't care to know if something happened to me. I hadn't seen or talked to her in years.

I hadn't ever thought to have Emily as an emergency contact, but she was the only one who made sense.

"E—Emily Wixom then," I muttered, my voice hollow.

The cop scoffed again, writing on a clipboard in her hands. "Because she'll *really* love you after she hears what you've done to her daughter. Phone number?"

I hesitated, the sting of her words lingering in my system like the scent of rotten tuna fish. "I don't know it off the top of my head. I don't exactly have a way to check either." That came out with a sharp glare in her direction. How could they expect me to think of things like phone numbers? I hadn't memorized a phone number since I was thirteen.

"Fine," she said quickly and dismissively. "Thanks for complying. Take him for fingerprints."

My brain finally began processing my situation when they took me for fingerprints and into the room for my mug shot. The striped walls made my eyes hurt. Too many contrasting colors too close together. Everything hurt my head. Remembering details of anything hurt. Mentally and emotionally.

The camera flashed, momentarily blinding me like lightning. Being fried with electricity, at that moment, seemed almost appealing. Anything to get out of the Hell I'd been thrust into.

"Turn to the left."

The woman behind the camera had her black hair pulled back in such a tight bun, I could almost hear each strand stretching like a rubber band.

I obeyed, still dazed.

Bea couldn't have died tonight. She was probably still being treated. She had to be. She'd be okay. I promised her she would be.

I should've been with her.

Why'd I run? More importantly, why had I shot that gun? Why had I punched that cop?

Stupid.

I would've asked someone about Bea's condition if they all hadn't acted so much like they wanted me dead too. Everyone there reminded me of zombies. They wandered the police station, dragging their feet like they were all half asleep. It'd been around ten o'clock when it happened. They probably really were half asleep.

I played it over in my head again. All I could seem to remember was her falling into me. And those words.

"It's not your fault."

I winced at that memory, a sting of emotion tightening unexpectedly in my chest. I cleared my throat of it, sniffing and pressing my lips together.

"Turn to the right," the woman with stretchy hair ordered, sounding just as impatient as the cop before.

"What?" I muttered, confused for a minute being yanked back into reality.

"Turn to the right, please."

Nothing about her startlingly bass-toned voice seemed polite when she snapped that back at me. Creasing my brow, I obeyed.

Sorry to inconvenience you with my girlfriend's murder.

No, she wasn't just my girlfriend anymore. She was my fiancée. I was going to marry her. . . Emphasis on was. I wasn't anymore.

I could've said that to anyone dragging their feet to get me through the procedures.

My body felt tense as Bushy Brow guided me with my hands behind my back toward the interrogation room.

FIVE
Bianca Wixom

A whistle blew and Dave shouted, "Okay, this is the tiebreaker round. Whoever wins this one wins a special prize."

I was grateful for the distraction. Will's question left me a bit wary. I didn't like talking about my decision to stay home from missionary service with just anyone since it was kind of personal.

"Let's see who wins," I exclaimed enthusiastically, though I honestly couldn't care less what the volleyball score was.

Reluctantly, his attention diverted away from me and to the game again. From the corner of my eye, I noticed the nervous expression on his face as he swallowed.

Nicole, a petite, feminine girl in shorts and a cute blouse, missed the volleyball and the other team cheered. Everyone on Isaac's team erupted in a unanimous outcry of, "No!"

Isaac, however, approached her and gave her a hug as sweet as he was.

"It's just a game, Nicky," he said over the crowd. "No one really cares all that much."

He flinched and his focus flicked behind him for an instant. Nicole blushed, flirtatiously touching her hair and giggling. Girls often had that reaction to Isaac. I thought it was silly. Shaking his head, he turned back to her with a reassuring smile. Patting her arm, he stepped away, heading for me and Will.

"You getting cozy with my girl, Will?" he teased, grabbing me by the waist and playfully kissing my cheek.

I smiled and pushed him away as he laughed. Will shot a glare in Isaac's direction before his expression fell into a frown again.

"Isaac, get off me," I laughed, wriggling from his grasp.

Casually, he leaned his hand behind me on the counter, wiping the sweat from his brow. "C'mon, Bea, I know you love it."

"Not in this lifetime," I laughed, pushing myself away from the counter and shaking my head.

"BB, c'mon, I was just kidding," he jeered lightheartedly.

"Isaac," Will growled, a disapproving and protective scowl on his face. His narrowed eyes warned him to back off. "Get off."

That surprised me. The fire in his tone suggested a deeper meaning, though I didn't quite understand what it meant. I smiled a bit, a little grateful for the intrusion. Isaac was easy egged-on, especially if you tried rejecting him in a more subtle manner.

His playful flirting didn't really bother me much, but it was nice to have someone stand up for me like that. No one had really done it before.

Flinching, Isaac paused before blinking hard with a nonchalant shrug.

He sniffed, swiping his finger briskly across his nose and scratching at his facial hair. "Fine. Apparently, someone's a little too sensitive tonight."

Will's jaw set. I could sense the tension in the air between them before he sighed deeply, relaxing his shoulders.

"Hey, anyone up for a little movie night at the apartment tonight?" Isaac offered cheerfully.

I was grateful for the mood change.

Will stood from the countertop, closer to me than he'd been before. I felt myself blush as his shoulder brushed lightly against mine.

"I don't really have a choice, dude," he remarked.

Matt came up from behind Isaac, punching his arm and breathing heavily, beads of sweat on his dark forehead.

"Whoa, some game, huh?" he said, resting his hands on his hips. "I'm sure you two didn't notice though, right?" He gestured at me and Will, a wink in his mischievous eye.

I grinned through embarrassment, lightheartedly shoving my forearm into his chest.

"Shut up, Matt," I said, fighting back my smile as I pulled out my phone to check the time.

I gasped and my heart sank with dread. Daddy texted me a half-hour ago?

"When are you coming home? Mom and I need you."

My shoulders sagged slightly. *Again?* "Duty calls, guys. No way I'm doing anything more tonight."

Isaac moaned, placing himself between me and Will and draping his arms around our shoulders. "C'mon, Bea. The party's only where you are," he whined, pushing out his pouty lower lip.

I chuckled, noticing Will's hopeful gaze on me. I could see how much he wanted me there.

My phone vibrated, belting out a ringtone version of *Uptown Girl* by Billy Joel.

Daddy.

Suddenly frantic, I ducked around Isaac's grasp and squished the phone between my ear and shoulder.

"Hi, Daddy," I said brightly. Grabbing my bag from the counter, I rushed toward the door. I noticed Will scramble to catch me but was gone before he could grab my attention again.

"Hi, Honey Bea, are you on your way home yet?" he asked, his tone worried.

I smiled at his concern. He always worried too much.

The hall left a few stragglers lingering after the activity ended. Part of me daydreamed of Will chasing after me, but a more dominant part of me worried about making it home as soon as possible.

"I'm coming home now. Sorry I didn't answer earlier. I just got your message." A bite of summer night met me in a gust of air when I opened the door to exit the church. The fresh air felt nice after being in the crowded gym for the last hour and a half. A shiver rolled up my spine as I headed for my car, a scent of sweaty bodies still potent in my nostrils.

"That's alright. I just worry about you being out after dark," he said, though I heard an underlying tone of distrust and disappointment.

"I'll be fine, Daddy. I'm a big girl," I teased, though his tone stung a bit. Why didn't he trust me to be out at night? It was just a Young Adult activity; I went to them nearly every week. It's not like I was out drinking or gambling at the Peppermill. "I'll be home in a second, okay? I'll talk to you when I get there."

"Drive safe. I love you, Bea."

I smiled, repeating the sentiment back and pulling the phone away from my cheek. When the screen locked again, I let my head fall back, gazing up at the sky.

The blackish-blue universe seemed dim by the lights of the city. Hardly any stars dotted the darkness, though the light of a full moon bathed the world in serenity. Street lights lined the small parking lot of the church. They provided enough light to make me feel secure, but not enough to make it safe to walk any farther than the building. Thankfully, I'd parked on the line of spaces in front where at least two lights illuminated the area.

I clicked the unlock button on my car key as I approached my black Mazda.

"Bianca," a familiar voice called from the church doors. I turned around, my dark, reverse ombre hair flipping into my eyes with a wind that picked up. I swiped my side bangs off my cheek and held tightly to my favorite fedora.

"Will," I said, amused by the fact he'd followed me outside. He sprinted to me, skipping stairs to get to me faster. "What's up?"

He hesitated, a bit winded. Probably from running.

"I was just . . . I wanted to ask—" he fumbled, raking his fingers through his hair.

I smiled, charmed by his nervousness. I'd seen that kind of behavior before. The nerves guys got while asking me out could be either sweet or creepy, depending on how they went about it. I didn't like to turn down any offers for a date, but I judged how the date would go based on how the guy asked.

His approach struck me as pretty cute.

Letting my head fall to one side, I bat my eyelashes at him and leaned into my hip, urging him to continue. I knew that would distract him, but I kind of enjoyed seeing his breath quicken as a grin flicked at the corner of his mouth.

"Uhh . . ."

"Wow, I've rendered you speechless," I teased. "That's impressive. I must be pretty intimidating."

I winked subtly, tossing hair from my eyes. He breathed an exasperated laugh, resting his thumbs in jeans' pockets, separating his legs slightly, and standing straighter. "A little."

Smiling, I quickly patted his forearm. "It was nice to meet you, Will. I hope you had enough fun tonight to come again." I headed for my car. If he was going to ask me out, he needed to do it quicker. Daddy already waited up for me. The last thing I wanted was to make him wait longer. "Have a good night—"

"Wait," he called.

I turned to him but continued walking backward. "Yeah?"

If I was any later, especially on account of a guy like him asking me out, I'd be in serious trouble. I was supposed to be there for

Convicted: 25 to Life

my family whenever they needed me, but he wasn't letting me. I was supposed to lead by example. What kind of example would I set if I let Will keep me at the activity later than he should've? Especially after telling Daddy I'd be home in a second.

Get on with it, Will.

"I was wondering . . . I'd like to visit that art gallery sometime. Wh—where's it at again?"

I chuckled, opening my car door. "Reno Epic Mediums by the Truckee River. See you there." I raised my eyebrows with that invitation and got into the driver's side.

Will's grin stretched broadly across his face, growing so wide, his teeth peeked through. I backed out, pausing to watch as he stepped backward until he reached the stairs leading to the church.

The whole drive home, I thought about him. Would he actually go to the gallery? If he did, hopefully, he wouldn't come while Daddy brought my lunch. That wouldn't end well.

• • •
71

SIX
William Markus

Bushy Brow led me to a small room, the tan, narrow walls squishing it together. One of the walls was made of one-sided glass. A long table with two chairs took up the majority of the room. In each corner, security cameras recorded my every move.

I looked straight into one of them as I sat in one of the chairs, leaning against its hard back and resting my cheek on my knuckles. What kind of things would they try to get out of me? They clearly didn't believe that I could possibly be innocent. My fingerprints were the only ones on the gun. How could that have happened?

"Wait here," Bushy Brow said.

"No promises," I mumbled, but he'd already left the room. How could I go anywhere? I had nothing to do but *"wait here."* That was such a stupid order.

I doubted the security cameras could hear me either. I'd said it too quietly. It was probably for the best they didn't hear me. They already had about three people outside standing guard to make sure I didn't somehow escape through the steel door that was locked with seven different types of locks. It was a little over-kill, but the security in Reno was always on high alert in case there was another shooting like there'd been three months ago in Scheels. Were they scared that I'd be another one to go on a psychotic rampage and kill everyone in my wake like the guy in that case had?

The light above me flickered and buzzed. I looked up at it and noticed two flies hitting against the rectangular fixture. I almost wanted to laugh at their stupidity. If they got burned once, wouldn't that make them realize that it's dangerous to fly into a light?

They were a lot like me, actually. I knew what I was doing when I hit that cop, yet I did it anyway. And now, everything I said or did slowly burned me.

What would Bea think if she saw me, sitting in an interrogation room, waiting for a cop to come in and pressure me into admitting to a crime that wasn't my own? She'd tell me to get through it.

"Everything always turns out better in the end. Everyone has adversity, but what matters is what you learn from it. It'll always be better in the end if you've learned something."

I could almost recite those words by heart. But she didn't understand sometimes. Adversity was sometimes just too difficult to handle on my own.

If I'd told her that, she'd just tell me to rely on God. What could *He* do for me now?

I was alone.

I looked at my reflection in the one-sided glass, my hair a messy crow's nest on my head. My eyes were bloodshot. Bea always said that her favorite physical quality of mine was my hazel eyes. She wouldn't like them right now. I hardly recognized the guy staring back at me. He looked haggard and angry.

The door burst open and an officer came in, his hand resting on the pistol at his boney hip. He towered over me like a hungry hawk glaring at his dinner. I didn't let the distrusting gleam in his eyes scare me.

I wanted to make a snide remark about how well-kept his mustache was but held my tongue. The *last* thing I wanted to do was make a bad impression on a cop who already seemed to hate everything about me. What would he think of my character if I said something about him being such a perfectionist that he even had to keep his thick, bushy mustache in order?

"Will—i—am Mar—kus," he announced too loudly, annunciating every syllable of my name with a fake smile hidden somewhere beneath all that mustache. "My name is Officer Todd. I have a few questions that need solid answers. I've heard a great deal about you, my boy. I understand this isn't your first run-in with the law."

I watched him for a moment, eyebrows raised as I tried not to think about the large, fish-shaped birthmark on his neck.

I shrugged. "My reputation precedes me then . . . It's nice to know I'm popular."

Officer Todd slowly made his way around the perimeter of the room, swiping his finger across the tabletop and brushing off the dust from his fingers.

"I don't like to believe that the criminals I confront are innocent because I know there's evil in us all. You are no exception to this, though you are just a boy. And quite the rebellious young man, I think. Most kids your age are. Now . . . What were you thinking when you *shot* Bianca Wixom in the Grand Sierra parking lot tonight?"

Fire sparked in my core at even the mention of her name pronounced by such a distasteful specimen as Officer Todd.

I was innocent. Just because I was there to witness her getting shot didn't make me the criminal. Or a rebellious young man, for that matter. I wanted to see him holding his wife—if he even had one—the way I'd held Bea, drenched in her own blood with a bullet hole in her chest. Then maybe he wouldn't think I was so rebellious.

I hadn't seen the man's face that'd done it to her. The night was too dark to see anything but the girl I loved crumbling to the concrete like a puppet suddenly relieved of its strings. I saw him run, dropping the pistol into a puddle. Not much else.

"Well?" Officer Todd pressed.

I hesitated, avoiding eye contact with him. I had the right to remain silent until an attorney was present. They hadn't believed me so far. Why try convincing them of my innocence now?

I cringed at the memory of her blank stare, straight forward and unblinking. She'd looked like one of those porcelain dolls that always freaked me out as a kid, their beady eyes staring into the soul as if to suck the life right out of you. I couldn't get it out of my head. Forcing myself to walk through the scene again seemed surreal. As if it would suck out what light I had inside me to think about it too hard.

Being there felt like being forced to watch my least favorite scene in a movie again and again and again to the point it was so engraved in my thoughts I couldn't un-see it. I'd gone over it in my head hundreds of times that night. It was absolutely impossible to forget at that point, though forgetting was exactly the thing I needed. I just wanted it to stop. Stop reliving the memory of her warm blood seeping between my fingers and the metallic taste it left in my mouth. I could still feel the sensation that prickled my nerve endings like needles.

Officer Todd leaned against the opposite wall and pressed his fingertips together.

"Let me repeat the question, William." He lowered his head slightly, challenging me to keep quiet. "What were you thinking tonight when you shot Bianca Wixom in the parking—"

"I didn't do it," I growled, my teeth clenched. I'd said that phrase so often it came out before I'd even realized it.

"How did it feel? Having her warm blood on your hands? Were you finally satisfied with yourself after she lay dead on the pavement? Or did you still want more and that's why you assaulted Officer Morrison?"

"I didn't mean to hit him," I said in weak defense. Immediately, I realized how much I sounded like a whiney child crying, *"He started it!"*

I cringed. I wasn't making my case any easier. Why did I keep talking? *Moron, shut up.*

"What were you doing there with her? She was certainly a looker. No young man goes out that late with a pretty girl like her with good intentions. Why did you have the gun in the first place? Were you going to use her then leave her for dead? You murderers make me sick. You're all sick, twisted, immoral—"

"Shut up," I growled, blood hot in my veins as I resisted the urge to punch him too for accusing me of such horrible things. I'd never take advantage of Bea. She'd never let me, even if I wanted to.

Why would I want to shoot her? She was the best person I'd ever known.

"Filthy, rotten, blood-thirsty—"

"I didn't kill my girlfriend," I bellowed, my shaky voice booming through the room.

"Then who did?" He slammed his hands on the table and leaned toward me.

I leaned across the table, fury controlling my actions as I stared him straight in the eye. "I'll know the answer to that question if it's what puts me at God's feet."

His spine stiffened as I glared at him, daring him to challenge me anymore. The sound his neck made when he cracked it made me shudder. "You believe in such a being?"

I hesitated. Bea taught me to believe in Him. Or at least something resembling God. It really didn't make much sense to me. If He was as good as everyone in her church proclaimed of Him, why'd she been taken away from me in such a cruel way? Obviously, something was wrong with that picture.

I slowly leaned against the metal chair, cold against my back.

"Aren't you gonna answer me, boy?"

I narrowed my eyes at him. "I have the right to remain silent, don't I?"

Officer Todd sniffed. "You're not afraid of me. I like that. You say you didn't kill her. There has to be someone who did."

SEVEN
Bianca Wixom

I slowed down as I passed the temple on my way home, *the Church of Jesus Christ of Latter-Day Saints* strewn onto a plaque in front. The golden Moroni statue atop its steeple faced toward the city below, the entire building glowing like a beacon of hope in a world so clouded with cigarette smoke and gambling. I didn't believe in such activities so rampant in my hometown, though I'd played poker for fun several times with Isaac, Matt, Natalie, and whoever they dated at the time. It wasn't my favorite pastime, but I did it because I loved their company.

"What do You want me to do, Father?" I asked God out loud as I passed the temple. My fingers tightened around the leather, maroon steering wheel cover when the image of Will's smile involuntarily popped into my head. The memory made me want to smile. "I wasn't even planning on going tonight, but you urged me to . . . Did you mean for me to meet him?"

I waited silently for any sort of answer from the Spirit. I felt nothing in particular. His answers usually came in the form of a feeling, a calming thought, or, on rare occasions, a sensation of touch. Right then, however, I felt nothing in response. I knew He heard me. I could sense that. But His hesitation to respond was also something I'd grown accustomed to over the years. He wasn't ignoring me. Probably just expected me to figure it out or something like that. I never really questioned if He could hear me or if He was listening because I knew He loved me. Regardless, the air in my car filled my lungs with heavy silence and the familiar scent of my Mazda.

Hating when He didn't answer me right away, I sighed. "Guess you expect me to figure that out on my own then."

Instantly after I said that, my chest warmed with reassurance. I smiled, recognizing His influence when I felt it.

Don't be afraid of him, Bianca. He's my son and I trust him.

The thought entered my head so clearly, I felt as though He sat in the passenger seat beside me. It was a feeling I relished in when it happened and would stop anything to experience. I loved feeling Him there with me. I smiled. His presence made me feel lighter and happier. Though I couldn't see Him, I knew He was there.

My car's headlights illuminated the darkness in front of me, lighting up the islands of tiny trees separating the lanes. Passing the large houses leading to my cul-de-sac, I glanced out my passenger side window. The world was awake in a skyline of city and lights. My world, however, was quiet and asleep with a peaceful silence that could only be found in the solitude of my mountainous home.

My thoughts wandered toward the way I'd felt when I first saw Will and how he had to double-take. He clearly liked me, but I didn't know him well enough to warrant the feelings I had upon meeting him.

Mom and Daddy always taught me to love everyone. Did that mean dating someone who wasn't a member of the Church? Members in Reno were sometimes more accepting of things like that than some I'd met in Utah. The general population there seemed swamped with Latter-Day Saints, though I never complained. I liked having a community of close friends and family who all shared my beliefs, for the most part.

Still. Living in Reno was different as far as the culture was concerned. It was a little more acceptable to see women in skirts that cut above the knee here or to see girls with pink hair. From what I could tell, they were rarely frowned upon.

Daddy grew up in a strict family and led ours with a bit of an iron fist because of it. His parents were some of the most loving and charitable people in their neighborhood back in Utah. They spent most of their time volunteering for the buildings on Temple Square and the rest of their time was spent in service to their family and community. Daddy tried emulating that example, though often fell short. He was only human, though he expected himself to somehow be more.

I'd heard Mom telling him several times that he wasn't Christ. He couldn't do everything. His response was always the same. *"No, that's your job. I'm just trying to keep up."*

The sentiment made me smile. My parent's relationship was sweet, though imperfect. They still fought every now and then, but always came together stronger in the end.

I wanted to be like them more than anything.

If I dated a non-member, would I ever be? Or was that territory that came with shared beliefs?

"Well," I began again. "If You trust him, guess I should too. There's really only one way to know. Besides, he hasn't even asked me out yet, so what am I so worried about?" I laughed at myself. It wasn't the first time I'd gotten carried away after meeting a cute guy. I could imagine God smiling at me too, shaking his head at my silly worries. With Him on my side, I didn't need to worry.

The second cul-de-sac approached and I pulled in. The wide driveway in front of my house left room for the many cars my family either owned or rented. My parents preferred renting over buying since they could afford to jump from car to car. I, on the other hand, became too attached to my Mazda to give her up. I'd had her since I was sixteen and couldn't part with her. Love at first drive, I always said.

I got out, locking the doors behind me and tossing my keys between my hands. Our house was fancier and larger than most I'd seen closer to downtown by Truckee and around the casinos. The brick and cobblestone structure towered over me, four stories and triple-car garage. The walkway toward our front door was lined with flowers and luscious greenery, a fountain trickling by the steps. Mom was a landscape designer, so our house had always been something of a showcase.

I smiled, remembering how much I used to hate the gnomes along the flowerbeds lining our porch. Their blank stares into oblivion always scared me growing up. It didn't help that Dillon Parker back in Utah used to tell me they'd eat my eyeballs from their sockets while I slept if I didn't kiss them every day.

I rolled my eyes at the memory and sprinted to the front door past them, gently pushing it open. It was late enough that Liana would be asleep. Milo would probably be in his room with a video game. Cannon and Julia played Mancala on the floor in the living room, looking up when I came in.

"Bea," Julia cried, springing from the floor to give me a hug.

"Shh. . ." I scolded gently, kissing the top of her head with a laugh. "Hi, Jules. Where's Mom and Dad?"

With a wide, toothy grin, she looked up at me, her arms still wrapped securely around my waist.

"You can't know until you say you love me first," she bribed.

I smiled, stroking my fingers through her stringy, brunette hair, and kissing her forehead. "I love you, Jules. Can I be released now?"

"No," she said, pressing her cheek against my stomach again and clinging to me tighter.

"Fine." I laughed, trying to walk into the kitchen with her hanging on my hips. She screeched with laughter and wrapped her legs around my knees. Cannon laughed, hopping onto my back. I grunted from the impact while he laughed.

"Doggy pile," he laughed heartily.

I moaned. "I'm being attacked from every angle. Must persevere," I moaned. Somehow, I managed to drag Julia as she slipped down my legs and onto my ankles while Cannon still clung to my shoulders and neck.

Mom stood by the kitchen island, wiping off the granite countertop and placing a vase of red roses as a centerpiece. Her eye for landscapes tended to make its way inside as well.

"Hey, Mom," I greeted. She whirled around, a hand to her chest, bright blue eyes wide and stunning.

"Oh, Honey Bea, you scared me," she exhaled. "How was Family Home Evening?"

The weight of my brother and sister hurt by then, so I made them let go of me, prying their grip off me and telling them I needed to talk to Mom. Reluctantly, they dispersed when Mom stepped in. With a hand on her hip, she gave them a sharp look that she'd used on us several times before.

"Go get your pjs on," she ordered in a gentle tone that only she had mastered. As the kids passed her, she gave them pats on the bums and they both bolted up the spiral staircase leading to the second floor.

I grinned, remembering all the times she'd done that to me as a kid. Sighing, I felt my shoulders slump a bit as I leaned my elbows on the island countertop, clasping my fingers together and staring thoughtfully at the bottom of the roses' vase.

"There was a new guy with Isaac and Matt tonight," I said as nonchalantly as I could, though my nerves jumped with anticipation of a bad reaction.

She stopped wiping down the other countertops for a second. I could almost see the wheels turning in her head before she began cleaning the already spotless surface again.

"Oh, yeah? Isaac's always been kind of a social butterfly, hasn't he?" she asked. "It's not surprising he'd have someone to invite."

"His friend seemed pretty interested in what I had to say." I winced, trying to think of the best way to describe what happened without raising suspicions. I probably wasn't good at it.

"Oh? How so?"

"He spent pretty much the whole activity talking to me."

She smiled slightly, wiping her hand across her apron. "Sounds promising. Is he a member of the Church?"

I groaned internally. Hesitantly, I shook my head. "Doubt it. He had a tattoo."

She raised her eyebrows at me with a knowing look.

"Honey Bea, that doesn't mean anything. He could've gotten it before he joined."

I sighed. "That's true. Still, I doubt it."

"Does he seem like a good person? Was he nice to you?" she asked, tossing the cleaning rag into the sliding garbage under the sink.

I nodded, the corners of my mouth tugging upward when I remembered his charmingly awkward mannerisms. "Like I said, he seemed interested in everything I said. It was kind of cute, actually. I thought he was sweet and endearing, but Natalie doesn't seem to think so."

Mom scrunched up her face and gave me a look. "Well, that's not saying much. She thinks every boy is bad. Did he ask you out?"

An unexpected giggle sprang from me with the relief of Mom's apparent acceptance of the prospect of me showing interest in a non-member.

"Not really, but seemed like he wanted to."

She grinned, light wrinkles framing her eyes as she removed her *Kiss the Cook* apron and leaned her elbows on the island beside me.

"Did he try to?"

I started to answer before Daddy's voice echoed from downstairs and jolted me out of the conversation.

"Honey Bea, is that you?"

My eyes widened and my spine straightened instantly. "Yes, Daddy. I'm in the kitchen."

He emerged from the basement and ascended the small staircase to the lower level. His stern expression softened some when he saw me, the crease in his brow relaxing. His button-down, black shirt was untucked, dangling onto the top of his slacks. I smiled, walking into his open arms. He embraced me tightly for an instant, kissing the top of my head.

"What did you need me for?" I asked, walking out of his arms and clasping my fingers together.

"We were going to ask you to babysit while we went out, but you weren't home and didn't answer in time. What were you doing?"

I swallowed, guilt weighing heavily on my conscience. "I'm sorry, Daddy. I was just at an activity."

He grunted slightly, swiping a finger across his nose with a disapproving sniff. He did that when he was disappointed in something. I sighed, picking at my fingernail polish with a frown.

"Really could've used you. What was the activity?" he asked passively as he walked away.

It stung a bit that he was so passive-aggressive, but it was expected of him. I glanced at Mom, quietly pleading with her not to say anything to Daddy about Will. She smiled, subtly zipping her lips while he wasn't looking. I sighed, relieved.

What was I so worried about? It wasn't like he'd actually asked me out. He wouldn't end up going to the gallery . . . would he?

* * *

EIGHT
William Markus

Officer Todd finally released me after he realized I wasn't going to answer any of his accusations. Why should I? Anything I say can and will be held against me. Why say or do anything while alone with the guy? He grabbed a handful of hair and yanked me from the chair. I gasped but didn't react much outside of glaring darkly at him. If I could've given him a black eye too, I would've enjoyed it. My blood burned through me when I stood. I knew there was a reason I hadn't liked him since the moment I saw that monstrous mustache eating his upper lip.

"Back to your cell until you learn some manners. If you refuse to talk, we'll just have to get an attorney here," he barked. He sounded like a drill sergeant. Spittle landed on my cheek and I winced. It wasn't the worst he could've done. "Do you at least have an attorney to hire?"

He let go of my hair after standing me up.

I shook my head. "No."

With a firm pat on the back, he grinned, though I could hardly tell other than the awkward smile lines around his cheeks.

"We'll have to assign you one then," he chuckled. "And I know just the one for ya."

Something about the way he said that made me uneasy. His hostile behavior shifted so drastically once we stepped out of the interrogation room.

What happened?

Everyone we passed kept their distance as Officer Todd led me to a cell in the back of the jail, secluded from everyone else. It was almost like they'd saved it for someone special.

I'm . . . honored?

Once in the cell that would house me for the night, he unlocked the handcuffs. I breathed a sigh and rubbed the marks on my wrists from them. He led me to the darkest room I'd ever seen. I couldn't see anything except what I caught from the light of the hall, which wasn't much.

He flipped on the lights and pushed me between the shoulder blades before the blue, cell door slammed shut. Claustrophobia instantly kicked in when I saw my new living space. I imagined Harry Potter might've lived more comfortably under the stairs. A musty cot crammed itself into one corner beside a metal toilet. Disgusting stenches radiated through the air with foul odors I didn't recognize. They were so potent; I scraped my tongue against the roof of my mouth in an attempt to get the taste out of my mouth.

I glanced back at the door behind me. At least he turned on the lights so I didn't have to stay in the dark. Husky coughing came from the cell next to me. I heard the deputy on the other side of the door spit something condescending at my neighbor.

These people must've seen a lot of crap in their lives to see the world this way. Are they all like this?

I'd always had a general respect for cops. Once, at Isaac's apartment, they pounded on the door in the middle of the night in search of someone. Regardless of it being so late, they were pretty respectful as they searched the apartment. I'd never thought of seeing this side to policemen before.

I cringed looking at the poor excuse for a bed, inmate clothing placed at its foot. At least they took the time to fold it. Remembering the neatly trimmed mustache on Officer Todd almost made me laugh. He must've had Obsessive Compulsive Disorder.

"Does everyone get this kind of treatment?" I asked the congested atmosphere as I slowly sat on the cot, wincing at the odor. It creaked beneath my weight. I wondered if I'd end up on the floor by the end of the night because it collapsed. I was tall but fit. Most of my body mass was muscle.

With a deep inhale, I caught hold of the stench that drenched my ragged clothes. I looked down at my shirt collar where a yellow, puss-like stain reeked like vomit. The smell left a disgustingly nauseating taste in my mouth that reminded me of the bad aftertaste of spicy, gas station nachos. Dried blood still stained my shirt from Bea's body. Something tickled the back of my throat, stinging as those oysters at dinner threatened to manifest themselves outside my stomach.

Bea's blood . . .

I fell to my knees, the full impact of exhaustion throwing itself on my shoulders. Once I had a minute to think, I couldn't hold myself together anymore.

She's likely dead right now. What have you done?

I stared blankly at the floor, cold, hard, and unforgiving. The only thing holding me up was my hand on the cot. I gasped for air. Every beat of my thrashing heart brought with it burning pain in my chest. I felt empty. Yet, as I crumbled into a heap in that small room, I felt everything.

Bea is dead. You didn't protect her. You didn't listen when you were warned to get into that stupid car. Now she's dead. And there's nothing you can do about that. You'll never see her again.

Panic settled in as I looked up at the blue door of my cell. What was I doing there? I shouldn't have been the one in that rank cell. I was innocent. I didn't do it. The walls seemed closer than before. The false lighting of the windowless building sucked out any hope I had.

"It's not my fault," I screamed at the discouragement shoving their accusations down my throat like poison. "It's not my fault."

All at once, I broke down. My muscles became so tense I couldn't feel anything in my body. I clenched my fists so tightly my fingernails indented my palm. My knuckles turned white. I didn't even realize I was sobbing until the tears doused my face. I might've cried out her name a few times in my agony, but couldn't tell what sounds were what. My brain couldn't make sense of anything. Everything was foreign, even breathing. I couldn't figure out what that noise in my head was. I mixed it up with my rapid pulse.

My shoulders quaked. My fingers trembled until I couldn't feel them anymore either. I wondered if I'd died and gone to Hell while Bea was in Heaven.

Would even God separate us in the afterlife?

If I could've described the fiery pit of despair, it wouldn't have even come close to this. Hell seemed appealing over *this*. I wished I'd died with her. I should've taken advantage of that gun while I had it. Taken myself too. That way, I could've escaped. It would've been over. I could've been with her if it was true. If there was an afterlife, I wanted it.

"Anything is better than this, God," I wailed, my voice muffled into the sheets as I gripped them between my fingers. "Take me with her, please." I let my head fall back to stare at the ceiling. "Why'd you do this to her if You're her Father? She believed in You and You *killed* her. You're a monster. *I'm* a monster."

I flinched when I felt something touch my shoulder. I didn't dare look back but straightened with a jolt. My spine stiffened with a tingling feeling that ran from my shoulder down into my tailbone. My breath halted for an instant and the sensation was gone. The touch brought a sliver of something pleasant with it. What that was, I couldn't tell, but I liked it and wanted more. It stopped my cries of agony with a clear message in response. Bea's voice came to my thoughts.

It's not your fault, Will.

"B—Bea?" I asked, gathering the courage to turn around, hope gleaming in my soul. Maybe I'd wake up and it'd all be over. Maybe everything would be okay after all. Maybe she was alive and it was all a nightmare.

That was a vain hope.

My cell was empty. I was thrown back into the harsh reality. Bea couldn't talk to me. She was dead. And I was in a dank cell that reeked of sweaty bodies.

I pressed my lips together, resisting the anger flowing through me. I wanted to punch something. I wanted to make someone else hurt as I did. Exhaustion kicked in again, however, and I slumped against the cot, out of breath.

"Some Father you are," I growled at the ceiling.

NINE
Bianca Wixom

I walked backward, leading a group of four tourists from Toronto through the gallery. "This villa was built soon after Reno was founded in 1869 and turned into an art gallery when its owner, a young widower . . ."

My voice faded when I looked up just in time to see Will walking through the doorway of the gallery, hands in his pockets and eyes scanning his surroundings. The world seemed to move slower.

He came, I mused, the thought bringing a smile with it.

His eyes met mine and he returned my smile, subtly waving as he wandered further into the building.

"Sorry, the art gallery came to be around 1901 when the widower sold it to a man named George Wixom. This piece," I paused, gesturing to the painting of a girl in a field of wildflowers I stood beside. "This is an original by a local artist named Maybelle Sullivan. She comes in every so often to see if any of her art has sold. She painted it as a symbol of . . ."

Will stood in the distance, stroking his chin as if deep in thought, a perplexed look on his face that made me giggle at its silliness.

"Of her childhood. Each flower represents a memory she experienced."

I was grateful to get that out. I turned to Will who grinned and winked at me. My heart leaped and I cleared my throat immediately to make it settle down.

"You're distracting me," I lipped to him silently.

He bit his lip, pulling a funny face again before nodding and heading the other way while I finished my tour. I chuckled, appreciating that he didn't persist.

The tour wasn't anything special, but Will's presence in the background made it hard to focus on the scripted details I'd memorized.

When I finally dismissed the group and allowed them to wander the building on their own and admire paintings they wanted to, I approached Will who stood before the painting by Maybelle Sullivan. He seemed genuinely enthralled in it, standing with his arms folded, brow furrowed, and head tilted.

I smiled, standing next to him and mirroring his stance. Rocking back and forth on my heels, I waited for him to notice me. For a solid minute and a half, he didn't but stared at the painting with rapt attention. He seemed to breathe in every detail of the vibrant paint strokes.

"It's beautiful, isn't it?" I observed. He flinched, whirling around to me. His eyes widened at first before he breathed an exasperated laugh.

"I—I've never seen a painting like this before. Just look at the detail. The artist took the time to paint every cherry blossom and strand of hair and blade of grass." He reached out to rest his fingers against the frame's base, leaning in to get a closer look. "It's exquisite. You can feel the emotion and depth she put into each brushstroke. You said that every flower represents a childhood experience but clearly, not all of them were good. See the lilies?"

I nodded, entranced by his descriptions.

"They're dark and sagging in comparison to the bright daffodils and roses. I wonder if there's more darkness in this woman's history than she lets on. It makes me want to know what happened."

"She did have a hard childhood as far as I know."

Will looked at me in surprise. "Really? You can't tell. Look at the colors . . . I've never seen an artist use such brightness without making it seem like a cartoon. It's vibrant but raw and heartfelt."

"That's why I always make it a point to talk about it with people. Maybelle spent most of her time inside doing hard labor on a farm just outside of town where her uncle abused her most of her life. She said this painting is meant to teach something."

"What?" he asked, letting his hands fall at his sides.

"There's a lesson in everything, especially trials. There's always more goodness in the world than evil. There are lots of things to take from it. It's an art form. It's whatever the viewer sees that counts, not necessarily what the artist intended."

"I know how that feels," Will mused thoughtfully. "Maybe that's why I'm drawn to this piece so much."

I tilted my head, wanting him to continue that level of vulnerability but not expecting it. "Do you mind me asking?"

"It's just . . . You never really know what it's like until you experience it, ya know? Family and love and companionship. If you never really know what that's like, you can't recognize truth even when it hits you across the face. She redeemed herself and came out of abuse with her head held high like the girl in the painting. It's almost like she . . ."

Will glanced at me, his cheeks reddening slightly. He shifted uncomfortably, pushing his hands into his pockets again. He must've assumed that stance when he found himself in situations where he was nervous.

"I mean . . . It's cool," he muttered, shrugging nonchalantly.

I laughed aloud. "Cool, huh? You go from describing a piece of art in detail to *that?*"

He chuckled, relief apparent on his face. "Yeah, what's wrong with that?"

I turned and headed for another painting. He followed close behind me.

"So, you're an artist?" I asked, adjusting a piece that'd gone lopsided.

I could hear the embarrassment in his tone when he spoke. "How'd you guess?"

I flashed a knowing look in his direction. "I'm around them a lot. Not many people who aren't artists themselves can go into that deep of a trance by simply staring at a painting. What's your favorite medium?"

His expression lit up slightly. "Chalk pastel and charcoal, mostly. I like graphite too, though that one's not my favorite. It's harder to get off my hands than pastel, I've found and it's not as easy to blend together. More time consuming too. I *can* paint, though I often choose not to. I can't control a paintbrush like I can a pencil or pastel. I don't understand it as well."

"What made you interested in art?"

He sighed. "My mother used to tease me that I was born with a pencil in my hand. I've been drawing since I can remember, but it really became something serious when I was in high school. I entered one of my pieces in a contest and won. That was when people started commissioning me to do portraits and things like that. It wasn't anything I ever wanted to do professionally since there's not much money involved in it. Every once in a while, I make some good money, but nothing really sustainable . . ." His eyes met mine and he laughed under his breath. "Wow . . . While I'm at it, why not just mention that I secretly like broccoli and chick flicks?"

I laughed, snorting. "Aren't you always this reserved?"

With a coy smile, he looked at his combat boots as he moseyed beside me. "That's usually what people say about me." His tone changed as he continued in a whiney, raspy sound like he imitated my Grandma Wixom. "I can't tell you how many times I've heard things like, 'William, speak up more. You'll never get anywhere if ya don't,' or, 'You're never gonna find a girl if ya don't talk to 'er. Get off that God-forsaken couch and talk for once.'"

My laugh echoed through the studio and I bent forward. I never would've expected that voice to come out of him, his voice was normally so smooth and easy-going. I covered my mouth with the back of my hand, trying to stop, though it didn't help much.

"You sound like my grandma," I chortled. Will's laughter was softer, yet proud as he continued.

"That was me impersonating *my* grandma." He pressed a hand to his chest. "She told me that kind of crap all the time. Drove me nuts."

"Well, I can't see what she's talking about. I've known you, what, almost twenty-four hours and you've already done most of the talking for me." I nudged him with an elbow. He smiled and nudged me back.

"Anyway, I'm curious about something," he said, pushing his hands into his pockets. "You said you can't draw worth squat, right?"

I hesitated, creasing my brow and trying to remember saying that to him. A vague memory came to me from Family Home Evening the night before. I had mentioned it but it was in passing.

"Good memory," I commented.

He grinned, beaming with pride. "Thank you. Now you owe me some information about the girl behind that pretty face."

My cheeks flared with heat and my heart thrashed against my chest. I gasped a bit from the sensation, but shrugged, brushing my fingers across a credenza under one of the paintings.

"You know, for someone as quote-un-quote 'reserved' as you, you sure can be smooth," I retorted.

"I try." His smirk was playful as he brushed off his jacket's collar. "So, if you're not an artist, why volunteer at an art gallery?"

"I volunteer here because it's my great grandfather's. He bought it from his uncle before he died of scarlet fever during its epidemic. My family has owned it ever since. My aunt from Daddy's side runs it now, though she'll accept anyone who wants to volunteer. It's nonprofit and all the money we get from people buying the artwork goes to various charities."

He listened intently, his expression soft. I glanced at the door where another group of people came in. Holding up a finger to Will to indicate him to wait for me, I approached them.

"Welcome to Reno Epic Mediums, may I show you around?" The greeting rolled off my tongue without any forethought.

"No, we're good, just here to look," the mother pushing a stroller said.

Typical response. I smiled, part of me grateful for it. "Okay, let me know if you have any questions or if you're interested in donating today."

The woman nodded once, moving on to browse.

I turned back to Will who watched me with a content expression. I walked back to him, twisting a loose curl onto my collarbone and clasping my fingers together in front of me.

"Where were we?" I asked.

He frowned, glancing at the wall clock above the donations desk. Muttering a curse under his breath, he pulled out his phone. Frowning with concern, I flinched a bit at hearing him swear. I was used to hearing it, but it still made me a bit uncomfortable. Did some part of me hope he didn't swear? I felt thrust into a reality I hoped wouldn't exist. I was reminded of the boundary Daddy would put between us if he ever found out. Maybe I'd hoped he was secretly a member or something. It seemed pretty obvious now though. I'd yet to hear a Latter-Day Saint spit out the 'S-word' so casually before.

If Daddy knew . . .

"What's wrong?" I asked, worried that something had happened.

"I'm gonna pay for this one," he muttered, suddenly frantic. "I want to keep talking, but I only meant to come here on my lunch break. Are you free tonight, by chance?" He cringed, seeming nervous for my response.

I sighed. I didn't want him to leave so soon. He was fun to talk to. "It's family night tonight since I'm hardly home on Mondays. I work or go to school every night except Thursday."

* * *

"Oh," he muttered, glancing at the clock again.

Panic pricked my skin and I reached out for him without realizing it. When my fingers skimmed his forearm, my heart leaped into my throat, causing my cheeks to burn. "But I liked talking to you."

He shrugged one shoulder, rubbing the back of his neck and glancing at his phone again as if it'd hide the nervous grin stretching across his face. "Could you spare a Thursday night?"

I smiled as he watched me with worried eyes.

"Maybe next week," I said, tilting my head. "If you think you can handle an entire evening with just me."

A nearly indistinguishable laugh bubbled from his throat before he cleared it and straightened. "H—have you been to the Grand Sierra Buffet?"

My mouth started watering at even the mention of it and I nodded enthusiastically. "Absolutely. It's pretty expensive though, isn't it?"

Will guffawed. "I just got paid on commission. Don't worry about it."

I smiled at his offer, though I made a mental note to bring my wallet. Daddy always taught me to help pay on dates whenever possible. He told me it was one of the things that impressed him most about Mom. Grabbing his hand, I plucked a pen from the donations desk and wrote my number in his palm. I felt his heart beating rapidly in his trembling wrist. My own heart thumped just as much being so close to him, though I tried not to let it show as I closed his hand into a fist, patted it, and backed away.

"Thanks for coming, Will."

The broad grin on his face seemed completely involuntary as he continued to stand there for a minute before shaking his head.

"T—thanks," he mumbled before backing into the wall.

A sound between a snort and a laugh burst from me. I covered my mouth as he blushed and stumbled out the door and toward a vintage Mustang parked on the street.

I watched him drive off with a deep sigh before directing my attention back to the tourists.

The rest of the day, I tried focusing on my volunteer duties, but then I'd think of Will and I knew it was no use.

Next Thursday couldn't come soon enough.

TEN
William Markus

How long did it have to take to get one public defender to come? Wasn't it his job to defend me? How could he do that if he didn't even take the time to see me?

I leaned my elbows on the table with an exasperated sigh. If I had to wait one more minute for the lazy butt to come, I would've ripped my hair out. The warden watched me as I played with a small screw that'd fallen loose from the walls put there for privacy.

That seemed pointless. It wasn't like it prevented anyone from hearing me. The guy in the stall next to me talked too loudly. You'd think the person on the other line was deaf.

I flinched and sat up straighter when a stocky man with flaming, red hair curling on his head like someone plopped a bird's nest on his head sat across from me. He wore a brown blazer and bright blue tie with neon green polka dots on it. I sat up straighter and blinked at him a couple of times. When he didn't disappear after I opened my eyes, I leaned back against the stiff chair and cringed, picking up the phone.

You've got to be kidding me, I thought, wanting to sink to the floor and hide under the table. *This* was the public defender representing me for a murder trial? He looked like a clown trying too hard to be taken seriously. And failing. Miserably.

I glanced toward the warden who watched me from the corner of his eye with a snide grin on his face. He thought it was funny, huh?

Reluctantly, I turned back to the public defender.

He adjusted his position at least ten times over before making eye contact and grabbing the phone on his side. I'd never seen more blue eyes in my entire life. I usually didn't notice eyes very much, but his were hard to miss. His eyebrows were so light they almost looked nonexistent. Vaguely, I wondered if they'd been burned off by his hair. Same thing with his eyelashes, though they were long and thick.

"William Markus?" he asked, his voice deeper than I'd anticipated. I almost expected Goofy's voice from the Disney cartoon. Laugh and all.

"Will," I corrected, shifting uncomfortably in my seat. When I thought about how my lawyer would look, his appearance didn't even match my most outrageous description.

He wouldn't stop touching his blazer. I wanted to hogtie his hands together with his neon necktie just to make him stop moving.

"Will . . . Odd name. It sounds like the start of a question." He sniffed, smashed the phone beneath his bulky jaw, clasped his fingers together, and flipped his orange curls off his forehead.

"What's your name?" I asked after a minute of waiting for his introduction. He just sat there scrutinizing me like a hawk debating its next move on a mouse. He wasn't intimidating in the slightest, yet I found myself staring back at him. Mostly in bewilderment.

"Huh?" he asked, raising his brow.

"Your name?" I urged, tempted to add an insult on the edge of it. I dreaded the answer. I pictured something as ridiculous as his appearance.

"Oh, you need that. My name is Smith Nathaniel Edwards, public defender for the state of Nevada. I've been dealing with cases like yours for over three years now. I have a lot of them, but I try my hardest to put another above one . . . Or one above the other. Either way. I believe everyone is equal in their rights to happiness and freedom as well as the right to their own voices. When defending the criminals, I do my very, very best to make the best of it and make it fun for everyone. With the case of some who have committed crimes such as killing puppies or eating bagels with cream cheese instead of butter and syrup. Those people deserve a death sentence. I prefer the name Smitty, though it's a little more informal. I've been also referred to as 'Gingerhead Man,'" he said in seemingly one breath.

I choked back a laugh, covering my mouth so it couldn't sneak out. I'd never seen someone so emotionless when making fun of themselves. I wasn't even sure if he was serious or not.

"I can see how that nickname would suit you," I said, trying not to stare at his hair.

"I know. They could've at least come up with something clever," he said. I bit my tongue. Had he never looked in a mirror? "You can call me whatever you want, I don't care. Just as long as you call me by my real name in court. Don't want people looking at me like I'm a fool," he said, pulling on his collar.

I coughed to cover my laugh.

And you think your hair and ties aren't making them think that?

Biting back the snide remark on my tongue proved extremely difficult. He made it *way* too easy.

"So, Will," he started, "The state has assigned me to be your defender and I'm prepared to defend you as best I can. But I can't do that unless you're *willing* to cooperate." He winked at me with a nod, his eyes wide with excited anticipation of my response. I glared at him briefly and his smile cracked his face in half with its size. "Do you get my joke?"

"My name's not *that* weird, Gingerhead Man." A smile cracked through at hearing myself say it.

Smitty chuckled, but it sounded more like he was choking on water. Or his own spit. "You're a funny guy. I like you already. Which isn't saying much, I like everyone."

He was probably too oblivious to realize that most people were probably making fun of him.

"I wanted to formally introduce myself. I'm known in my elite community of public defenders as—"

A total moron?

"One of the best. It's because I care an inordinate amount about each of my clients. Most public defenders have too many cases on their hands to really take time to know their clients individually. I try my hardest, however, to go above and beyond the call of duty. I've made it a point, a promise to myself. When I first got my license, I said to myself, 'Smitty, you can make a difference here or you can make yourself look like a total idiot—'"

I pressed my mouth into a straight line and bit my tongue to stop it.

"'But no matter what, people come first.' It's the people who matter to me, Willy Boy. And if the people matter to me, well then I'm gon be just fine."

A strange hint of an accent gave his voice a different tone. Southern, but not too much.

He cleared his throat, his voice going back to normal. "Most clients we work with are criminals," he said again, sitting up taller in his seat.

I frowned. He didn't even know me ten minutes and already he assumed I was guilty.

"Of course," he continued, rolling up his sleeves to reveal frilly cuffs like the ones in the romantic classics Bea loved so much.

The memory brought a fleeting smile with it. *Pride and Prejudice* was her favorite. With her family, it was impossible not to be cultured, since they all were practically forced to read classics like it as young as ten-years-old.

"That doesn't mean I assume anything," Smitty said.

I'd forgotten his presence for a minute. Remembering only shoved me back into reality.

"Everyone is innocent until proven guilty." He cleared his throat loudly. It echoed so much I heard it through the thick glass separating us, even if he hadn't nearly burst my eardrum through the phone. He coughed and gagged like trying to gather enough saliva and mucus in his throat to spit.

I winced, taking the phone away to rub my ear before reluctantly putting it back. He kept talking.

"Excuse me. Anyway. Is there anything I can do to help. . ." He moved his hands around in front of him, reminding me of the DJ at a club. "Ease your burning soul?"

I hesitated. *Burning soul?*

"Uhm . . . Knowing exactly how bad the situation is would be nice. I don't exactly get a whole lot of exposure to the outside world here."

Smitty sniffed again, his nose scrunching up for a second as he swiped his fingers across it. That gesture reminded me of Tom and I cringed. He hated me before. What would he think of me now?

"Well, you've been arrested, your girlfriend's dead, and you've as good as lost everything from your car to your job," he stated, the words rolling off his tongue like it wouldn't completely crush me happened every day.

Aren't you supposed to make me feel better?

"But as far as I see it, everything points away from you. Since you're the only one who was there in the eyes of detectives, however, there's not much I can do to prove it *wasn't* you. What have you done to defend yourself thus far?"

I hesitated, waiting for him to continue rambling. When he didn't, I groaned, my shoulders slumping.

What more could I do to prove my innocence other than telling the truth? I didn't kill her. Simple as that.

"I don't know," I mumbled. "There's not much I can do."

"*Wrong,*" he barked, pointing a sausage finger at me. His abrupt overreaction made me jump and almost fall off the metal stool. If I wasn't awake and alert before, I was after that.

"O—okay," I said, blinking and switching the phone to the ear that wasn't ringing. "What can I do?"

"Are you telling the truth?" he asked.

I glared darkly at him, my blood boiling with frustration. *What a stupid question, Gingerhead Man.* I was sick of people not believing I told the truth. "What do you think, Smitty?" His name spat from my lips.

He guffawed, waving a dismissive hand at me. "Innocent until proven guilty, silly gosling."

I opened my mouth to respond but lost my train of thought when I realized he'd called me a gosling.

"There are a few pieces of evidence that the next detective to interview you will ask about," Smitty said.

"Don't you mean interrogate?" I asked, raising an eyebrow at him.

He scoffed. "Same difference. That word sounds so intimidating and skeptical. I prefer to think of it as an interview."

My eyes scanned his ridiculous appearance again and I groaned inwardly. He couldn't really be a public defender. How had even made it past the first day of law school? Or college, for that matter? He didn't even know the jargon.

I'm doomed.

ELEVEN
Bianca Wixom

Morning air seeped through my sheer, maroon curtains as they blew in the wind of the furnace vent. My alarm buzzed relentlessly from my phone on my dresser across my room. With a groan, I rolled over onto my back, squinting at the organza canopy over my bed. The night seemed too short. How could it be morning when I hadn't even really dreamed about anything?

I sighed, rolling lazily off the edge and slipping on my favorite fuzzy slippers as I trudged over to my dresser. Even through my slippers, the oak wood floor made my toes curl with its chilly surface. I sniffed, unable to smell anything except the sleep still lingering in my system. My phone's robotically charming song echoed in my head and pounded on my eardrum like a woodpecker.

Finally, I picked up my phone and switched off the alarm.

"Okay, I get it. I'm up," I moaned, though my body refused to believe me.

I combed my fingers through my dark hair, stingy from sleep and glanced in the mirror through blurry vision. I glanced at my contacts on the dresser and sighed, grabbing my glasses and slipping them on instead. No way was I going with contacts that day. It was a day to be lazy with my appearance. I knew it from how much my body didn't want to wake up. I'd doll myself up before the date with Will.

With a long yawn, I scratched my head and began intertwining small braids with the rest of my hair and plopping my fedora on my head. I glanced in my vanity mirror just long enough to adjust my bangs and fix the curls from yesterday. Wiping at the mascara and eyeliner from the night before, I got dressed for another day at the gallery.

Once my denim jacket was thrown on over my T-shirt and ripped jeans, I thrust myself back onto the bed, grabbing the Book of Mormon on my nightstand. I was to Alma, the longest section in the whole thing.

Something about reading the scriptures before leaving my room in the morning gave me a sense of security. I liked to believe that, whenever I did that, I was given a host of guardian angels to protect me throughout the day. I noticed a stark difference in how my days played out when I didn't read in the morning as opposed to when I did. Most would call it coincidence, but I felt like I knew better.

When I was done, I got out of bed and went downstairs where the rest of my family gathered around the kitchen table. All except Mom, who flipped pancakes and cut fruit.

"Good morning, Honey Bea," she greeted brightly. She'd always been a morning person. As a kid, it used to bug me. Now, I thought it was cute how chipper she was.

I glanced at the clock. I'd be late if I didn't start driving in the next few minutes. Kissing the top of Daddy's head and Mom's cheek, I threw open the door to the garage, grabbing a pancake as I passed.

✳ ✳ ✳ ✳

I leaned over my vanity as I applied neutral lipstick and mascara. My hair was still curly from earlier that day, though I'd fixed it up a bit more, re-tying the small braids laced throughout my loose curls again.

I'd always liked the way I looked and felt comfortable in my own skin, but tonight, I felt raw and exposed. I wanted to hide the small imperfections I saw in my skin. Dates always made me nervous, but at least before, I knew I'd be dating someone Daddy would approve of. I wasn't sure with Will. All I knew was that I wanted to go out with him. That should've been all that mattered, right?

Still.

Nerves bubbled in my stomach and my heart thrashed against my chest when my phone went off. Flinching, I picked it up and held it between my cheek and shoulder as I adjusted the bracelets on my wrists, the charms dangling from braided leather jingling like bells as they clashed together.

"Hello," I said into the receiver.

Will's voice greeted from the other side. "I was getting ready to pick you up when I realized you never told me where I should do that."

I sighed, my mind scrambling for a suitable place where Daddy wouldn't see. He couldn't come here. He was home and if he saw Will, he'd never let me go.

"Do you know where the temple is?" I asked.

He hesitated. "The Mormon one?"

"Latter-Day Saint, but yes," I corrected. I never had liked the term, 'Mormon' when describing the Church. It often was associated with the Broadway musical, which didn't accurately represent our beliefs at all. In fact, it was a flat-out mockery of our faith.

"Any reason you want me to pick you up there?" he asked.

I hesitated. "I just . . . want to spend some time there. It's beautiful."

Someone shouted in the background and I heard him pull the phone away and shout something back before returning. "Sorry, I just got off work. Okay, can't argue with that. I'll see you in an hour then."

I smiled and hung up the phone after saying goodbye. The prospect of spending time on the temple grounds brought a sigh of relief. That building was sacred to me as well as several other members of our faith, even though I'd never been inside it. I'd seen pictures of the inside but never entered its walls. I'd heard people make fun of our religion and call it a cult because of only those who had been interviewed by someone with authority to grant a recommend, or pass, could enter temples to perform ordinances. It wasn't like people thought though. We weren't trying to keep secrets from the world. But it was like having something really special that you want to keep to yourself because it was very personal. Most people wouldn't want to flaunt something so personal in everyone's face, yet our temples were still seen as a cult's secret meeting house or something.

I wonder what Will's perspective is.

The thought made me sad to think too hard about.

Plopping my fedora on and shrugging into my favorite, denim vest, I headed for the door.

"Where are you off to?" Daddy asked before I could escape. I sighed, cringing slightly as I turned to him.

"I'm gonna go grab some food down at the buffet," I answered. I wasn't technically lying. That was what I was doing.

"With who?" he asked, his tall frame extended across the length of the couch. He didn't look at me but kept his eyes pasted to the book in his hand.

"No one." I didn't like lying to him, but I just wasn't ready for him to know the whole truth yet. I smiled, tilting my head to one side and batting my eyelashes playfully. "Just thought I'd take myself on a little date."

He grunted, his hazel eyes disbelieving as he turned back to his newspaper.

"You know the rules, Honey Bea."

"Back before nine, no later. Nothing even resembling gambling, unless it's with friends you know and trust, no drinking."

He knew I did none of those things and had no desire to. I didn't understand why he had me rattle off that list every time he caught me going out.

"And?" He peered over reading glasses, looking at me for the first time in the whole interaction. His scrutiny made me swallow nervously.

"No dates without your permission. Especially if you don't know them."

He smiled approval and turned back to his book with a raised chin. "That's my girl. Have fun."

Phew. I threw open the door, pushing the button to my car as I approached it. *He bought it.*

Will didn't arrive for another half hour, but I didn't mind. I liked looking out over the loud city from the solitude and peace of the temple. It sat on the hill I called home, separated from the Reno that seemed so distant and foreign from where I sat. A stone bench sat outside the small temple. My soul filled with peace as I imagined what went on inside the building beside me. It seemed so wonderful, the way my parent's and missionary brother and sister described it. It'd always been a dream of mine to be married in a temple one day. I'd been taught since I was a little girl about the sealing of husband and wife, but never knew exactly what that meant. All I really understood was the generally accepted idea of eternal families in the Church. And that concept had always been beautiful to me.

I breathed in a deep sigh, the air cool and fresh on my tongue. Serenity filled the universe and it seemed as though nothing could go wrong with the world at that moment.

"You ready?"

Will's voice yanked me out of my stupor and I stood, whirling around in surprise to see him standing a few feet away. His eyes widened slightly and he laughed.

"Didn't mean to scare you." He slung his jacket over his broad shoulder and pushed his other hand into his jean's pockets. His hair was slightly wet, implying he'd recently gotten out of the shower.

"No, it's okay." I walked to him, giving him a quick hug. Will didn't have time to react other than awkwardly placing a hand on my waist with a nervous laugh. He bit his lip in a feeble attempt to hide his smile when I pulled away and headed for the parking lot.

I gave everyone hugs upon seeing them. It was something I'd done since I was little. My family were very affectionate people.

I wondered, based on his reaction, if it wasn't something Will was used to.

"C'mon, slowpoke," I teased, twirling on the balls of my feet to walk backward. "You coming or not?" He smiled broadly before jogging to my side.

I'd waited a week and a half for that date. And even though it went against one of Daddy's biggest rules, I didn't care. He'd never find out if I had anything to say about it.

TWELVE
William Markus

Smitty sat in the chair beside me in the interrogation room, clearing his throat far too much and adjusting the front of his blazer again. I swallowed, watching him expectantly and wringing my hands in an attempt to stop myself from grabbing his wrists and pinning them to his sides. He turned his chair toward me, tucking it against the table in front of us.

His tie was yellow today. Lime green spots.

I shook my head. "Why the crazy neckties, man?" I asked, unable to contain the question anymore. It'd bothered me since we met.

He looked at me quizzically, his nonexistent eyebrows pulled together. "Who said they were crazy? They're lucky."

I stared at him. "Lucky?" Was he serious? I looked him over again, his stocky frame hidden beneath his brown blazer and distracting tie.

His blue eyes brightened with enthusiasm and he bit his lip as if he couldn't hold it in anymore. Throwing his leg with impressive flexibility onto the interrogation desk, he tugged on his pant leg to expose knee-high socks of the same clashing colors as his tie. I winced at the bright colors as little fairy lights blinked in the center of each polka dot.

"*Lucky!* Haven't lost a case yet while wearing these babies," he exclaimed, letting his foot plop back onto the tile with a significant *thud.*

I glanced at the camera in the upper corner of the room. What could the cops have been thinking as they observed this strange man without context to his weird behavior?

They were probably all laughing at me.

Shaking my head, I rested my elbows on the desk. What was it about strange people that drew me in so much? Isaac was definitely quirky and he'd been my best friend since middle school. Bea had a unique style all her own, not caring what others thought of her appearance. Now, Smitty. No words could describe accurately in my brain where his head was half the time. There was something endearing about his odd behavior, though. I'd found myself trusting his advice more often than not. We'd known each other for almost a week. He'd come to visit pretty often. Even as

● ● ●
133

weird as he was, I'd begun preferring his company over any cop.

He adjusted his position again, not surprisingly, his chin in the air as he sighed deeply.

"You ready for another interview?" he asked.

I smiled at the word, not bothering to correct him again. "No," I muttered. "I wish they could just figure it out already and either convict me or release me. It's starting to mess with my head, Smitty. I don't feel like I really know what's right or wrong anymore. This place stinks."

I sniffed, the overpowering scent of sweaty bodies and angst made my tongue moisten in the most uncomfortable way.

He gave me a half-hearted grin, patting me firmly on the back. "I understand. It stinks being in your shoes."

I snorted, wondering if he realized how that seemed. "Well, I haven't exactly changed my own socks in nearly three days. Sorry if I offend."

He narrowed his eyes at me, confused, before shaking his head. "So, there are a few things I want you to steer clear of, here as well as in court," he continued, clearly not getting my sarcasm. "One, control your emotions. The last thing you want to show these guys is anger. They're looking for that. You know this already, I'm sure."

I rolled my eyes, avoiding eye contact by looking at my clasped fingers, wrists bound by the handcuffs I grew to hate almost as much as the officer who put them there. Officer Todd was an extremely distasteful guy. If I never had to see him again after all this was over, I'd be a happy man. My memory flashed back to my first interrogation with embarrassment. I really wasn't good at controlling myself when I was angry.

"Two," he said, crossing his ankle over his knee and placing a hand on the back of my chair. "You don't *have* to answer every question they throw at you. You have the right to remain silent, remember. Don't feel the need to give them whatever they ask for."

I sighed. That was difficult for me too, unless they treated me like Officer Todd. Then I kept my mouth shut. I proved when I met Bea that I could run my mouth too much and get myself into trouble. She brought that out in me. I thought it was a good thing . . . until now.

"You got it, Willy Boy?" Smitty asked, leaning forward to see my face through my grungy hair that hung over my eye. I turned to him, flipping my hair back.

"Willy Boy? Why can't you ever just call me Will?"

He guffawed, waving a dismissive hand at me. "I already told you. 'Will' sounds like the start of a question."

"Just don't ever call me 'Bill,' please," I muttered, shuddering at the thought of my father. The door burst open after that and we both looked up. Smitty jumped so much, he scooted his chair back.

"Alright, Mr. Markus, I'm Detective Tess Cole. Let's settle one thing right off the bat, okay?" a woman said as she entered. She leaned against the interrogation desk, her low-cut shirt catching me by surprise. I expected another large woman with the mole as big as her nose but saw instead an attractive woman with dark hair and curvy figure. I tried not to stare and blinked hard, making myself look away from the cleavage staring me in the face.

Thank God Bea never dressed like that.

Pretty or not though, she was still my enemy.

"What's that?" I asked, genuinely curious what she meant.

"I don't think you're guilty," she said softly, her blue eyes sympathetic as she shook her head.

I narrowed my eyes suspiciously. It was the first time a detective had ever said that to me. Part of me wanted to believe her, just for the sake of thinking someone, *anyone*, thought I was innocent. She smiled, her full lips dark.

"You don't?" I asked, confused.

She shook her head. "No." She straightened and leaned into her hip, the handgun on her belt hitting against her thigh.

I was grateful for her change in posture. It hid her chest from view again. I never really liked when women flaunted those things to get attention. Seemed a little shallow for my liking. Unfortunately, I lived in the wrong city for that opinion. I didn't mind it as much, however, before I met Bea. After her, I couldn't understand its appeal. I saw what true attractiveness was. Class and modesty won me over after her influence.

"But I have to bring you into questioning since you're currently our only suspect,"

Detective Cole continued, circling the table with her fingers skimming across the surface.

"Just about everyone thinks I'm guilty. Why not you?" I asked, genuinely curious. Hearing some reasons for my innocence might've been refreshing after all the accusations and judgments on my character.

"For one reason. I think the evidence points to someone else. Have you ever seen this glove before?" Out of her shirt collar, she pulled out a Polaroid of a black, leather glove and handed it to me.

My brow creased. "I—I think I saw a friend of mine wear it once. He gave them to me as a good luck charm when I inherited my father's mechanic shop. But it was a long time ago. It was in my office, though I never paid any attention to it."

"What was your friend's name?" she asked.

"Matt Young."

"Did he ever own a gun?"

"He was a hunter, so yeah, he owned a *lot* of them. He was kind of obsessed with them."

A memory of going shooting with Isaac, Matt, and Natalie came to me. Matt was the one teaching everyone how to shoot. His favorite were handguns, in particular, his dad's Browning Hi-Power.   Bea didn't go because Tom hated guns.

She pushed her knuckles off the table. "Interesting. This glove was found near the crime scene with traces of gun powder from a Browning Hi-Power pistol on it, the same gun used to kill Miss Wixom. Close enough to be suspicious, but not enough to technically be included with the initial vicinity. Did he own this gun?"

I hesitated. "Um . . ."

"Out of curiosity, *you* weren't wearing this glove to cover your tracks after Bianca Wixom was shot, were you?"

Hearing that phrase stunned me. Subconsciously, I lifted my cuffed hands to rub the spot where a sharp pain pricked my chest like a needle. I'd never get used to hearing that phrase. *'Bianca Wixom was shot.'*

A shudder rolled up my spine and I glared darkly at her. *"No.* I haven't seen that thing in months. I *said* that."

"Willy," Smitty grumbled.

I shot a look at him, remembering his advice about not losing my temper. Closing my eyes, I inhaled deeply. "I was by the car, telling her to get in."

Smitty cleared his throat beside me.

I glanced at him, trying to figure out what I was doing wrong now. One leg crossed over the other as he casually picked at his fingernails. I sighed, dragging my elbows onto the table as I begrudgingly relived that night again.

"I was behind her. She stood by the car, staring out at the Sierra Bay. I told her to get in the car, but she didn't listen," I answered.

Smitty sniffed.

"That's interesting. Autopsy reports say she was shot once from the front," Detective Cole said, folding her arms. "They found traces of gun powder on this glove from the same gun used to kill her. It was found right by the bay. Right along the same path where you were running from our officers. Did you shoot that gun?"

Smitty leaned toward me, uncrossing his legs. "You don't have to answer that," he whispered.

My eyes widened and I leaned forward, ignoring Smitty and listening more intently to Detective Cole with renewed interest. "Yes, I shot the gun."

"Willy Boy," Smitty groaned.

"Why?" she pressed.

"Yes, I shot it. No, I didn't shoot *her.* It was after she was shot and I, stupidly, tried getting the coward who killed her to come out by shooting it into the air. It knocked out one of the street lights, but didn't hurt anyone."

Detective Cole straightened her spine, a sly grin on her face. "Well then . . . My work here is done. We'll see about this glove and your friend. Thanks for your cooperation, Mr. Markus." She winked at me, shooting a glare at Smitty, before leaving the room.

I breathed a sigh of relief, grateful the interrogation was over for now. I didn't dare hope for freedom. They wanted me guilty. Seemed like they'd find any reason to come to that verdict. What was the use in even asking me questions?

Smitty rubbed the bridge of his nose. "I told you not to answer questions that incriminate you," he moaned, annoyance in his tone.

I turned to him, surprised before anger flared in me. "You told me I didn't have to answer questions."

"That was one where you should've taken advantage of Miranda Rights," Smitty responded, surprisingly calm as he let his hand slap onto his leg. "She was baitin' you. They'll do anything to get you to talk. Did you not feel that something was off about her?"

I paused. *Other than her inability to button up her shirt?*

"Not really."

"She was . . ." Smitty glanced up at the cameras and cleared his throat, leaning in farther. "She was trying to get you to let your guard down. She was good at it too. You're too trusting." He grabbed his briefcase and stood, pulling me up with him. It occurred to me how tall he was. He stood at eye-level with me. That wasn't something I was used to.

"Here's another word of advice, free of charge."

"I'm not paying you, Smitty," I pointed out.

"Potato, tomato," he scoffed. "Try to recognize when they're baiting you. It'll make all our lives easier . . . except theirs. It'll make their lives significantly harder and more miserable. That's what we want."

I never thought I'd hear that making someone else's lives harder was what we wanted. The thought made me hesitate. *What goes on in his head?*

With a firm pat on the shoulder, we left the interrogation room where another officer waited to escort me back to my cell. Before I couldn't, however, I turned back to Smitty who waved at me, his thin mouth tight in a straight line.

My head spun trying to understand everything that'd been thrown at me as I walked and eventually sat in my cell. All that I had to do now was wait for my first court hearing to begin.

Matt's glove was found at the scene? How did that happen? And how'd he even get it? The last time I saw that glove was hanging on my office wall behind locked doors. Was he trying to frame me? Maybe he'd gotten another pair just like it.

He wasn't a suspect. He enjoyed hunting animals but wasn't a murderer. Then again, I wasn't either. I didn't really know him *that* well. Maybe he wasn't as trustworthy as I thought he was.

THIRTEEN
Bianca Wixom

Will seemed so nervous, though he gazed lovingly at me as if I were the only thing that mattered in the entire world to him. I sipped my drink nonchalantly, trying to distract myself from his scrutiny.

He gave me a playful smile before putting a corner of an oyster shell to his lips and spooning its contents into his mouth. My gag reflex activated and I winced, imagining its slimy texture on my tongue. He looked back at me, eyes bright with enjoyment.

"I hope you weren't hoping for a kiss at the end of the night," I teased. "You're not getting it now."

He threw his head back laughing. "Damn, that's harsh."

I shrugged, picking up my root beer and batting my eyelashes at him as I sipped. "Sorry, you lost your chances of a kiss the moment you let that oyster touch that cute little smile of yours."

A challenging grin pulled on the corners of his mouth as he leaned his elbows on the table. "Why's that? It's just a fish."

"I'm not kissing fish lips."

An amused snort burst from him as he let his head hang forward and shake. "You know, it wouldn't be so bad if you'd try it yourself. You could literally eat anything in this buffet and it would probably be amazing."

I shook my head, yanking off a piece of chicken leg in defiance and chewing it hard.

"Okay, you're asking for it." Grabbing another oyster, he got up from his side of the booth and settled into mine. Covering my mouth to shield the chicken still between my teeth as I swallowed, I gaped at him, scooting to the other side of the booth. *He's not going to kiss me anyway, is he?*

"Don't worry, I'm not making moves on you," he assured.

A startling amount of relief swept over me when he said that and I relaxed, watching him shock the oyster again, seasoning it with salt, pepper, and dousing it in lemon juice. He held it up, offering it to me as a peace treaty.

"I promise it's not going to hurt you. Unless you're secretly allergic to shellfish. Then it might. But unless that's the case, you'll be fine."

"I don't want to, Will," I said, meaning it.

His eyes met mine, searching my expression. Fear of being forced to do anything tingled in my stomach. Silently, I pleaded with him not to push me. After a minute, he cleared his throat and set the oyster down on a napkin.

"Alright, I won't make you."

I hesitated, surprised and trying to figure out what'd changed. Would he really not make me eat it? My chest felt warm with gratitude.

"Though, you really should be less picky," he retorted playfully. "I really do think you should give it a try."

I laughed, feeling significantly more at ease. The respect he showed for my boundaries notably impressed me and I scooted a bit closer to him, feeling safer than before knowing he wouldn't force anything on me.

"What did you order as a drink again?" I asked.

"Vodka Diet Coke," he answered, picking up his glass and sipping it. "Want some?"

I laughed. "I'm good, thanks," I answered, slightly embarrassed I'd even asked. How'd I end up going out with anyone who would dream of letting that roll off his tongue like it was second nature? And yet, something about him drew me in. I felt comfortable talking to him and he was easy to get along with.

He winced, swearing under his breath and chuckling nervously. "I forgot Mormons don't drink. I'm sorry."

I smiled, munching on a French fry. "So, besides work on commission for random businesses, what do you do?"

He pointed a finger at me. "You're not getting me this time," he said, narrowing his eyes at me.

"What do you mean?"

"It's my turn to get information out of you. It's your turn to be in the spotlight."

Remembering how many times he'd caught himself oversharing made me giggle lightly and I bowed my head. It was adorable.

"What do you want to know?" I asked, tucking my hands between my knees and turning to him with raised eyebrows. Part of me dreaded him asking me anything. I didn't like talking about myself too much. I always felt like I came across as arrogant or self-righteous.

"Everything," he said, letting his arm rest behind me again. I smiled at his casual gesture and how natural it felt. "Have you always lived in Reno?"

I shook my head. "My family moved here from Salt Lake City, Utah, about six years ago. My dad got transferred to a more prestigious law firm here where he'd get paid better. We moved into a nice house by the temple and my parents go every weekend."

"Is that when you babysit?"

He remembered that?

I nodded. "They ask me to babysit all the time. I don't mind, Daddy's generous with his rate, but sometimes I kind of wonder what it's like to have a *real* job, you know?"

Will squinted slightly and straightened, renewed interest in his expression. "You've never had a job outside of that?"

"Well," I corrected. "Unless you count the art gallery as a job."

"That's volunteering, isn't it?"

I sighed. "Yeah, I guess. Even that's still family-based. I have a very family-oriented life."

Will's eyes downcast and his expression turned sullen. "That must be nice," he mumbled.

I flipped my hair from my eyes and leaned on the table. "What do you mean?"

He sighed, shifting uncomfortably. "Family's never been so . . . forgiving for me."

I thought of the rumors Natalie told me about him. He came from a bit of a broken home.

"What does that mean?" I asked, curious to hear the real story as opposed to rumors. I wanted to know the real Will Markus, not a misconstrued version of him told by gossip. He didn't seem at all like the guy Natalie described.

'Doesn't he just seem surrounded by darkness?'

I shuddered to think of that description. She was wrong. I wished she could see that.

He breathed a soft chuckle, not taking his dazed eyes away from mine as he sipped his drink, wincing a bit as he swallowed.

"Can't I have *some* secrets?"

He clearly wasn't willing to share that side of him yet.

"I'm sorry," I said, realizing how much I'd been prying.

He broke eye contact with a significant frown. "It's your spotlight, remember?" Will said, bringing the conversation back. "You said you came here six years ago. Were you still in high school then?"

I sighed. I hated answering that question. "Everyone in my family is home-schooled until they reach high school. I was sixteen, so I barely got a chance to go."

"You're twenty-three then?" he asked, surprised.

I nodded, chuckling at his tone. "Yeah, is that bad?"

"No." He smiled. "I'm just surprised. You look and act more mature than I've seen a lot of twenty-three-year-olds act."

I smiled at the compliment. "How old are you?"

"Twenty-five."

I laughed, nudging him playfully. "Aren't you all high and mighty?"

He laughed, nudging me back. "Hey, I'm not saying *I'm* mature. Far from it. I just expected you to be older. You seem very classy and down-to-earth. That's hard to find in a city like this where women seem to think they have to flaunt to get attention."

My cheeks burned at the thought. A flash of memory haunted me of a practically topless woman I saw walking downtown, men gaping at her as they passed, some of them stopping to hit on her. I never wanted to be that. Subconsciously, I adjusted the collar of my denim jacket over my high-necked T-shirt and folded my arms.

"I dunno, Will, it's only the first date," I said slyly. "For all you know, I'm psycho."

He laughed. "Bianca, I live with Isaac. My definition of psycho has been entirely redefined."

Embarrassment left me and I laughed aloud, causing people in the buffet to turn and stare. Their critical glares sent a burst of insecurity through me, though it diminished when I saw the broad grin on his face. Everything from his eyes to his mouth beamed.

"I'm serious," he said, repositioning so he faced me instead of lounging beside me. "This morning, the guy sorted his sock drawer because he wanted to make sure they didn't touch. He said they didn't want to be that close together and it would make them uncomfortable. Then he made eggs and sang to them about how much he loved them. The guy's completely nuts."

"Oh, Isaac," I chortled. "I can totally picture him doing that."

"You gotta love the guy though," he observed. "He may be weird, but he's got a heart of gold."

I nodded. "Definitely."

Isaac had always been the weird one, but everyone in the ward adored him. Will was right. He had a bigger heart than anyone I knew and always wanted to make sure everyone felt welcomed and included.

Will grinned, leaning his cheek on his knuckles.

"What're your parents like?" he asked, seeming a bit distracted, though he stared at me with rapt attention. No one had ever made me feel so much like I was in the spotlight, yet content to be so.

I scoffed, thinking of the stark contrast in my parent's personalities.

"Well. . ." I glanced at a clock on the wall and my eyes widened. How had it gotten so late? Forgetting his question, I stood from the booth. My curfew was in ten minutes. It took about fifteen to get back home. The last thing I wanted was Daddy waiting up for me ready to prod me with questions.

Will looked up at me with confusion. "You okay?"

"I have to go," I said, frantically grabbing my purse on the seat and heading for the exit into the casino. Will followed after a minute, probably trying to figure out what happened.

"Bianca," he called, finally catching up to me after I was already half-way through the endless array of slot machines. I slowed down, walking backward to face him. "What's wrong?"

His hand landed on my forearm and I flinched, smiling in spite of myself. His eyes glittered with concern.

"I'm sorry, I just didn't realize it was so—"

My back slammed into the squishy belly of a man with a cigarette in his mouth. His appearance startled me. Dark circles lined his tired eyes as smoke puffed from between his lips and into my face. I coughed, turning away from the foul stench. I couldn't decide, however, if it was the smoke or his horrid body odor that burned my eyes and nostrils. He glared down at me, his grungy tank top stained with what I could only assume was a mixture of sweat and nacho cheese.

"Watch where yer goin' . . . little . . . missy," he growled, his voice deep and menacing. It caused a shrill ringing in my ears as danger loomed in the air around us.

Hands landed firmly on my shoulders and I jumped, turning around to see Will feigning a smile toward him.

"Sorry about that, Jack. We'll be more careful next time." With a firm nod, he narrowed his eyes at the man, apparently named Jack.

He grunted, glaring darkly at me as he walked away. His eyes held my gaze as he disappeared into the mess of blinking lights and slot machines.

The unease I felt from the interaction faded into vague curiosity as to how Will knew him, then back to urgency.

"You okay, Bianca?" Will asked, his fingers gently rubbing my shoulders. My breath quickened and I kept walking, making Will release his grasp on me. All I could really think about was getting home in time.

Will came after me again, walking beside me as he slipped on his jacket. I watched our feet move in unison as I cantered toward the glowing, red exit.

FOURTEEN
William Markus

My cell felt as wet and groggy as I always imagined palace dungeons. The air itself seemed to weep with the burdens carried on the backs of inmates. If I could've picked the most depressing atmosphere to drive someone to insanity, that jail would've suited the job description perfectly.

Artificial lighting amplified the general lack of sun and happiness, sucking the life out of every room. Officers laughed outside the blue door trapping me in, occasionally shouting something at one of the other inmates. I hated when they yelled because most of what they said was derogatory.

I didn't understand. Any experience I'd had with cops previous to this was pleasant, for the most part. Even when I was arrested for that DUI a few years before, they were at least respectful, though a bit condescending. The only time Bea got pulled over for speeding, the cop let her off with a warning and a smile. She had a way of charming everyone around her though, so that wasn't a surprise.

With a heavy frown, I adjusted positions in an effort to be more comfortable. Nothing was comfortable about that room. The people beside me talked too loudly. The place reeked of angst and sweat. I hardly wanted to think of my appearance, which I was sure looked as awful as I felt. I didn't really care all that much about it before, but now, the smell of my body repulsed me and my hair flattened against my scalp like I'd never bathed before. A shower sounded Heavenly at that point.

There were a lot of things I missed about normality. Like having a phone to distract myself when I couldn't stand my own thoughts anymore. Or a pencil and paper to at least write them down so I wouldn't have to endure them in silence for so long.

I lay on the cot that squeaked beneath me as it cried for help under my weight.

"Come on, I'm not that fat," I muttered, wishing someone could hear me. The silence of my cramped cell left my thoughts screaming at me. "I'm turning into Isaac. Talking to things like they can hear me."

I decided to stop then. The thought of becoming like him felt weird. At least I hadn't sung to inanimate objects yet.

Over and over again, my mind clouded with visions from that night. For the life of me, all I could really remember was her dying and me shooting that gun. Had there really been another person in that parking lot?

A flash of memory appeared behind my eyelids when I blinked. An empty parking lot of cars but vacant of people. Massive casino lights illuminating the night in eerie darkness.

No, there wasn't anyone else there.

But you didn't do it, so who did?

I sighed, tempted to answer those questions aloud, but refusing to go there. I wouldn't talk to myself and try answering my own questions. That was stupid and would get me nowhere.

Glancing around the room, my head spun with similar variations of the same questions.

No, someone had to have been there. Obviously. I didn't have the gun with me and it wasn't even my gun. It was Matt's. And that glove. Where'd that come from? The rustling bushes. Had I imagined it?

Think about something else, for once, Will.

I yearned to forget about that night for one minute and have a moment of peace amid all the turmoil. Desperately, I combed through my memory, tucking a hand behind my head, my wrists rubbed nearly raw from wearing handcuffs outside my cell. At least I had that to look forward to with solitude.

My memory could only seem to remember the incident. Couldn't I think of *anything* else?

My mother's voice. Telling me she didn't know me anymore.

I shook away that one and searched for another, squirming uncomfortably against the cot that seemed to twist my back muscles in knots.

My father yelling at me to get out of his office so he could focus then hearing him through the door, talking to someone on the other line about secret rendezvous and true love.

I never told anyone but Isaac and Matt about that one. Bea would've gotten scared I'd do the same thing to her and my mother was too brainwashed to think for herself. I wondered about my mother sometimes, though I knew I'd never see her again. I remembered seeing something about her in the newspaper about a stripper who'd been nearly raped to death.

No one knew what my father was really like. *He* was the one who drove her to madness. I hated him for it. And because of me, he got away with cheating as well as everything else. Nothing I could do.

Part of me wanted to scoff. How'd I keep finding myself in these ridiculous predicaments where I was the one getting the blame for stuff I didn't do?

Officer Burns was on my side, at least. He'd treated me with respect, in comparison, and snuck in a chocolate bar with my food one night, though he didn't say a word about it. I was sure I hadn't done anything to deserve that and he probably could've gotten fired for it. Still, the change from the disgusting food served here was a welcomed one.

I couldn't lie down anymore. The close quarters of my cell felt stuffy. Seemed if I didn't move every so often, I'd become part of the air or something. I sat up, running my fingers through my hair. It'd grown some since the night I lost her. I usually styled my hair to be away from my face, but after all this, the last thing I thought about was fixing my appearance. It still felt grungy after I'd spent so much time in a sweaty environment.

I glanced at the door. Any minute, an officer would come in, cuff me again, and take me to talk to Smitty again. Vaguely, I wondered what ridiculous accessory he'd have on him today.

All I could do was wait.

FIFTEEN
<u>Bianca Wixom</u>

I paused to breathe fresh air after being bogged with cigarette smoke. Will halted beside me and I continued forward silently.

"Hey," he said. "What's going on?"

Finally, I sighed, slightly embarrassed. "My curfew is in seven minutes."

His hand landed on my back and he turned me a different direction, toward his car parked close to the building. That gave me pause. My family never parked close to buildings. Mom swore that the little bit of exercise from parking in the back of a lot was utterly necessary.

"Okay, I'll take you home. You'll be fine."

I glanced at Will, his expression genuinely concerned as he led me back to his car. With his hand on my waist, a strange and overwhelming sense of security swept over me like a gust of wind.

"Sorry," I muttered, self-conscious about how quickly I'd raced out of the buffet. I just didn't want to see Daddy's reaction when he found out I was late, even by a minute. His by-the-book, plan out *everything,* personality gave me very little leverage in life.

"Don't apologize," Will said. "Matt and Isaac are probably dying to know where I am too. Those eggs and socks of Isaac's will be missing me."

I snorted, grateful for the distraction as Will opened my car door for me. I smiled at the gesture. It was nice when a guy did that. Natalie would've glared and scolded him for not thinking she could open the door herself. I, however, liked feeling like a proper lady getting into the passenger side. He flashed me a smile and shut the door. I inhaled the musty smell of his Mustang and watched him circle the front of the car, nearly hopping over its hood to get to his side.

He threw open his door and plopped in, rubbing his hands together before turning the key. The car's poor muffler caused the engine to roar to life and Will bit down on his smile as a shudder rolled up his spine.

"Man, I love this car," he muttered, shifting the stick into reverse and backing out.

"I bet you do," I said. "What's a man's car without a roaring engine?"

He glanced at me and chuckled. Shifting gears again, the car's engine continued to roar as we made our way out of the parking lot and onto 2nd Street.

"You'd think, owning a mechanic's shop, I'd have a nicer model, but unfortunately, my 1995 Mustang has seen better days. The muffler on this baby busted ages ago. A customer sold it to me three years ago when Dad still cared." His voice deepened when he continued. "He told me, 'If you can fix it, you can have it.' It was an easier fix than either of us anticipated and I ended up paying the guy for it anyway even though he tried to refuse."

I smiled, my attention caught on one phrase. *"When Dad still cared."* I wanted to know more about that but didn't dare ask. He'd said it so flippantly, yet it still felt like too personal a question to ask on a first date. So, instead, I glanced nervously at the clock. I was already past curfew. Hopefully, Daddy wouldn't notice. Maybe his clock was slow back home.

Who was I kidding? I was going to be in so much trouble.

"What is it about you?" he muttered, his cheeks reddening slightly as he shook his head.

"What?"

"You make me talk way too much and share my deepest thoughts without even doing anything. I don't know how you do it, Bea."

The nickname surprised me. "You just called me Bea," I observed. Only my closest friends and family called me that.

His eyes widened and he stumbled over words, hitting the breaks too hard at a stoplight on account of looking at me. I laughed after my heart rate calmed down and he rubbed the bridge of his nose.

"I'm sorry," he moaned. "I swear, I'm not trying to kill you."

I laughed again. The clock and curfew faded into the background as I smiled at the awkwardly charming guy at my side.

"Are you sure? You seem pretty set on it," I teased.

He shook his head. "Swear on my life, I don't want to." A nervous laugh tinted his voice and he leaned forward until his forearms rested across the steering wheel. "Anyway, back to what we were talking about before that little burst of excitement . . . Isaac and Matt call you Bea all the time, so it just slipped. I'm sorry if you're uncomfortable with it."

I shrugged. It sounded nice coming from him. "I don't mind. It's a common nickname among family and friends."

He pursed his lips with an unamused smile. "Yeah," he answered slowly like he didn't know what else to say.

For the first time that night, silence hung in the air and I realized how much I missed his voice. He didn't seem to know how to proceed. I hadn't realized how easy he was to talk to until he wasn't speaking anymore. The air seemed heavier as it pressed against me. I didn't like it.

I turned to him, trying to understand what he was thinking based on his expression. His expression was serious and focused as he stared at the road leading back to the temple. Was it something I said? Maybe he thought I'd friend-zoned him or something. I didn't want that. Internally, I tried guessing how I could get something more out of him. A joke, a smile, anything. I played over in my mind what I'd said, kicking myself for practically referring to him as nothing more than a friend.

"Take a right here," I said after he'd nearly missed the turn.

He chuckled airily and flashed his blinker before turning. "I've lived in this city my whole life, you'd think I'd know every corner of it by now. I still find myself getting lost sometimes. It's called 'the biggest little city in the world,' yet its many facets still confuse me. Guess it doesn't help that I'm a little distracted right now."

He flashed a teasing, sideways glance and grinned as silence filled the car again. I was grateful for him talking, though he still seemed a little distracted. He was probably focused on driving so he didn't almost cause another accident.

As we approached the temple, I hoped I hadn't just completely ruined our chances together.

He pulled into the parking lot where my car still sat. I sighed with relief, grateful they didn't shut the gates until ten. Anticipation threw me out of the car once he'd turned the key. I'd completely forgotten about letting him open my door. Embarrassed, I headed for my car. I felt like I'd buried myself in a hole and I didn't really want to think about anything but getting home before nine-thirty.

"Bea," Will called after me. I spun around, half-way to my car. His mouth twitched into a lighthearted smile. "I'll call you tomorrow?" His brow furrowed like he dreaded my response, but hope gleamed on his flushed cheeks.

Before I could stop myself, I sprinted to him and threw my arms securely around his neck. I couldn't contain my relief that he hadn't completely written me off as I squeezed tighter. I had to stand on my toes to reach him, he was so tall. It took a second for him to hug me back, but when he did, he held on securely with both arms. I gasped a bit and caught the scent of his clothes, strangely inviting with a mixture of mustiness and clove.

His embrace was warm and safe. I didn't want to let go but held onto him a moment longer than I probably should've. I wanted to bask in the wonderful feeling of his body pressed to mine. I squeezed my eyes shut, trying to stick to memory how his jacket felt against my fingertips. The gentle feeling of his hands rubbing my back.

All at once, I pulled away, planting a kiss on his cheek as I passed. My cheeks flared with excitement as I adjusted my fedora and ran back to my car. I didn't look back before heading home.

* * *

SIXTEEN
William Markus

Waiting for them to answer the video call was agonizing. I wasn't even sure why they wanted to still keep in contact with me after I'd been accused of murdering their daughter. That was something I would've deemed unforgivable. But how did they feel? I found myself wondering as I held the phone to my ear if they wanted to talk to me so Tom could tell me how right he'd always been about me. The man hated me, though I never quite knew why, other than I wasn't what he wanted for his daughter.

"Will," Julia cried as the screen appeared. I flinched, nerves pricking my senses when I saw her.

"Hey, Jules," I muttered lifelessly. My voice reminded me of Bea when I'd call her too early on Saturday mornings. Groggy and exhausted. I managed a smile.

Those large eyes bright with excitement as she bounced on her heels reminded me of the night we met. How sweet and innocent she was. How she'd hang on my every word like she did Bea's ankles.

Her parent's bed creaked under her weight. It was nice to see someone enthusiastic for once . . . Aside from Smitty who seemed a little too enthusiastic about things like crazy socks, suspenders, and neckties.

"Why is your hair so long?" she asked, tilting her head as she sat on her ankles. "You look different."

I hesitated. I couldn't play off our little inside joke about me owning a secret agency. I was on a monitored and recorded line and in enough trouble as it was.

My shoulders felt a little lighter seeing Julia smile again. "I . . . haven't gotten it cut in a while. Where's your mom?"

She looked past the camera, waving a hand quickly. "Mommy, Will wants to see you."

Emily said something in the background. I frowned hearing her voice again, a jab of pain in my gut with the guilt she reminded me of. Emily sat on the bed beside Julia who wrapped her arms around her mother's neck in a loving embrace. I missed her hugs. She was the most affectionate girl I'd ever met.

"Hi, Will," Emily greeted, her tone weighty and unenthused.

I did that to her.

The thought haunted me on a daily basis, though I knew it didn't make much sense.

"How are you holding up?" she asked, running her fingers through her blonde, shoulder-length hair. She seemed older. Dark circles rimmed her normally warm eyes and I noticed a few graying hairs around her widow's peak hairline.

I almost scoffed at her question. How good could I be?

"Shouldn't I be asking *you* that? I lost my fiancée, but you lost your daughter. Why do you care about how I'm holding up?"

She shrugged. "I care about you, Will. She loved you, so I love you too."

The sentiment would've made me tear up if I hadn't known better. It was an honor hearing her say something like that. I felt undeserving of her care before, but now, the prospect seemed unfathomable to me. She couldn't have really felt that way. No one ever had before. How could she possibly love the man suspected of killing her daughter? It didn't make sense.

"Where's Tom?" I asked slowly, knowing the answer.

Anywhere but where I am.

Emily hesitated, hoisting the rambunctious Julia onto her lap so she wouldn't jump on the bed anymore. "He's . . . not here."

At that moment, I noticed him walk across their bedroom doorway. My shoulders fell slightly, pursing my lips as I looked down at the cuffs around my wrists.

What did I ever do to you, Tom?

"He thinks I'm guilty, doesn't he?"

"He's still a bit . . . suspicious. But he's a prosecutor. It's his job to think that way. Guilty until proven innocent is the way he sees it."

I rolled my eyes, trying to be subtle about it. It was no use since she noticed everything, but I didn't care. With a half-hearted scoff, I muttered, "You don't have to cover for him, Emily."

"Well, people don't understand him like I do. Sometimes, I feel like I do need to cover for him. He's a good man, Will, and he cares about you in his own way. He just . . . had a different plan for his daughter than the one she followed."

"In other words, he didn't plan on me," I grumbled. "I remember when I asked for permission. He never wanted me to be part of the family."

Emily was silent for a bit before telling Julia to go practice the violin so she could talk to me more privately. Julia turned to me, blowing a kiss into the camera.

"Love you, Will," she cried as she scampered out of the room.

Emily followed, shutting the door behind her daughter, before sitting on the bed again.

"How is she so happy?" I asked, confused at her undying enthusiasm.

She smiled. "She's still a little too naïve to really understand what's happened, I think. Plus, we've all been taught that families can be together forever, so it brings comfort during times like this."

"Families together forever, huh?" I asked doubtfully. It was a phrase I'd heard thousands of times while attending church meetings with Bea, though the sentiment never really brought me comfort. No way I ever wanted to face my father again. The thought of being with him for eternity made my stomach curl. "How can you still hold onto that?"

She looked at me, her eyes sad, but empathetic. "Will, Bianca wasn't the first child we lost. She had a younger brother who passed away when she was about Julia's age. His name was Marcus."

I flinched. Bea told me about it briefly, but not much. She decided to tell me little details of his struggle with cancer then pronounced that she'd see him again, so she wasn't worried. I could see through that façade instantly, however. She never told me his name was Marcus either. Maybe that was a reason Tom hated me so much.

Emily continued, wiping tears from her eyes as she pressed fingers to the bridge of her nose. Seeing her like that hurt. I wanted to help her feel better somehow, but couldn't think of anything to do.

"I remember the day Bea told you about him because she came home crying after one of your dates. She spent the night looking through pictures with him. This isn't the first time we've lost a child. But that doesn't make it any easier. I'm sorry."

She cried silently for a moment and I frowned, not knowing how to react through a computer screen. Her poise and elegance slipped away for a bit when I saw her in such a vulnerable state.

"But I know, despite all of this, God still loves our family and He loves *you*. He needed them in Heaven with Him and He's provided a way for us to be together again."

I stared at her in disbelief. How could she still believe so fervently that He loved her? It felt surreal hearing her speak like that. Almost like it wasn't really her talking, but words borrowed from . . . Someone else. God? The church leaders?

Something in the way she said that gave me pause and I felt like I couldn't speak anymore.

She sniffed, wiping tears from below her wet eyes.

"You're going into court tomorrow, right?" she asked, her voice strained, but less so than it'd been before. I sighed, thrust back into reality. I glanced around the room. Dull and gray with other inmates on their own visiting calls with nothing separating them but two dividers on either side.

I hated this place.

"Yeah," I mumbled, unsure how to proceed after the feeling that seemed to pulse in the universe after her comment about God's love. "Y—yeah, I'm kind of terrified. My whole life is riding on it, so I don't really know what to think right now."

Emily's expression softened into a half-hearted smile.

"I wish I could bring you some of those caramel apples you loved so much," she said, obviously trying to lighten the mood.

I returned her unenthusiastic smile with a lifeless chuckle, my mouth watering with the memory. She'd made them when I spent Halloween with them. Bea and I dressed up as pirates. I had no idea someone so girly could've had such an obsession with Halloween.

"I wish you could too. The bailiff is giving me the stink eye though which means visit's over." I watched her carefully as she adjusted her position. Something in her expression made me wonder if she realized then the reality of her situation. I wanted to be with her rather than a dank jail cell. "Are you and Tom going to be in court tomorrow?"

She nodded. "Of course. We love you, Will. Good luck. And remember that God's aware of you and He loves you too."

The thought should've brought me comfort. Instead, it filled me with anxiety as the screen shut off and the bailiff led me back to my cell.

I knew it wasn't true. I was nothing to Him. Just a worthless prisoner blending into the background of a world He'd created. He didn't care about me. Who would?

SEVENTEEN

Bianca Wixom

Carefully, I slipped through the front door, squeezing it shut as slowly as possible in an effort to not draw attention to myself.

"You're late, Bianca."

A jolt of shock made me flinch and spin around, hands pressed to my heart. "Daddy," I gasped, genuinely frightened by his unexpected presence. He was mad. He didn't look mad, but he never used my formal name unless he was really upset.

Daddy sat on the couch still. Instead of the book he'd been reading before, however, he held the Bible between his separated knees. He leaned forward, resting his elbows on his knees and removing his glasses.

"You know," he began, casually flipping through its thin pages, crinkling in the otherwise silent house. I swallowed, knowing what was coming. "I was just reading in Ephesians. I came across some *interesting* passages I wanted to share with you."

I cringed. He was about to use scriptures against me. I hated when he did that.

"'*Children, obey your parents in the Lord, for this is right. Honour thy father and mother; which is the first commandment and promise. That it may be well with you.*' Of course, I'm paraphrasing a bit, but I think you understand my point."

I refrained from rolling my eyes. "What's the next line?" I asked, knowing exactly what came next.

"Irrelevant," he barked, anger flaring in his eyes for an instant as he snapped the Bible shut and slammed it on the side table.

I winced, shrinking against the door a bit. I hated when he yelled like that. His prosecutor's voice came out when he did that. I didn't like feeling afraid of him.

"'*And, ye fathers, provoke not your children to wrath: but bring them up in the nurture and admonition of the Lord,*'" I spat back at him. He used that scripture a lot and it often backfired. I didn't understand why he kept using it.

"Where were you, Bianca," he growled, standing to approach me.

"I told you, Daddy. I just went to the buffet, sat in front of the temple, and lost track of the time."

He softened a bit, his shoulders relaxing as he placed a hand on my forearm. "It's forty-five minutes past your curfew. You've never been that late before. I worry about you, Bea. I thought something had happened. I thought . . ."

I shook my head. "I'll be fine, Daddy. I appreciate your concern, but I'm almost twenty-four. I'll be fine."

He sighed, his brown eyes shutting as he pulled me in to kiss my forehead. Part of me thought of shrinking away from him, but that wouldn't be a good idea.

"I'm sorry I yelled at you, Honey Bea. You know I just worry, that's all."

I scoffed. "Yeah, I do. I appreciate the apology. But . . . I *am* an adult. I'm not sixteen going on my first dates anymore. I think I'm old enough to stay out at least a half-hour later than nine o'clock."

"Out of the question," he said sternly, shaking his head without a moment hesitation and letting go of me.

I sighed. "Why? If I'm out for FHE, I'm allowed to stay out until midnight."

"Because I know you're safe with Natalie, Isaac, and Matt. Anywhere else, I don't know."

That seemed ridiculous to me. It was half an hour. What could possibly happen in half an hour that wouldn't happen before nine o'clock? But, instead of arguing, I nodded. It was better to just agree than it was to argue with someone who literally did it for his profession.

"Yes, Daddy," I muttered, feeling like a ten-year-old again, complying with whatever he said just to avoid that disapproving grunt.

His expression relaxed into a smile as he brushed another kiss across my forehead.

"Go upstairs and get some sleep. You have school tomorrow."

Now I really feel like a kid again. I didn't go to school growing up, yet he'd say that to me every night regardless.

I sighed, giving him a swift hug before running silently up the stairs. Sometimes, I felt like I'd never grown up in his eyes. I'd always be a sweet little girl who looked to him for guidance in everything I did. I felt like he'd never see me as a grown woman, but a naïve girl whose innocence allowed him to bend me like a reed. And yet, at the same time, he wanted me to act older than I actually was. He expected me to play as Mom while they were away, but he didn't trust me to be out for a half-hour after a childish curfew. He wanted me to know how to act like an adult when he didn't really believe I could be. He wanted me to have obtained the same level of knowledge he had, without any sort of acknowledgment of my actual age.

I'd heard that a person's twenties were a time to make mistakes. It was a time to learn about yourself and what you really want out of your life. I never really had that choice, since he expected me to grow up too quickly while still wanting me to retain the innocence of a little child.

I shut and locked my bedroom door. At least he'd given me the privacy of a locked door in a house swarmed with siblings. I loved everyone in my family dearly, but sometimes it was nice to have a moment of peace among the chaos.

I loved him, but sometimes, when I'd stare at the canopy of organza over my bed at night, I wished God had given me a different father.

A knock came at my door. I opened my eyes, startled, but not necessarily surprised. When I unlocked my door and peered through, Julie stood with her favorite toy penguin tucked behind her back, bare feet curled around her pigeon toes, and pjs hugging her thin legs. She gazed up at me through her eyelashes, almost as thick as my own.

"Jules, are you okay?" I asked, opening the door all the way.

She didn't say anything before reaching out for me. I smiled half-heartedly and rested her against my hips as I shut the door. She cuddled her head into the crook of my neck, hugging my neck tightly.

"What's wrong?" I asked again, rubbing her back as I brought her to the bed. A mischievous grin stretched across my expression as I tossed her onto the bed. She erupted in a fit of giggles as I fell on the bed beside her, giving raspberries on her stomach in an effort to hear her laugh more. She did, rolling across my bed with a giggle that made my heart swell with joy inside me. I tickled her belly as she screeched a bellowing laugh.

I ran out of breath just watching as she threw her arms to the sides, gasping through laughter. I tucked my hair behind my ear with a wide grin.

"What're you doing in here so late, you should be in bed by now." I glanced at the clock. It was past ten.

She sighed, her laughter dying down pretty quickly. "How was your date?"

I froze. *How'd she know?*

"What date?" I asked, sitting on the side of my bed.

"The one you tried hiding from Daddy. Mommy was fighting with him again about your curfew," she explained, letting her legs dangle off the side of the mattress beside me.

I frowned. "Oh . . ."

"Plus, you don't get yourself all dolled up like that unless it's to impress some boy," she said, flinging one of my curls in the air and nearly knocking off my fedora.

"Hey," I cried, holding my hat tightly against my head and poking her stomach. She giggled again and covered the spot with her hands. "Does Daddy know it was a date?"

I dreaded the answer.

She shook her head. "Mommy knew though, I think. Daddy was just upset you were out so late."

I rolled my eyes, tucking my legs into my chest. "Ain't that the truth."

"So, who's the dude?" Julie asked, copying my position. I eyed her suspiciously, trying to gauge whether I could trust her or not. Her large, blue eyes gazed up at me with a curiosity I'd always admired in her. With a burst of affection for my little sister, I wrapped my arms around her and gathered her into a cuddle.

"You'll find out someday, I'm sure," I muttered. "But his name is Will."

EIGHTEEN
<u>William Markus</u>

People in the courtroom chattered, though it all seemed a bunch of nonsense to me. I overheard two women in the congregation. The one in a bright pink hat that seemed like it belonged in the nineteenth century and a plain, gray dress didn't seem to realize how loudly she voiced her opinions. The other stared at her with bug eyes that bulged from their sockets as if her eyes were simply too big for them to fit properly. She nodded so quickly at everything the woman with a poor fashion sense said I thought her head might pop off her neck.

"Just look at the way he's sitting," the pink-hat lady blabbered loud enough for everyone to hear, though she leaned over to bug-eyes as if it'd been for her ears only. The man seated next to her raised his eyebrows and glanced awkwardly around the room. "You can tell by the way he's staring at us that he's positively murderous."

I swallowed and blinked, realizing how intently I'd watched them, and faced forward again. How could I not stare at that unfortunate hat she wore? She should've been

used to it if she dressed that way on regular
occasions.

The seat beside me swiveled, startling
me enough to make me flinch. Smitty tossed
his briefcase onto the table in front of us,
causing a commotion that echoed through the
entire court when the chains holding it
together rattled like the shackles holding my
wrists together. The loud *thud* that proceeded
the chains silenced a few people behind us. I
cringed, subtly lowering myself into my seat.
Why hadn't I tried harder to get a *real* lawyer
instead of letting the state decide for me?

"You couldn't be quieter? We're trying
not to draw attention to ourselves here,
Gingerhead Man," I said as calmly as I could
through the anxiety rising into my chest like
lava from a volcano.

"Where's the fun in that?" Smitty
scoffed, waving a dismissive hand at me. He
fidgeted. So much fidgeting. Tugging on his
coat. Sniffing. Clearing his throat.
Tightening his bowtie then loosening it again.

Make it stop!

I let my head fall back against the chair.
"God, have mercy on me, just this once," I
moaned.

"What?" Smitty said, leaning toward me. I pulled away automatically. He just kept leaning until he practically laid his head on my shoulder.

"Nothing." I scooted farther away from him, tucking my clasped hands between my knees. "Got any extra neon ties or socks in that briefcase?" I asked snidely.

Smitty glanced at me, his bright blue eyes wide with questioning. "Why would I do that? I'm already wearing 'em." He pulled up his brown pant leg to expose blinding yellow, knee-high socks with purple polka dots scattered on them. At least they matched his bowtie and suspenders. The spots seemed unintentional and uneven. Like he'd gotten into a paintball war and lost.

The image of throwing paintballs at that clown of a man almost cracked me up. I would've at least smiled if I hadn't wanted to cry.

I shrunk into my chair, facepalming. Why did God give me such a hopeless defender? Why did He hate me so much? I could almost hear Him laughing at me.

"All rise for the honorable judge," the bailiff announced.

A general sound of bodies shifting echoed the courtroom as everyone from the congregation to the prosecutor stood and sat back down after the judge entered.

Opening statements drug on after that. If I were honest, all the legal jargon went over my head. I didn't pay that close attention until I was called onto the stand.

The prosecutor was a thin woman with short hair that spiked to one side, streaks of red amongst the piney, brown hairstyle. Her navy blazer looked smooth and professional, especially in comparison to Smitty's. She wore too much eyeshadow, making her appear like a raccoon got ahold of her makeup and tried to paint a self-portrait on her face.

"Mr. Markus, where were you the night of December 20th?" she asked, her voice booming through the courtroom.

I hesitated, shifting my eyes and trying to remember the significance of that date. Was I losing my memory? After being in the jail where any sense of time disappeared into the empty void of a windowless building, it was difficult to keep track of dates or time.

All at once, I realized that was the night Bea was shot. Five days before Christmas. We'd planned to announce our engagement

Christmas morning. Instead, I spent my holiday in the stony lonesome and on a courtroom stand.

"I was . . . at the Grand Sierra Resort and Casino."

"Who were you with?"

That seemed like a dumb question. She knew I was there when Bea was shot, right?

"Bianca Wixom. I'd proposed to her that night during a skiing trip with friends and we were out celebrating."

The prosecutor nodded. "Did anyone else know about this?"

I hadn't really thought of that before. It crossed my mind enough to feel a little bad for excluding Isaac like I did, but other than that. . .

"No," I said indecisively. The skeptical twitch of her eyes made me second guess myself. Suddenly, the collar of my shirt choked me. "I mean, a few people knew I was proposing to her, but no one was there with me."

"Had you talked to anyone about it afterward? Friends? Family?"

I shook my head. "We went straight to the buffet. If she told anyone, I didn't know about it."

"What did she say to your proposal?" she asked.

"Objection!" Smitty slammed his fist onto the desk, causing most in the room to flinch. "My client has already stated that they were celebrating. If they were celebrating, doesn't that imply that the answer was yes?"

I paused, staring at him in surprise for being so quick to respond. The judge sustained his objection passively, smacking her lips together like she was trying not to yawn.

"But then where's your proof, Mr. Edwards?" the prosecutor asked, folding her arms with raised eyebrows.

Smitty smirked. "Miss Bianca's finger, of course. Officials did say there was an antique ring on the victim's left ring finger at the time of death. They confirmed that this particular ring was, in fact, Miss Bianca's grandmother's ring."

"Through what source?"

"Emily and Thomas Wixom themselves." Smitty gestured toward them in the congregation. I tried not to make eye contact.

"Ah, yes, *that* ring. The one that, when taken to a local pawn shop downtown, had an estimated value of nearly ten thousand dollars." The prosecutor turned back to me, her grin conniving. I swallowed, leaning nervously against the witness stand. "Mr. Markus, you could've really used that money, couldn't you? What if you staged the proposal just to make yourself look good for the public when you were accused of the *murder*?"

My jaw dropped as I gaped at her in disbelief. "No, I would've never—" I interjected, trying to understand what was even happening. Everything happened too fast. I felt crammed in the middle of two political debates that quickly turned into a riot over something stupid. Both sides made sense in an illogical way that demonized the other. My brain wasn't prepared to piece it together yet. I was still back at the beginning.

"You were so desperate to get that money in your hands that you were willing to *kill* the girl you professed to love. But I question whether you ever really loved her at all." She turned her back to me to face the congregation as her voice escalated with passion.

"What?" I snapped.

"Mr. Markus," she said, spinning toward me again. "It's common knowledge that the victim, in this case, has very strong religious views, correct?"

I hated hearing her referred to as 'the victim.' She was a person, not a case.

"Yes," I spat, irritation and confusion raving in my stomach.

"Is it also true that her father disapproved of this engagement?"

I glanced involuntarily at Tom who scowled my way with fire in his eyes.

"Yes."

"And yet you did it anyway. Even though it would go against everything he'd dreamed of for his daughter and it would mean that she couldn't be tied to you beyond the grave?"

"Objection," Smitty cried.

"Overruled," the judge replied as she leaned forward with renewed interest.

The prosecutor smirked cockily. And I realized just how much I hated her.

"Answer my question, William. Did you go against her father's wishes and propose to his daughter anyway?"

I swallowed, trying to figure out how to answer the question in a way that didn't incriminate me. My eyes darted to Smitty who shook his head.

"I . . . yes, but—"

"And you crushed her aspiration with this selfish desire to marry someone who you knew you could never truly provide everything for, in turn crushing the lifelong dream of getting married in what she believed to be a temple of *God*."

"No," I shouted.

"You staged the proposal so you could get her alone and away from any witnesses, didn't you? You tried to get the ring off her finger but by then, it was already too late, wasn't it? That's when you decided to run. But let me tell you something, Mr. Markus, you'll never be able to truly run from the guilt inside you."

My palms felt sweaty. My body felt numb. If I had to endure one more minute of this. . .

"Furthermore, you say there was someone else there, but that's awfully convenient considering that Officer Morrison is an eye witness to the fact that no one else was around the scene of the crime."

"I did see someone else there."

"Really? You must've seen this so-called 'murderer,' so why not tell us what he or she looked like?"

"No, I didn't get a clear vision of the face, but I know someone else was there."

"How can you prove it?"

"I don't know. I don't know anything anymore. I don't remember anything clearly enough to tell you. All I remember is shooting the gun and running."

"Then how do you know you didn't do it?"

I hesitated, repeating her question in my mind until my temples throbbed. Maybe I wasn't as innocent as I thought.

NINETEEN
Bianca Wixom

My phone vibrated against my thigh. Mortified, I pressed my hand against it to hide it from Professor Workman who lectured at the front of the class.

"Stupid—" I breathed, desperately trying to find the lock button through my pant leg. It seemed like the more I tried to find it, the harder it was to locate.

Natalie looked at me with raised eyebrows, an amused smile on her face. "You okay?" she asked quietly, resting her pencil against her chin as she watched me.

"Why now?" I snapped in a hushed whisper. Slipping it from my pocket just enough to see the screen, I blushed. Will's name appeared above the two phone shaped lights flashing on the screen, one red and the other green. It'd been a week or two since our first date though we'd talked at least once nearly every day. He must've forgotten I had school on the days I wasn't babysitting or volunteering.

I sighed, rejecting his call for now. I didn't want to get in trouble because of him again.

It vibrated a few minutes later, implying he'd left a voicemail.

The whole rest of the class, I resisted the urge to look at my phone. The image of his name flashing across my screen left me wanting to blush and giggle. I couldn't do that, though. If I did, I'd get into trouble again. My eyes darted to the clock every few minutes.

I hope he doesn't think I'm ignoring him.

That was the last thing I wanted him to think. I bit my lip, shaking my head of the thought and forcefully leaning over the assignment in front of me. My attempts were futile, however. The more I tried to focus on the notes I'd written, the more I thought of his smile. His laugh chimed in my memory and I caught myself grinning from ear-to-ear with the realization that he'd called me probably the first opportunity he got.

Finally, the class ended. I threw my books together, hoisted my bag over my shoulder, and headed straight for the door.

"Hold on, Bea," Natalie called after me. I stopped, forgetting about her. "Where are you off to in such a hurry? Who called you?"

I flipped my hair from my eyes, facing her with an air of casualty, though I still had to bite down on my growing smile. I was used to Natalie wanting to know all about personal stuff. She was the master at gossip. I looked at her bouncy, platinum curls and thought of how many times Isaac and Matt referred to her hair as a storage bin for other's personal business.

"What do you mean?" I asked, touching my own curls in hopes of seeming relaxed. Instead, it probably just made it seem like I was hiding something. Part of me wanted her to drop the subject before it even really started. Another part wanted to be the giddy, girly-girl I'd been around her before, gushing about cute boys. I fidgeted, my fingers itching to call him back, text him, do *something*. I couldn't around her though. She'd read over my shoulder and pretend it was an accident.

"Come on," she teased, giving me a knowing look as she lightly slapped my arm with the back of her hand. "I know that giddy look in a girl's eyes anywhere. What's his name?"

I sighed, pulling out my phone.

"What're you talking about?"

She wouldn't like me talking to Will. I knew her opinion of him. That couldn't have changed in such a short amount of time, especially without having really talked to him like I had. She was a bit too judgmental to really give him a chance . . . unless she knew I cared about him. Then she'd *try* to be supportive through her little 'subtle' jabs. Ultimately, however, the fact of the matter was, she had a hunch and wouldn't be persuaded otherwise. I did care about Will, but that wouldn't have been enough to earn her approval.

"Bea, I've known you since we were sixteen. You're not fooling me. Unless it's just Matt or Isaac," she said passively. "Then I don't really care."

I grinned, seeing a loophole in our closest friends. Nodding, I shrugged innocently. "Yeah, Matt just wanted to know if my dad would let me go shooting this weekend."

It was an activity they'd already invited me to, but Natalie didn't need to know that.

"Are you going with us then?" she asked, excitement rising in her voice.

I laughed at the thought. "No way Daddy would want me anywhere near a gun."

"But it's with us," she argued. "He loves us. We could commit murder and he'd still practically worship the ground we walk on."

I laughed at the extreme sentiment. "That escalated quickly. Murder?"

She shrugged. "First thing that came to mind."

Interesting mind you got there, Natalie.

"Anyway," she continued. "You seem a bit too excited for it to just be Matt inviting you to hang out with us. It's that Markus guy, isn't it?"

"No, it was just Matt," I lied, my heart skipping a beat. I didn't like lying, but it seemed like the only way to protect from criticism and unwelcomed opinions.

She blew a bubble from the gum chomping between her teeth. "I'm bored now," she stated, blowing a kiss and walking away. "See you later, Bea."

I chuckled, shaking my head. That was definitely Natalie's personality. If there wasn't gossip involved in a conversation, she lost interest way too quickly. I didn't understand why she thought she'd get much enjoyment out of my friendship.

Grateful she'd left the conversation, I yanked my phone from my pocket, dialing his number and flinging my hair from my eyes as I held the phone to my ear.

As the phone rang, I tried to calm my heart rate by breathing slower. It didn't work. He didn't answer until the fifth ring.

"Hey, Will," I greeted warmly, my voice embarrassingly enthusiastic. I cleared my throat and sheepishly tucked my hair behind my ear. "Sorry I missed your call, I was in class. What's up?"

I could hear the smile in his voice when he answered. "Oh, I didn't know . . . uh . . . I just wanted to know if you'd want some lunch, but my hour's almost up now. I'm heading back to the mechanics."

My heart sunk with disappointment. Someone called to him and he pulled the phone away, shouting something back at them about the radiator in a Civic.

"Sorry I missed you," I muttered, a mischievous idea coming to me. "Where would we have gone?"

"I was thinking of ordering out a Pirate's Pizza."

Just hearing the name of that restaurant made my mouth water. "Oh, my gosh, now I'm *really* sorry I missed out."

He laughed and I found myself unable to fight my smile hearing it. He had a refreshing and infectious laugh that was as genuine as his smile. The thought of both made my heart leap into my throat.

"*That's* why you're sorry?"

I laughed, watching my feet as I made my way through the university's campus toward my next class. "Well, at least I know you'd be worth more of my time, with a taste like that."

I heard the surprise in his voice. "So, what would you have done if I'd suggested something else?"

"Probably dumped you on the spot," I teased.

His hearty laugh burst through the phone as noise accumulated in the background. Someone spoke to him on the other side.

"That car has to be made out of five other cars," he muttered. I laughed at the image. "Anyway, I'm glad I didn't make the mistake of picking something else then. You free again sometime to grab some of this life-altering pizza?"

I approached the English department, slowing at the door. "You sound like you're at the shop now, I better let you go."

"Wait," he cried. "You can't leave me hanging there."

"What's your shop called, anyway?" I asked, an idea coming to me.

"Bill's Mechanics." He hesitated. "I know, it's so original. My father was *not* a clever man. He enjoyed two things in life, liquor and buttering people up for a letdown."

I smiled, grateful for him sharing a bit more on his father. I wasn't sure if he'd fully realized how much he'd said, considering he spoke quickly around me without much forethought.

"He sounds like an interesting man. I'd love to meet him." I leaned against the brick wall of the English department, hoping to get a little more out of him.

His tone changed slightly. Sadder and almost regretful. "Yeah, that won't happen."

"Why the certainty?"

You don't think we'll get that far?

My heart sank a little at the prospect. I wanted to keep seeing him.

He sighed, reluctance evident in his hesitation. "It's just . . . Not important."

"Oh." Clearly, we'd reached a point where he wasn't willing to share any more information. We'd hit a wall he didn't want to break down just yet. Part of me felt relieved at that. "Bye, Will," I said, mischief gleaming inside me like the sun. "Hope you saved room for pizza."

TWENTY
<u>William Markus</u>

For the first time, the scowling eyes in the courtroom sunk into my skin. The prosecutor's accusations felt like a dagger ripped into my chest. I clenched my hands into fists, trying to see if any feeling still remained. The harder I squeezed, however, the more unfeeling my body became. I stared at a spot of wood on the courtroom floor. Breathing through my mouth, I hoped to drown out the demons shouting accusations at me from every corner of my thoughts. I'd been interrogated about that night for so long, I didn't know how to believe anything anymore. I couldn't feel anything. Desperately, I searched the numberless faces surrounding me from the stand. All of them seemed to be glaring in my direction.

I looked into the eyes of her parents. Emily's eyes were wet with tears of mourning. Tom sat with an expectant and hateful glare that made me feel three inches tall. Now, however, I deserved to feel that way.

I faced the prosecutor with a reluctant sigh. I couldn't handle it anymore. "I don't even know what my intentions were that night anymore. I hardly feel like I can keep anything straight anymore. The only thing I remember is shooting the gun and running. I didn't even realize I'd punched Officer Morrison in the face until the damage was already done."

I turned my attention to Emily and Tom again. They were the only real family I'd ever known. Even if Tom never approved of me, he still was more of a father to me than my own ever was. He cared about me in his own, weird way. And I'd hurt them beyond belief.

"Tom, Emily . . ." I began. "I loved your daughter. I wish I could bring her back to you. But I know I can't. I know it's because I wasn't there to protect her that she's not here today. It *is* my fault." The words didn't feel like my own. They were borrowed. Used. Stale as I felt. "It's my fault. I did it, alright? I'm guilty of the murder of Bianca Wixom. The gun was mine. Just *please,* make it stop. Get me out of here. I'm begging you, please. I'd rather rot in jail than have to face this anymore and relive that night."

A general gasp swept over the courtroom, but the only person in that room I cared to see, however, was Emily staring at me with a hand pressed over her mouth in an effort to fight sobs. With that distraught expression, I felt like I may as well have murdered her too. She'd been nothing but kind to me since the moment we met. She'd invited me into her home as if I were part of her family. I had betrayed her. She didn't deserve to mourn the loss of her beloved daughter . . . especially on account of my reckless and thoughtless behavior.

"William Markus, you are found guilty of the murder of Bianca Wixom. Convicted to twenty-five years to life in prison. Case closed. Take him away."

The judge's words faded into the background as bailiffs cuffed my arms behind my back once again.

Tears streamed from Emily's eyes as she gazed at me with heartbreak as pure as I'd ever witnessed. Tom gathered her to his chest, holding her as she sobbed. The last thing I heard before being shoved off the stand, hands cuffed, was the sound of the only true mother figure I'd ever had screaming in agony, asking why such a thing could happen to her baby girl.

She left, stumbling past Tom and out of the courtroom. Tom glared at me, his eyes as dark and murderous as if he'd enjoy wringing my neck himself.

I didn't care what happened to me after that. I couldn't do anything worse than what I'd done to destroy such a beautiful family.

"Objection!" Smitty slammed his hands on the table, commanding the attention of everyone in the courtroom. "What makes you think he's in his right mind? He's just been prodded about his fiancée's murder, for Bryce sake. I'm not done here and neither is he. He cleared his throat way too loudly as he stood, continuing to adjust that stupid blazer of his. I sat in dumbfounded silence, trying to figure out what'd just happened.

"I demand a cross-examination."

"On what grounds?" the judge sighed.

"My client just professed false guilt, Your Honor. But if you'll allow me, I can still prove that he is undeserving of such a harsh sentence for a crime he did not commit. Please, Your Honor, just let me . . ."

The judge glared at him with a reluctant sigh like she didn't want to be there anymore. "What kind of witness do you have to prove this man's innocence, Mr. Edwards?"

Smitty stumbled over words. Everyone watched him.

Please just let them take me, Smitty.

He made eye contact with me and smiled, nodding once in a reassuring gesture.

"As a matter of fact, when my client said there was another person at the crime scene, he wasn't lying. I can prove it. There are other suspects in this case if you're willing to let me show you."

The judge and prosecutor shared a look, though I couldn't decide what that skeptically lifted, pencil eyebrow on the prosecutor's face indicated. Fear? Determination?

I just want to be done with this.

"Very well," the judge said, pounding her gavel.

I stared, dumbfounded, as the judge suspended my sentence and sat me back on the witness stand.

Smitty sighed, obviously relieved, and thanked the judge before approaching me.

"Will, where were you when Miss Bianca was shot? In proximity to her?" Smitty asked.

I had to think hard for a minute before a flash of memory popped behind my eyelids. "She was looking out at the bay and I was behind her by the open car door." My eyes caught the gaze of the prosecutor who raised a cocky, knowing eyebrow at me as if to say, *'Don't remember anything, huh?'*

I swallowed.

Smitty nodded thoughtfully, taking his necktie and twirling it like a baton as he paced the courtroom. "Now, *that* is interesting, because, from the evidence found in the autopsy report, Miss Bianca was shot from the *front*. In her chest." He pointed to his own, jabbing his finger into his broad, somewhat plump, pectoral. "Now tell me, good people," he continued, turning to the jury. "How would such a thing be possible if my friend Will here was *behind* her at the time she was shot?"

He pursed his thin lips, shrugging as he casually walked the perimeter of the room, finally leaning a hand against the defendant desk and facing me.

I blinked in surprise. I didn't think he'd ever say something that actually made sense.

"Unless he had some sort of superpower where he could somehow freeze time and shoot her from the front—which would be pretty cool if you think about it—then it is virtually *impossible* for my client to have shot this wonderful young lady point-blank. Now—"

I sat up straighter as he approached.

"What were you doing with Miss Bianca that night at GSR?"

I hesitated. Hadn't I already answered that question?

"I'd asked her to marry me that night. We were celebrating."

"Where did you propose that night, if not at the GSR?"

"In the mountains during a skiing trip with our friends."

"And did you have anyone else involved in this plan, Willy?"

I hate when you call me that. "Yes. One of our best friends, Isaac."

"So, he knew you were going to propose?"

That goes without saying, doesn't it?

"Yeah, he did. Pretty much everyone did. They'd been trying to convince me to do it for months."

A sly grin slashed across his face for an instant as he tapped his index finger and thumb together. "One more question for you, buddy."

He paused, placing his fingertips on the stand in front of me and leaning in far too close. "Did you love her?"

For some reason, that question struck me deeper than it ever had before. In an instant, I saw our entire relationship pan out. All the beautiful moments we'd shared. How much she'd taught me, showed me. I remembered what it was like to hold her, the warmth of her body against mine. I remembered what it was like to kiss her. How, even when we fought, she was still kind and considerate of me. She understood me on a level no one ever dared try before.

My jaw set as I swallowed the emotion rising into my eyes. "Yes."

Smitty smiled. Something shifted in his eyes at that moment. He seemed to understand on a personal level what that word uttered through my teeth meant, the weight it carried with it.

"And did you kill her?"

The question startled me. I thought he was supposed to be defending me.

I shook my head. "No. I did not kill my fiancée."

"Ladies and gentlemen, Your Honor, and everyone else," he shouted, flipping around on his toes toward the congregation. He reminded me of a ballerina. "I'm sure you can hear in this young man's voice the depth of his affection for our leading lady. It's raw and heartfelt. He's clearly *shattered* over this. Do you really think that someone who cared for her this deeply would kill her in cold-blooded murder?"

The room was silent. So silent, I felt like the whole court heard me swallow. Smitty's brown shoes clicked across the floor as he paced the perimeter, facing his head toward the ground as he let the quietness continue.

"No more questions, Your Honor."

TWENTY-ONE
Bianca Wixom

"Isaac," I called, entering Bill's Mechanics, holding onto the pizza box tightly with one hand as I waved him down. His hand hovered over the doorknob of what looked like an office when he turned around.

He squinted at me for a second before his eyes lit up. "BB," he screeched jovially as he gabbed and spun me off the ground as usual.

I laughed, trying to hold the pizza upright. When he put me down, his eyes flashed toward the pizza box and he inhaled deeply, closing his eyes with a loud sigh.

"You brought Pirate's?" he asked, shaking his head through a shudder. I nodded. "Aw, you shouldn't have." He lifted the lid. Immediately, its delicious aroma wafted into the air, making my taste buds thirsty for it. Slapping his wrists, I yanked it away from him and snapped it shut.

"Hey, paws off, dude," I snapped with a snide grin. He met my eyes, confused and a little hurt before his expression melted into mischief. I could almost see the wheels turning in his brain as he gave me a knowing look, nodding his head slowly.

"Oh, I get it . . . You got this for—"

"Hold on," I snapped playfully, trying to avoid the subject of Will and me. "You work here?"

Since when?

He nodded, straightening his spine and saluting me with a hand dirtied with oil. "Yes, ma'am. I've been Will's assistant for months now. I practically manage this place when he's in that office of his."

I grinned at the thought. It still seemed strange to think of Will owning a mechanic's shop. He seemed too young and creative to do something so menial and professional. Still, it impressed me.

"Where is he?"

"Oh, I get it," Isaac teased, nodding slowly with a knowing look as he blinked rapidly. "The pizza's a peace treaty."

"What?"

"Don't try hiding it, Bea. I'm not blind. You missed a date with Will and now you're kissin' up to the boss. Well, I don't think so, Missy. That's *my* job."

I laughed at his silliness as he bopped the tip of my nose. "What're you talking about?"

"He skipped lunch today hoping you'd eat with him." He jerked his head toward the door with 'William Markus, Owner," written on a golden plaque across the top.

I smiled at the idea of Will wanting to see me. "And how would you know this?"

He guffawed. "I'm his best friend, Bea. He tells me everything."

Narrowing my eyes at him, I leaned into my hip. "Uh-huh. And what else has he told you?"

He wagged a finger, clicking his tongue, and leering at me as he bowed deeply. "Confidentiality is key here, Miss Bianca. I'm sworn to secrecy."

I shook my head at him, shoving his shoulder with a playful nudge. "Isaac, that's not fair."

With a smug grin, he slapped his knuckled on the door and opened it before Will could respond. When he let the door fling open, I entered.

"Got a delivery for ya, boss. Also, the last customer's taken care of. Insurance accepted his claim on that replacement radiator. Should I start closing now?"

Will looked up, his ear plastered to a corded phone the length of his face. His eyes lit up when he saw me and he grinned broadly, mouthing a greeting before pressing the phone between his jaw and shoulder as he typed on the computer in front of him.

"Yes, ma'am, we'll see you tomorrow then. Have a good evening," he said quickly before plopping the phone against the receiver and standing from his oak desk.

"Did you hear me, Will?" Isaac asked, a hint of irritation in his tone.

Will nodded at Isaac once, his eyes only leaving me for a second. "Yeah. Thanks, man," he said dismissively, either distracted by me or generally disinterested. I couldn't quite tell.

Isaac pressed his lips together. "Have fun," he mumbled before shutting the door.

"What're you doing here?" Will asked, approaching me with a deep inhale.

I grinned, presenting the pizza to him by opening the lid. "Surprise."

He sighed deeply, his knees seeming suddenly weak as he grabbed ahold of my elbows and bowed his head. "You are a saint. I had half a sandwich for lunch."

My jaw dropped as I remembered Isaac saying Will skipped lunch altogether. "No wonder you sounded so ravenous earlier. I thought you'd keel over at any second."

He stood straight again, his expression confused. "Really?"

I laughed. "Oh yeah, I knew I'd have to save you."

He glanced at the pizza then back at me with a perplexed raise of his eyebrow. "It's just for me?"

My cheeks flared with heat and my eyes darted across the room in an effort to avoid contact with his.

"You were the one who suggested grabbing lunch. I just saved you the trouble."

"You're eating this with me, aren't you?" he asked, his eyes glinting with a smile.

I shrugged and a crash came from outside. I flinched, though Will hardly seemed to notice. Suddenly, all I could think of was Isaac's face as he left, annoyed and slightly hurt.

"I probably should go," I said slowly, feeling a little self-conscious of Isaac outside.

Will followed me as I headed for the door, his concerned eyes meeting me with urgency. My chest burned when he grasped my hand as if in a panic and taking my hand was the first thing he thought to do. I stared at his fingers intertwined with mine and my breathing hastened. His fingers were warm and course. Safe and dangerous all at once.

"No, don't go . . ." he muttered, his tone unexpectedly soft and affectionate.

I lifted my eyes to his. My focus wandered to his mouth as it twitched into a saddened smile, one side lifting higher than the other. At that moment, we crossed into unknown territory. He pulled me a bit closer. I felt his heartbeat quicken in his wrist as his hand glided toward my elbow.

The warm sensation of his skin sent chills up my arm. I relished in it for a minute before meeting his gaze. My fingers curled around his forearm. His muscles tensed beneath my touch and I felt goosebumps rising to the surface of his skin. I watched him carefully as he gently pulled me closer.

"Don't go," he breathed, his voice low.

My heart thudded recklessly against my ribs, sending jolts of excitement through my body. My head spun, though I felt completely in control.

He brushed my hair off my forehead, his fingers stroking my jawline before tucking below my chin. My heart throbbed as he swiftly leaned forward, tilting my head as he aimed a kiss at my cheek.

I stared, dumbfounded, as a jumbled mess of incomprehensible words staggered from my lips in a sound between a giggle and sigh. He chuckled, his cheeks glowing a fleshy pink before his eyes wandered to my lips.

The world blurred around me and my eyelids fluttered in an effort to stabilize my vision again. I certainly hadn't expected my visit to turn out this way. But I loved it.

Three rapid knocks sounded at the door to Will's office before it flew open. I gasped, instinctively stepping away from him as soon as I saw Isaac.

"Oh," he mumbled. "I'm apparently interrupting a moment, sorry."

Awkwardly, I bowed my head, touching my hair more than necessary as I turned my back on him, my cheeks hot with embarrassment. Will breathed a nervous laugh and slowly let his hands fall to his sides.

"It's fine," he said. "What is it?"

Isaac ran greasy fingers through his cropped, black hair. "It's closing, Will. I've already finished everything. You stayed past hours and everyone else has already clocked out."

Will's eyes widened and he turned toward the digital clock on his desk, swearing under his breath. Grabbing the pizza, he urged us out of his office as he stepped out and locked the door.

Mortified by the look on Isaac's face, I ducked my head and went back to my car. Will sprinted after me.

"Bea," he called.

I turned, glancing at his belt loop where his keys were absent. "You need to lock up," I said.

"Isaac knows what to do."

"You left the keys with him?"

You must really trust him.

He shrugged. "When can I see you again?"

I hesitated, unsure how to answer the question. I wished I didn't have to say goodbye, but how could we. . .

Mom and Daddy wouldn't be home for another couple of hours. It couldn't hurt.

"Unless something unexpected happens, I'm babysitting tonight. My parents usually go out on Fridays. If you don't mind meeting my siblings, we could have a movie night at my house," I suggested.

What was I saying? I was bringing him right into the belly of the beast. Daddy would kill me, then him, then me again just to make a point. I hesitated at that thought, almost laughing at how ridiculous it sounded. Daddy hardly ever went into the theatre room anyway. He wouldn't suspect Will if I drove and we were with my brothers and sisters.

Will's eyes shifted suspiciously. "What happens when your parents come home?"

"You'll be fine, they won't be home for a while. Meet me at the temple and I'll drive."

He grinned, taking my hand for an instant and squeezing firmly. "Drive safe."

✳✳✳✳

"You're gonna be fine, Will," I said, slipping my hand into his as I walked him up the steps to my front door.

I doubted that sentiment myself, but couldn't help it. I wanted to spend time with him and trying to arrange anything around my schedule was nearly impossible.

Once Will and I crossed the threshold of holding hands, it felt as natural as breathing. I found myself missing the security of his hand encompassing mine when he wasn't there.

"Daddy shouldn't be home for another hour. He's the only one you should be afraid of."

The nervousness in his countenance grew intensely as muscles in his jaw jumped. "Afraid of? You mean I have a reason to be this scared?"

I sighed, squeezing his hand again. "You'll be fine. They'll think I'm just babysitting."

Opening the door, I was swarmed by Julia as always, squeezing me so tightly I gasped for air. "Bea," she screamed, her face nuzzled into my stomach.

I laughed and pried her off me with a kiss on the forehead.

"You brought pizza," she shrieked, jumping up and down before thrusting it from my grasp and running to the kitchen.

"Good thing we ate some in the car," I retorted mostly to myself.

Will stood behind me in the doorway, keeping his distance just in case. His fingers gently brushed across my back, jolting excitement through my system as I took his hand again and slowly led him into the house. I looked back as he gawked at our front room with pure amazement.

Liana meandered down the stairs, her phone in hand.

"You watched them while I was gone, didn't you, Liana?" I asked cautiously. The dazed look in her eyes screamed indifference until she looked up. She flipped her blonde hair over her shoulder and leaned against the railing.

"Yeah, yeah . . . Who's the guy, Bea? You know you're not supposed to have guys over here while Dad's not home. He's gonna be mad when he finds out," she said casually, raising her eyebrows as her focus wandered back to her cell phone.

"He's just here to help me watch Cannon and Julia, sis," I sighed, growing a bit irritated at my sister's snarky tone.

"Oh, look," she said, flashing her phone screen at me, Daddy's name across her messages. "It's Dad wanting to know how things are going."

"Liana," I snapped.

"What're you gonna pay me?" she bribed.

I moaned. "Twenty and a free movie."

"Which one?"

"Your choice of Disney?"

"Done." Her blue eyes brightened with elation as she slid down the banister, sprinting to the basement with Julia who raced after her, pizza box in hand. I laughed, towing Will behind me.

When we reached the theatre in our basement, Will stopped in the doorway, leaning against the frame as if his knees went weak.

"Holy mother of—" he muttered. I flinched, hoping he wouldn't swear in front of my little sisters and brother. He didn't, thankfully.

My siblings sprawled across the brown, microfiber sectional, fighting over who got the LoveSac.

I pulled down the projector screen, looking at Will with amusement. He slowly approached the couch, his fingers brushing across the back of it longingly as if he wandered through a dream.

"What?" I asked.

"I've just . . . never been in such a big and beautiful house before. What did you say your dad does again?" he muttered.

I laughed. "He's a prosecutor for the state and Mom's a landscape designer. They're incredibly generous with donations to the Church and the Lord has definitely blessed us for it."

"No kidding," Will mumbled.

"Okay, Liana," I said. She sprang up from the cushion and began rummaging through the Disney movies, eventually picking *Lady and the Tramp* and setting it up.

"Why this one, Liana?" I asked, a little embarrassed that she'd picked a romance.

She winked at me. "Set the *mood*."

I rolled my eyes.

"So, this is considered babysitting?" Will asked, hands in his pockets as he approached me. I leaned my backside against the couch, folding my arms as he came closer. His smile was relaxed as he gazed at me, eventually leaning against the couch beside me. Our arms brushed against each other, making my heart flutter.

"Yeah, I get paid to watch movies with my family," I bragged as the Walt Disney

Studios logo boomed across the screen, panning out to show the castle and fireworks.

"So, you're Will, right?" Julia asked, leaning her head against her palm. I blushed, realizing I'd told her his name the night of our first date.

He nodded. "Yup. You're Julia, right?"

She narrowed her eyes at him. "Have you ever killed anyone?"

I stared at my sister, silently ordering her to shut up and not ask questions like that.

Will blinked, hesitating before clearing his throat and kneeling before her. "You know, between you and me, I'm completely harmless. But don't tell the people at my agency. They won't like it."

I chuckled. *His agency?*

Julia's expression gleamed with sudden interest as she sat back, a dazzled look in eyes. She clearly believed him. He nodded, raising his eyebrows in mock seriousness.

"The agency doesn't know that I've never actually killed anyone, so it has to be kept top secret. Can I trust you with that?" he asked, watching my sister carefully as if gauging her trustworthiness. She leaned in with rapt attention, nodding enthusiastically.

"What does the agency do?" she whispered, cupping her hands around her mouth as she spoke in his ear too loudly.

He glanced around the room as if for eavesdroppers, his eyes meeting mine enough for him to wink at me. I smiled, enjoying the interaction. Something about seeing him act this way melted my insides with joy. He was good with her which was a trait I hadn't quite found before.

"They gather information on vehicles and confiscate them long enough to turn them into time machines. I'm their leader. No one else knows about this though. Not even Bea. So, you see, Julia, you're the chosen one."

I snorted with laughter, covering it up with a cough. Cannon popped in, having eavesdropped the entire conversation.

"That's not true," he bellowed. I hushed him immediately as Liana shot him an annoyed glare. "Time travel isn't possible because time is only something that some dude made up to trick us into thinking we're late all the time. I learned it in Sunday School last week."

Will's eyebrows pulled together, bewilderment and confusion evident in his eyes when he looked up at me. "Umm . . . Okay?"

I smiled at Cannon's misunderstanding. "What Brother Madsen was referring to, Cannon, is the scripture about how God is one eternal round, meaning that time doesn't mean to Him what it does to us."

"Oh . . ." Cannon muttered thoughtfully. "But time travel is still impossible."

"Cannon, *stop*, Will's not supposed to tell anyone but *me*," Julia whined, pushing Cannon's shoulder.

"You guys are missing the movie," I observed, trying to divert their attention away from Will. He laughed, a refreshing sound that sang in my ears, as he stood and let his head shake.

"It's okay, Julia. He can keep a secret, right?" Will grinned at Cannon who grunted and flipped in his seat toward the screen.

Will whispered in my ear, "I don't think he can."

I laughed until the door to the basement opened, Daddy's silhouette easily distinguishable in the now ominous flashing lights of the movie.

TWENTY-TWO
William Markus

"Defense calls Matt Young to the stand, Your Honor," Smitty announced, pronouncing the words too loudly.

As Matt approached the stand, he seemed nervous, though I would've expected it of him. He was quiet around strangers like me and did terrible under pressure. Once, he'd been under so much pressure to do well on a test, his blood pressure got so high he passed out and was nearly hospitalized. I wondered if they knew about that as he placed his hand on the Bible and vowed, he'd tell nothing but the whole truth.

I feared for him as perspiration formed on his dark forehead and his breath hastened.

"Mr. Young, where were you the night of December 20th?" Smitty asked. I'd heard that question so many times it went in one ear and out the other.

"In the mountains of Lake Tahoe for a little skiing trip," Matt answered, his eyes flashing toward me for an instant before he straightened his spine.

"Who was with you, exactly?"

"Well . . . Isaac Petersen, Natalie Bowmen, and—" His voice cut short and he swallowed, gesturing vaguely to me.

My brow creased. Did he have a hard time saying her name too?

"Were Miss Bianca and my client with you?" Smitty asked, sympathy in his tone.

Matt hesitated then shook his head. "They disappeared and didn't tell us where they went. Next thing I knew, I was getting calls from police askin' me to testify against Will's character. I couldn't do that though. He's one of my best friends."

My thoughts wandered after that. Hearing him speak only brought back memories too painful to relive. He was one of my best friends, but that didn't stop him from saying he would testify against me.

"About what time did you notice that Miss Bianca and Will were missing?" Smitty sniffed, pacing in front of the witness stand.

Matt shrugged, leaning back against his chair. "It was right around the time we were gonna head back home. So, maybe eight-thirty. We looked for 'em, but they had a tendency to disappear from the group. Isaac left early too, but he said that was because he was supposed to meet Will and Bea at the GSR to take pictures of Will proposing."

"How did he feel about taking those pictures?"

"I don't know, he was acting kind of weird. Well, weirder than usual. Talkin' to himself, going into corners by himself. . . Weird stuff."

"Objection," Prosecutor Brown shouted.

I glanced at her, disinterested. What could she possibly have to say now?

"What relevance does this serve? We're here to talk about Mr. Markus, not his friend."

"Overruled," the judge said. "Mr. Edwards, do you have a motive for this line of questioning?"

Matt's hands trembled as he scratched the back of his balding scalp that glinted in the light above him.

"Indeed, I do, Your Honor," he said, turning on his heels toward the congregation. "The way I see it," he shouted suddenly, making me flinch from the interruption of his moment's hesitation. "We have another suspect on our hands. Your Honor." Smitty whirled on the balls of his feet to face the judge. "The defense would like to request a brief recess before I call my next witness."

"Sustained."

✳ ✳ ✳ ✳

Smitty patted me on the back. "We'll find out who did this, Willy, I promise."

I looked at him, a glare in my eyes I felt to my core. How could he make such a ridiculous promise? He couldn't keep it.

"Is there anything I should know before we go back into the courtroom? For instance, Prosecutor Jane mentioned at one point you'd already served in jail once before?" Smitty asked, his brow furrowed as he leaned his elbows against the briefcase on his lap.

I hesitated. Somehow, I knew that skeleton in my closet would manifest itself during all of this. When she had Officer Todd testify at the very beginning, I wasn't paying much attention. I couldn't think straight at the time.

Smitty didn't know about the incident. I didn't want anyone to know about it. Telling Bea was hard enough. But if it'd help me. . .

With a reluctant sigh, I stared at my fingers. "Yeah, this isn't the first time I've spent time in a jail cell."

Smitty blinked and sniffed, a wet sound that made me want to blow my nose. "Oh?"

I nodded as the memories flooded back to me, weighing on my soul like the shackles around my wrists.

"It was on account of my father's abusive behavior. I got in his way once when I was barely eighteen and he made me pay for it, beating me practically senseless then calling the cops to tell them I'd beaten him when I tried to defend myself. The cop happened to be a long-running customer at the mechanic shop we owned. He'd told him before about how awful I was. He lied, saying I'd been on medication that I'd just quit, cold turkey, and gone ballistic. The cops believed him until they looked into my medical records and found I never took the medication he claimed I did. He was then charged with domestic violence and jailed for a minute. My mom bailed him out before he could be really charged with anything too serious because he had a *lot* of other skeletons in his closet. My dad killed himself not long after Mom bailed him out. I inherited the shop, but she cut me off, blaming me for his suicide and saying I only wanted the shop and I never cared about him."

● ● ●

Smitty was silent, sitting more still than I'd ever seen him. His eyes downcast as he cleared his throat, solemnly leaning his elbows on his knees. "I'm so sorry, Will."

I glanced up at him, surprised by the genuine tone in his scratchy voice. His eyebrows pulled together sympathetically and he gave me a reassuring smile. For some reason, hearing him say that did something to me. I found myself smiling for the first time in what seemed like ages. When he apologized, he meant it with everything in him. I could tell by the look in his bright, blue eyes.

The memory of when I'd told Bea that story flashed across my memory. She reacted in a very similar way to Smitty. Compassionate and understanding.

Something dawned on me then that never had before.

He really does care about me.

I wasn't used to that idea anymore. I adjusted my position, the handcuffs uncomfortable against my skin. "Yeah, but it was six years ago. I'm fine." The crack in my voice surprised me as the memory tightened my stomach. I stared at my hands, not wanting to look at him.

"How did he do it?" Smitty asked. I swallowed and kept my eyes downcast. "If you don't mind me asking."

"Gunshot after a failed attempt at overdosing."

"Miss Bianca's passing must've been all the harder for you because of that, I bet," he muttered, mostly to himself. I met his gaze again. "You must have quite an aversion to guns now."

I shook my head. "I meant to get a concealed carry permit after it happened, but couldn't bring myself to carry the gun he'd shot himself with. It was the only one we had and I couldn't exactly afford another at the time. He was never much of a dad, but he was still my father. You know what I mean?"

Smitty nodded, clearing his throat and tugging at his blue necktie with yellow polka dots. I chuckled a little at the clashing colors. Those neckties had become something I almost looked forward to when seeing him now. They became a symbol of his generosity and quirkiness.

"I think you said it best, Willy. Sometimes, people disappoint you, even family. Sometimes, even when you hate them, you still can't help but love them too. Family dynamics are weird like that. Unfortunately, some folks turn away from family and swear it off. Other ones grow closer together with adversity. But even though they're family, sometimes it's important to realize that they're just as human and individual as you. As much as it may hurt, you may need to let go the dreams of what you wish they could be and accept a harsh reality. Some families just aren't good for each other. And that's okay. It's not anything *you* did or didn't do."

I hesitated. "I don't know how to let go of that ideal, Smitty. I've longed for a loving family my entire life. I finally find it and screw that up too."

A sharp pain sprang at the base of my neck, lurching my head forward. Smitty dusted off his hand before resting it back on his knee, leaning forward. *He hit me.*

"Oh, stop it. You screwed up nothing . . . except when you shot that gun . . . and ran from the cops . . . and punched one of them . . . Okay, so you've actually screwed up a lot."

I squinted at him, trying to figure out what he meant by bringing any of that up.

"But I don't think you screwed up your relationship with Miss Bianca's family," he continued.

Part of me wanted to smile at him but didn't quite feel up to it yet. Thinking of the pain I'd caused the Wixoms made me want to bury myself in a hole so I'd never have to face them again.

"You know," I began before I could stop myself. "Her family was kinder to me than my own ever was. Why? I'm not related to them, yet they loved me. They *still* seem to love me, even with everything that's happened. Why?"

Smitty shrugged, casually swiping his finger across his nose. "How should I know? I'm a lawyer, not a therapist. It could just be that you're a great guy and you didn't deserve poor treatment."

I scoffed at that. "You don't even know anything about me."

"I can see it in your eyes when you talk about her, Willy. It's why I asked how you felt about her in the courtroom today. You never would've hurt her, even if you did have a motive. You loved the girl too much."

My chest constricted. Involuntarily, memories of Mom hungover on the couch, bruised and withered, appeared behind my eyelids when I blinked. I saw Dad guzzling beer in front of the TV and not giving a crap about his son cowering behind the refrigerator. Anger boiled inside me as I clenched my fists tightly.

"He beat her every night, Smitty," I muttered, my jaw set as another flash of memory came back to me. "I remember Dad's fingers clenched around Mom's throat as he screamed at her for something as *stupid* as forgetting to pick up milk at the grocery store. I tried to intervene but ended up being thrown into the couch, breaking my collarbone. I was nine."

I didn't mean to share the memory aloud, but it poured out of me like a waterfall. I couldn't stop myself once I'd started. I didn't realize how much I was still affected by it.

"I'm sorry, Will. Truly," Smitty said, sincerity in his voice. "I can't imagine what that must've been like for you."

I didn't look at him, still trying to push away my anger.

"Now, about your friends," Smitty continued.

I cringed slightly with the force of an abrupt subject change.

They must've hated me by now. "What about them?"

"Anything suspicious you've noticed about any of them?"

Before I could answer the question, we were summoned into the courtroom again. Spikes of anxiety fired off inside me at the prospect of entering again. I wished I could've escaped just so I wouldn't have to endure any more of those stupid questions. I looked to Smitty who gave me a reluctant grin and patted me on the back again. I must've looked as terrified as I felt.

TWENTY-THREE
Bianca Wixom

Daddy stopped when he looked up and met Will's mortified gaze.

"Tom, do you think—" Mom's voice cut off as she came up behind Daddy, both of them staring, dumbfounded. "Bea, who's . . ." Her eyes met mine. I shook my head. She nodded, understanding quickly what happened. "Let's go upstairs, Tom," she muttered, patting Daddy's chest and subtly tugging on the collar of his shirt. His hand landed firmly on her shoulder and he held her back. Her eyes met mine with a concerned and regretful gleam that frightened me. She knew what was coming just as much as I did and dreaded it even more. The apology in her expression said it all.

"No, I don't think we should go anywhere," Daddy said, his voice monotone as his eyes glued to Will like he'd watch every move he made. I noticed his eyes dart toward Will's tattooed wrist and he scowled.

"Daddy, I can explain," I lied. I couldn't excuse my blatant disregard for his rules with a pathetic lie. He held a hand up to me without making eye contact. He looked like he was trying to protect me from a wild beast. His movements were deliberate and calculated as he approached Will.

"I'll deal with you later, Bianca," he growled beneath his breath.

Instinctively, I stood between him and Will. Once I stood close enough to him, Will's hands landed on my shoulders. I cringed, loving the support I felt from him but hating the anger the gesture fired in Daddy's eyes.

"Who are you and why are you touching my daughter?" Daddy's fists clenched.

I folded my arms, the awkwardness and terror I felt tangible in the air.

Will's hands lifted off my shoulders and he held them in the air like he was being arrested.

"I'm sorry, sir. You must be Bianca's parents." Will stepped away from me, approaching Daddy with surprising confidence, his hand outstretched for a handshake. "I'm William Markus, sir."

Daddy's eyes flashed toward him again, something strange in his expression. "Margret and Bill Markus' son?"

I tilted my head. Daddy knew his parents?

Will hesitated, adjusting his position with his hand still reaching for a handshake he'd probably never receive. "Yes, sir, I am. You knew them?"

Daddy's countenance grew more guarded as he folded his arms across his broad chest, standing taller. I stood behind Will, sliding my hand into his as I tried pushing past Daddy to go upstairs. I passed before he grabbed Will's arm with an amount of force I hadn't seen him exhibit before. Fear pricked my skin as I flinched away, clinging to Will's hand.

"Wait," he said, his voice unnaturally calm. "I have a few questions for him before you leave so soon, Honey Bea."

I moaned, dreading the interrogation which inevitably followed a statement like that. My voice burned with a warning. "Daddy . . ."

Will's lips pressed together uncomfortably. "Ask away."

I swallowed nervously, rubbing the bridge of my nose as anxiety rose into my stomach.

"How did you meet my daughter?"

"A . . . mutual friend."

"Who?"

"I—Isaac Petersen. I'm sure you know him."

Daddy's eyes narrowed suspiciously and he grunted. "Good kid. Comes from a good family, from what I've heard. A stable, kind, active member of the Church. Are *you* a member of the Church?"

My heart raced as I watched Will's forehead beaded with perspiration. "No, sir."

Daddy's scowl deepened as he stepped closer to Will, his voice lowering. "Then what makes you think you're good enough for her?"

"Daddy," I snapped, appalled.

"No, Honey Bea," he bellowed, turning to me with indescribably dangerous explosions of passion and disappointment flaring in his nostrils. His shoulders sagged slightly as he shook his head at me. "You already didn't serve a mission. Why couldn't you have just married Jace?"

"Tom—" Mom interjected, sitting on the steps behind me. He held up a finger to silence her before thrusting it toward Will and staring him directly in the eye.

"No Markus boy is going to be involved with my family. Now go back home and *never* reach out to my daughter again."

Any light Daddy possessed vanished in that second.

I glared at him. My heart burned with his distrust in my ability to choose a good guy, as I drug Will silently back up the stairs and out to my car. Mom called after me, chasing us to my car until I shut myself in. Will stood awkwardly outside my door after closing it behind me to speak to her. Through muffled voices, I heard some of their conversation.

"Tom's bark is worse than his bite. He doesn't mean half the things he says most of the time. He usually comes back to me after an outburst like that and talks about how much he hates that about himself. Please don't think too harshly of him," Mom said.

"I'm sorry I caused this, Mrs. Wixom—"

"Please, none of that. Call me Emily. So, you're Will? Bea told me about you the night you met. She spoke highly of you. I just want to let you know that you don't have to be afraid of Tom. He seems like a grizzly bear sometimes, but give him some time. He'll warm up to you then you'll see he's nothing but a big teddy."

My heart softened a bit seeing Mom being her sweet and welcoming self toward

Will. It was refreshing after seeing Daddy's reaction.

I could hear Will's weighty tone lighten a bit as he continued. "Thank you . . . Emily."

She smiled regretfully, pulling him in for a hug. Will stood awkwardly, obviously confused by such a gesture. He didn't seem like the hugging type of guy, so the sight almost made me smile.

"Drive safe, you two," she said, pulling away with a broad smile as she patted his back. She looked at me and blew a kiss, waving.

Gratitude for her swelled inside me, momentarily replacing my frustration and humiliation.

Will laughed silently then circled the car with a confused expression as Mom went back inside, probably to calm the beast raging in Daddy.

I rolled my eyes at that thought. Before, I looked at my father with respect and a loving eye. Now, I saw him as nothing more than a judgmental man who spoke in the name of religion as a form of manipulation. He knew nothing about the kind of person Will was, yet he acted as if he understood everything about him simply at a glance. How could he pass such harsh judgment on him without knowing a single thing? Being a member of the Church wasn't enough to know if someone was worthy of my attention or not. He was a liar and a hypocrite.

I started my car when Will plopped into the passenger seat, remaining silent for the most part as I drove. I found myself hating the fact that, even though my heart throbbed with anger, I still loved him so dearly. I still wanted nothing more than to be good enough for him.

Maybe I never truly would be.

Tears burned behind my eyelids at that possibility and I pressed my lips together in an effort to hold them at bay. I couldn't cry. I wasn't allowed to. I was the example of strength. Weakness was showing how I really felt. No one really wanted to see what I had to show as far as negative emotions. Crying was a weakness. I had family who counted on me to be the best version of myself possible. Daddy counted on me. Mom supported me. What was I doing? Driving through Reno with Will in an effort to escape them. How could I do that to them? I wasn't a rebel. I'd never considered myself to be so. I just wanted to know what it was like to date Will. He made me feel deeper than anyone else ever had. I cared about him.

Something touched my knee and I flinched, my eyes flitting toward Will's hand resting over my kneecap. I didn't dare look at him as I felt a tear slip from my eyelash and down my cheek.

"Bea?" he muttered, his tone sympathetic and understanding. "You okay?"

What was it about someone asking that question that made me want to crumble at their feet and bawl through all of life's woes? I felt like I held onto my emotions with nothing more than a thread which grew thinner and thinner as the seconds passed.

Will's fingers squeezed my leg comfortingly as if to tell me he was there if I needed him. The thread snapped.

My fingers trembled. I gasped through the flashes of memories. Words used against me. Terror and anger coursing through my system as I thought of running. *Really* running. Back to the familiar. I bit down on my knuckles in an effort to slow down the panic of cars behind me possibly being *him*, following me as I'd dreaded for years. Hearing Jace's name again from Daddy sent shocks of adrenaline and anxiety through my system I wished never existed. He'd never leave me alone. He'd always haunt me. Finally, I pulled into the only place I knew where to find true peace.

The temple shined a light into my soul darkened by anxiety. Will was silent, waiting for me to be ready to talk. I covered my face, my breath hastening as I envisioned Jace's car pulling up beside us. I pictured him throwing me out of the car, demanding to know once more why I'd left him behind. Telling me about how much I never really loved him. How worthless I was. How I'd never be as good enough if I didn't achieve. I needed to work harder to be worthy of love. God wouldn't love me otherwise.

Daddy didn't know that about him because he threatened me not to tell anyone about what he'd done. If I did, I'd never be forgiven and I'd be lost and unlovable.

I wrapped my arms around my torso as I rocked back and forth, trying to calm the frantic feelings causing my nerves to prick with anxiety.

Somehow, my face ended up buried into Will's shoulder, his arms securely around me as my shaking fingers clung to his denim jacket, prodding at his collar frantically as if it would save me from the memories. My thoughts thrashed against my head, seeming to ricochet recklessly against the insides of my temples.

I couldn't go through this again. I couldn't have panic attacks again. I hadn't experienced one since I'd left him. I was stronger than this. Why did my past still bother me so intensely?

Will hushed me, his fingers lovingly stroking my hair.

"He's coming after me," I groaned, my voice muffled by his shirt.

"Who? Your father?"

I shook my head quickly.

"Jace. He knows where I live. He knows I spend time in front of the temple. If he sees me here, he'll . . ." The possibility of him seeing me with Will dawned on me in a panic and I yanked myself out of his arms, turning my car's key with a sniff.

"Whoa, whoa," Will said, grabbing the gearshift before I could to stop me. I stared at him, terror shooting through me. His eyes were calm as he gazed at me. "Calm down, Bea. You're safe with me. Nothing's going to happen to you while I'm here. Now, breathe."

I obeyed, though hyperventilation made it difficult. Once my breath quickened, it felt impossible to stop. My muscles felt like I'd worked out too hard for too long, even though the panic attack only lasted a little over five minutes. Finally, Will's hand in mine registered in my brain, giving me a sense of security that relaxed me against the seat. Exhaustion swept over me and I let myself melt into the seat, my head nothing but dead weight as I let it fall toward him.

He smiled reassuringly, squeezing my hand. Once I could find an even breath, I returned his smile, my face tired.

"How'd you do that?" I asked.

"What?"

"No one's ever been able to calm down an anxiety attack like that before. How'd you know what to do?"

Will shrugged. "I've had my fair share of them myself. My parents never knew how to handle them and would scream and throw me out in the rain to calm me down. That worked, except when it wasn't raining. Something about water calmed me down. If it wasn't raining, my father would throw me into the bathroom and lock the door until I stopped. It did nothing good for my psyche, but it worked. What I just did is what I always wished they would've done for me."

I stared at him, pleasantly surprised as I shook my head. "Will, why are you still here?" I asked, my throat tightening from the strain of tears wanting to come through again. "I'm weaker than you think I am. I'm not perfect."

He chuckled half-heartedly, his hand lifting to caress my jawline as his eyes searched my expression. "That's why. You're human. I don't want perfect. Never have and never will. Perfection isn't attractive and neither is false strength. You're genuine in your individuality and that's hard to find. So, why would I ever want to run away from that?"

His words brought more tears with them. His smile broadened as he brought his other hand to my cheek, wiping my tears as he pulled me into him again, pressing a kiss to my forehead.

"Wanna get out and walk around the temple?" he asked.

Grateful, I nodded. *I don't deserve you.*

TWENTY-FOUR
William Markus

The courtroom bustled with a dull sound of conversation. I was long past listening to whatever was said by a gossipy group behind me. Any kind of sound gave me a headache. I groaned, rubbing my temple as my hair hung in my face. My facial hair had grown to an uncomfortable length, itching every five seconds. I tossed back my hair when Smitty flopped into the seat next to me.

"How ya holdin' up there, Wayne?" Smitty smacked me firmly between the shoulder blades. I grunted, lurching forward a bit from the impact.

In spite of myself, a part of me was relieved seeing him beside me. "Will, Smitty. You know my name is Will," I sat up straighter, my mouth teasing at a smile. Being around him made me feel a little more human. Probably because he seemed to be the only one who saw me as such anymore.

"I was experimenting a bit. You know that name was always weird to me." The fidgeting continued as I'd come to expect from him. It didn't bother me as much as it used to, however. I saw it more as an almost endearing quirk of someone I dared believe cared about me.

"My name's not Wayne," I said again, leaning my elbows on the table in front of me.

I shook my head with a small grin, glancing around the courtroom. It wasn't the weirdest thing he'd ever said, but it was still pretty weird.

A voice boomed through the courtroom. "All rise for the honorable judge."

We stood as the judge re-entered and sat on the stand, tossing her robes across her thick legs.

I wished I was just back in my cell so I could sit in peace. I hated that courtroom. I hated the people there. I hated the judge. I hated everything about reliving that horrible night over and over again as if something would change. Nothing would change. Why couldn't they just convict me and get it over with?

Why is Smitty doing this to me?

I shook that last thought off. It was Smitty I referred to, after all. Everything he did was a mystery to me.

"Defense calls Isaac Petersen to the stand, Your Honor," Smitty announced, standing from his seat again, his sausage fingers pressed against the cherry wood table in front of us.

I pulled my eyebrows together, surprised to hear Smitty calling that name.

"Smitty, what does Isaac have to do with this?" I asked.

He shrugged. "I dunno."

I hesitated, creasing my brow in confusion. "Wha—Then *why* are you calling him to the stand?" I demanded, trying to keep my voice low through the panic.

Smitty shrugged again. "I dunno. But there's one thing I do know." An unfamiliar determination flashed across his features as he gave me a sideways glance. He tugged on his blazer collar, winking subtly as he leaned toward me, muttering under his breath. "Where there's a Will . . . There's a Wayne."

He stood straight again, giving me a knowing look with a raise of his nonexistent eyebrows.

The air seemed to pause as Isaac stepped forward, making his way to the stand. They made him swear on the Holy Bible he'd tell nothing but the truth as I'd seen others do before. Something about seeing him do it, however, felt off.

He looked *awful.* Deep bags beneath his eyes blackened his countenance with darkness I'd never seen in him before. Bea's death must've been taken its toll on him as much as it had me.

"State your full name to the court, please," Smitty said, a confident smile on his face.

"Isaac Damon Peterson," he mumbled.

"Nice to meet you. Will has told me a lot about you."

I have?

"Cool, why am I here?" Isaac said, thrumming his fingers on the desk and twitching more than normal.

"Mr. Petersen," Smitty began, throwing one leg in front of him to practically skip forward. "How do ya know my client over here?" Smitty gestured to me for a second before turning back to Isaac with a clap of his hands.

Isaac didn't look at me, a bored expression on his sullen face. "We're best friends, roommates. He dated Bea for six months before jumping the gun to marry her. Then apparently used it to shoot her."

I cringed. *Et tu, Brute?*

"Well, that's what I'm trying to prove didn't happen, Isaac—May I call you Isaac?"

He shrugged carelessly. "Sure . . . He did it, why waste your time?"

Smitty sighed. "What were you doing the night Miss Bianca was killed?"

I noticed him swallow. "I was home."

"Did you have any family at home? Mother, father, brother?" Smitty asked, stroking his chin thoughtfully.

"I live alone. Matt lived with me before his lease expired, then he ditched me. Will used to be my roommate too before he decided to become a criminal and ruin everyone's lives." He scoffed. "Again."

I glared at him. *What the hell, man? Who are you?*

"Tell me about your family history. What's your father like? Do you see him a lot?"

Isaac's relationship with his dad was a sensitive subject. I never quite knew why, since he never talked about him more than a few passive-aggressive jabs. He usually avoided the subject like a germaphobe avoids people during flu season.

"No. He doesn't see anyone. He's kind of a recluse."

Smitty nodded. "I see. Any reason why?"

Isaac shook his head silently.

He won't talk about his dad in court, Smitty. Don't waste your time.

"Perhaps you can answer me a different question. My client, Willy, here," Smitty continued, gesturing to me again with a grin before turning back to Isaac. "Tells me you're quite the photographer. Is that true?"

Isaac frowned. I noticed a bead of sweat form on his brow. "Sure."

"You were meant to take pictures of his proposal to Miss Bianca the night she was murdered. Is *that* true?"

"Yeah."

"Where are those pictures?"

Isaac closed his eyes, rocking back and forth slightly before he breathed a hefty sigh and opened them again. "Yeah, I was supposed to take pictures for Will that night. He told me he'd do it at GSR, but lied about it and ditched me to do it somewhere hidden in the mountains."

"Hmm . . . But didn't you just say you were home alone that night? Our last witness did state in his testimony that you disappeared to take those pictures."

I leaned forward, eyes narrowed at Smitty. Where was he going with any of this?

"Well," Isaac said, tossing a hand in the air. His eyes scanned the room like he wanted to look at anything but Smitty. "I went home after Will abandoned me. What else was I supposed to do?"

"Ah, so you went home *afterward* . . . Alright. Well, if you went home that night, why was your phone tapped thirteen feet from where Miss Bianca's body was found in the GSR parking lot at exactly 9:15 PM the night she was murdered?"

My eyes widened and my jaw dropped as a general gasp waved over the crowd. Isaac fumbled for words, eyes frantic as he visibly shook. Smitty's voice grew in intensity the more he spoke.

"And what's more, why was a glove, which has several traces of *your* fingerprints as well as gunpowder from the very same gun used to kill Miss Bianca, found by the Sierra Bay an hour after the incident happened? Can you tell me more about that, Isaac?" Smitty shouted, raising his eyebrows as a snide grin played at the corners of his mouth.

Isaac's fingers gripped the witness stand, prodding and recoiling as his eyes darted frantically around the room.

Smitty pulled out the photo of the black, leather glove Matt gave me when I inherited the mechanic shop. How could Isaac have gotten it?

Immediately, a flash of memory came to me. The day I met the Wixoms, I left Isaac alone in the shop with the keys. I didn't think anything of it . . . Until now.

TWENTY-FIVE
<u>Bianca Wixom</u>

"I'm so sorry, Will," I said, my voice strained from tears. His eyebrows pulled together sympathetically as he kissed the back of my hand. We meandered the temple grounds, the skyline sparkling in the distance.

"For what?" he asked, looking at his combat boots as he walked.

"Nothing can excuse my dad's behavior toward you tonight."

He cringed slightly. "Yeah, that . . . I think I made a good first impression," he said, his tone completely serious.

I turned back to him, hoping to read his expression. He couldn't actually be serious. His face cracked into a poorly fought back grin before he laughed in his throat. A half-hearted laugh lightened my heavy heart and I walked closer to him, resting my head on his shoulder.

"I'm serious, did you see the way he scowled at me?" Will continued, obviously trying to get me to laugh again. "I think he was contemplating how he'd kill me, skin my body, and leave me in the darkest alley in Reno for buzzards."

I snorted, wrapping my arms around his torso and hugging him tightly. We stopped walking as I buried my face in the curve of his neck and breathed in the masculine scent of his skin. He encircled me in his strong arms and I felt his chin rest against the top of my head as I turned toward the skyline.

I'd never get over how serene and breathtaking the view was from the temple. The casinos and city lights glimmered under the haze clouding the air around it, stars dotting the night sky above. The temple grounds were the only place in Reno I could go to truly feel the silence around me. Warmth enveloped me with the smell of fresh air, tasting just as refreshing on my tongue as it felt.

I didn't feel deserving of the treatment he'd given me. He seemed to really care about me. No one had ever treated me the way he had before. I didn't understand how Daddy could think so little of him. He was better than any returned missionary I'd dated. And I liked it that way.

"Why are you so nice to me?" I asked.

He squeezed my shoulders in a cuddle, sitting us down on a bench close by. I shut my eyes, breathing in his nearness.

"Bianca, you're the best person I've ever known," he said matter-of-factly. My heart skipped a beat when I pulled away to look him in the eyes. The expression he wore showed vulnerability and sincerity. "I didn't even know there *were* people in the world like you."

I sighed, my focus wandering to his mouth. His lips pursed slightly, a grin tugging at the corners. Involuntarily, I imagined kissing that smile. I shifted slightly, too afraid to move away. He seemed fragile, like a butterfly. I feared that if I moved too fast, he'd fly away. I didn't want that. I didn't want to lose the way I felt with him close by. My eyes flashed back to his as they searched my soul.

His expression turned serious, his Adam's apple jumping as he swallowed the nerves evident in his eyes.

"Will, stop being so nice to me," I muttered, my voice constrained. "I don't deserve it."

His eyebrows pulled together sadly, though a smile still lingered. He lifted a hand to brush my hair away from my face, tucking it behind my ear. He leaned in closer. My heart pounded and my spine stiffened. I heard my breath as it puffed from between my teeth.

"No," he whispered, closing his eyes and brushing his lips gently against mine with a kiss so soft I almost didn't even notice.

For some reason, I wanted to cry again. Something in me snapped and I couldn't stop the tears welling my vision. My eyes fluttered, lashes wet with emotion.

"Will," I began, intending to stop him somehow. I could just imagine what Daddy would do if . . .

He kissed me again, his palm now pressed against my cheek, fingers in my hair. My head spun, sending jolts of dizziness through my body with an incomprehensible wave of excitement and joy. I kissed him too, trying to find my balance again. Vaguely, I wondered if this was something like intoxication. A rush of exhilaration so dizzying you feel like you've flown on the breeze. The scent of his skin sucked me in, masculine and alluring as it filled my senses with him. His lips tasted like desire.

I wanted more.

That was why I pulled back, breaking the connection between us with heavy breath.

I bit my lips to prevent my giddiness from shining through. I knew the attempt was futile. I couldn't stop myself from sighing like a girl falling in love for the first time.

Will's smile broke loose with an exasperated laugh as he melted into me, his nose brushing across my cheek. His body seemed to go limp as his tight muscles relaxed.

"Wow," he breathed, his tone lighthearted and airy.

I laughed too as he rested the bridge of his nose against my shoulder, slowly turning toward the curve of my neck. He sighed deeply, letting his hand drift onto my arm.

"I think I'm in love," he mumbled, though I got the feeling he'd said it on accident.

Joy drained from me with those words. How had I sunk so deep? He was like a tidal wave, pulling me in farther and farther with every passing second. Daddy would mount Will's head on the wall if he heard that.

"Oh, really?" I said, my voice teasing though part of me wished he was too. He nodded, his head still on my shoulder. I swallowed nervously.

He sat up straight again, gazing into my eyes with a peaceful grin relaxing his features. He brought his fingers back up to my face, caressing my jawline with his thumb.

"You're so beautiful, Bea," he whispered, the tenderness in his voice shocking my nerves with adrenaline. I wanted so badly to relish in that moment. I wanted to feel the same way for him too. But I was terrified.

I couldn't stand the thought of disappointing Daddy any more than I already had. Falling in love with Will would crush him. I'd already disappointed him by not getting married to Jace after deciding not serving a mission. I didn't serve a mission because I thought I'd marry him. I knew that broke Daddy's heart.

What would he do if I told Will . . . ?

"I love you." The words escaped before I could even think to stop them. I cringed, knowing how much I meant them.

Will pulled back, his expression stunned before lighting up with hope. "Really?"

I nodded. *What am I doing?*

The elation on his face was almost too precious to look at without melting. The fingerless gloves he wore felt warm against my face as he stroked my cheek, tangling his fingers into my hair again and pulling me in. He scooted closer to me, kissing me gently over and over. I giggled as every kiss he gave me tickled my insides. Joy replaced the anger and fear I'd felt earlier that evening. I only wanted to live in that place in my mind for as long as possible. It was beautiful.

His kisses were quick and simple, intentional and heartfelt, but fun and exhilarating as they teased me with their choppy spontaneity. It left me feeling refreshed and edgy in a way I'd never thought to experience before. It awoke my senses to the world around me. I could smell the crisp freshness of the air, sweet with the promise of life and excitement. I giggled, his lips tickling with happiness. I liked kissing him. He knew how to give me just enough so I'd want more.

"You're dangerous, Will," I whispered. My hand lifted to his face. He chuckled, leaning in farther before he quickly tucked his arms around my knees and behind my back, hoisting me onto his lap.

A strange sound between a screech and laugh burst from my mouth and Will laughed as he held me. He kept kissing me and I could feel his grin against my lips.

"I love you, Bianca," he breathed, his voice husky as he stopped for air. My breath huffed from between my teeth and I tucked my hair behind my ear, pulling back to look at him. His expression was dazed, his eyes darting between my eyes and lips. I pressed a kiss to his forehead. Wrapping my arms around his neck, I turned toward the temple glowing in the background, smiling up at it. For the first time that night, I felt real peace. I knew God smiled down on us. Somehow, I knew that, even if my earthly father would never accept Will, my Heavenly Father would.

Something about being with him felt calm. He made me feel genuine and safe. I liked it. My heart felt more alive in his embrace.

I turned to him as he gazed at the temple with me, his entire countenance glowing with inexpressible joy. He looked back at me and his smile grew bigger. I giggled again, nuzzling my nose against his.

"Bianca," a familiar voice boomed from the parking lot.

Will flipped around and I stood the instant we saw Daddy storming toward us. My heart fell.

"Daddy, what're you—" I stood between him and Will, hoping to protect him in some way against the rage that Daddy could exhibit.

"Get in that car right now and wait for me," he roared, thrusting a finger toward my parent's car in the parking lot.

Will awkwardly rubbed the back of his neck before his hands landed on my shoulders. "Mr. Wixom, I assure you I didn't mean any harm—"

"Don't talk to me, boy," Daddy snarled. "Get your hands *off* my daughter and go back to the slums you crawled out of."

"Daddy," I snapped, my hand landing over Will's. He'd never spoken like that before. I stared at him, appalled and disappointed. "Stop it."

Will opened his mouth to protest, but couldn't seem to combat my dad's inappropriate words.

"Remember whose property you're on, Daddy, and be careful what you say," I growled, protectively taking Will's hand and gesturing to the Lord's temple beside us. We stood on holy ground.

Swallowing nervously, he turned to look at the golden statue of Moroni atop the temple's steeple. The symbolic statue held a long trumpet to its mouth, sounding the day of Christ's second coming. But at that moment, it seemed to blow a bugle of warning against speaking guile on the property where harmony and peace should prevail. The fear of God struck Daddy's features as he trembled. Exasperated, he sighed and faced me again.

"Get in the car, Bea," he muttered. Though softer, his tone was still gruff with annoyance and barely concealed anger.

"No. Especially not after that display," I spat.

I'd never seen him act this way before. But I'd stand between the two as a defense for as long as I needed to. His behavior scared me. I felt safer in Will's arms than I did in his car after seeing this side of him. He'd never been so angry at me before, at least not this outwardly. What had gotten into him? It couldn't have been because I was dating Will. Something inside told me it was much deeper than the surface.

"You don't know this boy—" he protested.

"Neither do you. Stop talking about him like he's not here."

"He's a felon, Bianca. I was meant to be the prosecutor in his father's case six years ago for several counts of domestic violence, including the attempted murder of his wife. Before he could appear in court, he killed himself with a single gunshot to the head after an attempted overdose," Daddy said quickly as if he'd been holding it in for hours. His lips pressed tightly together, eyes wet with fury and terror. "I don't want my baby girl to be part of that. I don't want you to become like Margret."

I stared at him, my heart falling into my stomach with the weight of his words before I turned to Will who shot a menacing glare at him. All at once, Will's presence made me feel uneasy. Why hadn't he told me? He avoided the subject of his father like a disease. Was this why?

"Will?" I asked, scared of his explanation.

He looked down at me, his expression forlorn as he forced a smile. "Bea," he muttered in response, sarcasm in his tone.

Something of betrayal sparked in my stomach and I stepped away from him. This wasn't a time to be sarcastic. It stung and I stared at him intently, daring him to avoid the subject now.

"Is this true?" My voice was barely audible as I backed away from him.

His eyebrows pulled together and he reached for me as panic rose in his eyes. His hand felt like ice and I yanked mine away. The touch that'd sent exhilarating chills up my spine now felt foreign and frightening. I wondered if I really knew him anymore. How could I have gotten dragged so far into this without even realizing who pulled me into the deep end? I felt like I'd been thrust into a world where everything was confusing and wrong. We'd talked for months almost every day. How could I have let him avoid the subject so long without it raising a red flag?

"I'm not my father, Bea," he said, his tone suddenly desperate.

"Of course you are, boy," Daddy chimed in, a sickeningly satisfied grin fighting for dominance on his face. I glared at him, anger blazing inside me at his unwelcomed presence. "You have that same look of darkness in your eyes that your father had."

"Daddy," I barked. "Go home. Let me handle this alone." I paused, but he didn't budge.

"I'm not leaving until I know you're safe . . . away from him."

"Go."

He watched a minute, his focus darting between me and Will, his glare dark, before sighing defeat and perhaps beginning to understand my feelings.

"Fine. But I'm in the car and if I see anything suspicious," he said, thrusting an accusatory finger toward Will. "If I see you lay one finger on her, you're as good as rotting in a prison cell. Do you hear me?"

Will frowned, pressing his hands into his pockets. "Loud and clear, sir."

Daddy glared, finally heading for the car.

TWENTY-SIX
William Markus

"Do you recognize this, Isaac?" Smitty asked, waving the picture of the glove back and forth.

Isaac shifted almost as much as Smitty did, discomfort obvious on his face. "Y—yeah, it's a work glove. What of it?" He laughed, choking on air.

"Will has told me and the lovely Detective Cole that he never took this glove out of his mechanic's shop downtown. It was in his office which he's said he only granted access to two people, the victim, Miss Bianca Wixom, and *you*."

"Will let me borrow it. He said it wasn't something he cared too much about," Isaac said, beads of sweat on his brow. Smitty turned to me, a question in his eyes.

I shook my head. I never told him that.

It was true I hadn't cared that much about an insignificant glove until now. But I only granted him access when I asked him to grab something for me, which I never did for that particular glove.

"You worked with my client in his shop, did you not?" Smitty asked.

"Yeah, he was my boss. I was his assistant. He hired me when I didn't have anywhere else to turn."

That's true, I mused, growing more and more suspicious of my employee and best friend as he spoke.

"Will gave me access to his office in case he needed something. He did that a lot since I was the only one he really trusted there. He gave a *key* to Bianca though."

Something changed in his demeanor when he said that last thing. Jealousy? Bitterness? He twitched, his body tensing and flinching as his head jerked toward the ceiling. I'd never seen him act so jumpy.

Part of me wished I could've asked him about this before, outside of a murder trial.

"How did you feel about that?" Smitty asked.

Emotion drained quickly from his eyes, leaving nothing but a sullen, dark expression that left him appearing half-dead as he stared blankly at nothing. "Fine."

Were you jealous of her? Or jealous of me because I had her?

Smitty's eyes narrowed suspiciously as he wrapped his arms around his own torso like he gave himself a hug. "I see . . . Now, back to the subject of theft, what was it you were doing for Will in that office?"

"Theft? I'm no thief. He asked for that glove, I went and got it for him. It was something I did a lot. I was more like a servant than a manager. I did everything for him. I was the one who even got him the girl in the first place. She would've dated *me* if I hadn't introduced them."

Really? That's not what Bea thought.

"You must be pretty bitter about that," Smitty observed.

"I'm sorry, but this—this is stupid," Isaac objected, leaning across the witness stand with upturned palms. He reminded me of a drunk the way he moved, words slurring recklessly together. "I'm Isaac, I'm the good guy. I'm always the good guy. Everyone loves me."

"Frankly, Isaac, in this case, I don't think so," Smitty interjected. "You took that glove from Will's office and used it to cover your tracks so you could shoot Miss Bianca without a hope of getting caught, didn't you?"

His eyes bugging out, he stared at something at the back of the courtroom. He didn't seem to notice Smitty's accusation through the genuine terror striking his countenance as he trembled, grabbing the witness stand with a start.

"They're here. They've come for me. Not the bugs. No," he muttered, his eyes glued to whatever was in the back of the courtroom. Cautiously, I glanced behind me with everyone else. Nothing was there, yet Isaac gaped at it like something on the wall was going to eat him. "D—did Will tell you about how many times he's been caught drinking and driving? Or the time he beat his dad then killed him to get the mechanics shop? Yeah. He lies all the time. He's always been a criminal deep down. He killed his own father to get that stupid shop of his. He *shot* his own father. He's been to jail before. He's a bad person. He's the guilty one—*Not* me, *not* me. I—it was Matt's gun. *He* did it, not me. And Natalie. Sh—she wanted Will gone from the beginning. It was their fault, it was *them*. Not me."

Isaac's voice quickened with intensely the more he spoke. He put his head down, slamming fists against his head.

"Stupid, stupid, stupid, you're so *stupid*." He muttered the chant so low I could barely hear him. Unsettled by such a drastic change in his behavior, I watched him. I'd lived with him and I'd never seen him do this before. His tone shifted drastically as he muttered under his breath, hitting his head with both hands as he scrunched up his face as if in immense pain. "Stupid, stupid, stupid, you're so *stupid*."

"Mr. Petersen—"

Isaac curled into himself, gripping his hair and rocking back and forth, his muttering becoming more audible. "Shut up, stupid, They know. You know. They know. You can't keep this up. They know about you. They're coming to get you—*Gah*, get out, get out, get out—Leave me alone. What do you want with me? Stupid, stupid, stupid."

"Isaac," Smitty shouted over him. Concern brewed in his eyes as he backed away from the witness stand.

"*What?*" Isaac barked loudly, shooting his head up, hair matted and eyes wild and bloodshot.

His breath huffed through his gritted teeth and a dark grin gradually crawled across his countenance like a snake as his head tilted back and forth.

"You know, don't you? You all know. I'm never alone. They're always there with me, talking to me, yelling at me, comforting me." He moaned, gripping his hair like it was a life-source. "Stop, stop, stop."

He shut his eyes for a second, wincing and twitching before they opened again and his expression relaxed too quickly.

"They're my friends. They'd never tell me to do something *bad*. There's always something They know about everyone. They're always telling me. *Always*. They trust me . . . They trussst me."

His voice was nearly inaudible as he spoke. The darkness in his eyes as he glared at Smitty frightened me. He looked more like a demon than the friend I knew.

"*Gah*, just make it stop. Make Them go away. Just *make it stop*," he wailed in agony, smacking his head with both fists, clenched so tightly they almost bled.

Smitty hesitated, obviously as shocked by this display as I was. Somehow, he kept calm as he continued. "Isaac Petersen, did you shoot Miss Bianca and frame Will for—"

"Yes! Okay? Are you *happy?*" Isaac roared, leering murderously at Smitty.

Chewing his lower lip, he tilted his quivering head as a menacing grin made its way across his demonic face.

Bailiffs approached either side of the stand, poised to pounce when necessary as a general outcry erupted from the congregation. Isaac flinched at the sound but kept his gaze on Smitty.

"You'll regret this, Smith Edwards . . . They'll get you. They'll find their way into you. They're going to kill you. Beware . . . Beware the smoking gun," Isaac mumbled in a sing-song voice.

He shrieked. A sound that rattled my bones and caused Smitty to stumble backward. Everyone in the courtroom gasped in unison as his body started convulsing. He slammed his hands against the witness stand, his eyes wild with fury and confusion. "Stop, stop, stop, stop . . ." He continued muttering the word until his head flew up again and he flinched. "*No!* I killed Bianca Wixom. Will had nothing to do with it. It was all me. I stole the key from his office the day she brought that *stupid* pizza. I grabbed the first gloves I saw. It was me, me, me."

"Ah, hah!" Smitty cried, pointing at him with a grin as broad as his face, suddenly dominant over the surprise that'd been there before. "I got you."

Isaac leaned forward, gripping the wooden stand with bloody knuckles. "Killing her for Them was an *honor*."

Anger erupted inside of me at watching his disgusting display.

"Go to Hell, you psychotic bastard," I screamed before I could stop myself, my voice cracking from the emotion tearing me apart inside.

Smitty shot me a stabbing look, but I didn't care. It took everything in me not to go up there and beat the life out of him myself for what he'd done. He ruined my life and stolen hers. Without reason.

Any life he deserved to live was inside a straightjacket.

Isaac looked directly at me, standing slowly with his head bowed. Bailiffs stood behind him now, ready to grab him at the judge's orders or the first sign of violence. His body twitched, looking possessed as he glared, darkness surrounding his presence like I'd never experienced before.

"They're coming for *you* next, Will. Beware the smoking gun, my friend."

"Order," the judge shouted finally, pounding her mallet. "I've had enough."

Smitty stood in between us, approaching the witness stand and trying to speak calmly. "Your Honor—"

Isaac snarled like a rabid animal and climbed across the stand, grabbing Smitty's arm. I stood, prepared to do whatever proved necessary to protect him against my psychotic best friend. Smitty struggled as the bailiffs grabbed Isaac and drug him, kicking and screaming, out of the courtroom.

My heart pounded, but I couldn't decide what I was thinking. My head spun as I melted back into my seat. What had I just witnessed?

"Order," the judge shouted again. "In behalf of this court of law, I pronounce Isaac Petersen guilty of first-degree murder and sentence him to six months in the Renown psych ward then twenty-five to life for the murder of Miss Bianca Wixom. I pronounce the defendant, William Markus, not guilty. Mr. Markus, you're free to go. The court is adjourned."

TWENTY-SEVEN
Bianca Wixom

I breathed deeply, rubbing my temples as a headache formed. Slowly, I faced Will, unsure of how to approach the subject. When I met his gaze, I saw nothing but panic. His shoulders rose and fell quickly with the adrenaline in his expression. He watched me intently, his hazel eyes pleading for mercy beneath a sullen brow. I looked into those eyes and saw nothing but my own reflection. Somehow, without words, I understood everything.

He had nothing to do with his father. His father had nothing to do with him. And just because his father was abusive and violent, didn't mean Will would be.

My shoulders relaxed and I sighed, noticing for the first time a scar on his neck with what seemed to be scratch marks. From fingernails or an animal? My heart sunk as the realization kicked in. What would that have been like to live with such abuse? How many times had he suffered because his father couldn't control himself? What had that done to him?

Poor man. . .

I couldn't help it. In one, swift movement, I approached him and wrapped my arms around his neck in a sympathetic embrace. Standing on my toes to reach him, I closed my eyes, breathed him in, and held on tightly. He didn't hold me back. A stab of pain pranged against my gut with the realization it was because of Daddy. I hugged him tighter, not caring about our audience from the car.

Let him see, I thought. *Let him see the daughter he raised doing what he raised her to do. To love. To not care about a past or appearances. Let him see.*

I already told Will I loved him and meant it. Will's body trembled and quaked in resistance.

"It's okay," I whispered in his ear, hoping Daddy hadn't completely driven him away from me. "I'm not mad. I said I loved you and I meant it. I want to love all of you, but I can't do that if I don't know the truth. Please . . . Talk to me."

Will's breath shook slightly and he grabbed me, pressing me firmly against him in an embrace that seemed to suck out his pain and suffering. He held me for a long time, his arms wrapped completely around my waist.

His fingers prodded my jacket, his hands rubbing my back frantically as if he didn't quite know what to do through the panic in his quivering breath. I clung more firmly to him, hoping to be a source of comfort. Hiding my face in his neck, I whispered soothing words to him and stroked the back of his hair, coarse and slick against my fingertips.

"He choked her, Bea. He choked her until she passed out. I saw everything. Then he came after me. I was so scared. He swore he'd kill me if I said anything about what I saw. He still haunts me. I hate him so much."

Hushing him, I kissed his neck lightly, trying to comfort him as he had me.

"Is that why you didn't tell me?" I asked after his body relaxed into me and his breathing slowed.

"I didn't want to remember," he sighed, lifting his head to press his cheek against the side of my head as he gasped for air. "I guess I blocked it out."

I closed my eyes, savoring his smell and warmth and the security it gave me.

"I'm so sorry, Will. You didn't deserve that."

He squeezed me tighter. "Y—your dad—" he stuttered. "I don't want to get in trouble.

* * *

I don't want to get *you* in trouble. Don't let him take me to jail, Bea. I can't go there again."

I shook my head. "Again?"

"My father had me thrown in jail when he sweet-talked the cops after beating me. It's how he got caught. He told them I'd gone cold turkey on psycho meds I never took. They booked me then saw the cuts and bruises as well as medical records. Please, don't make me go back. Please, I can't go there again."

I hugged him tightly again before pulling away, my hands encompassing his face. "He's not going to actually do anything. I won't let him. If he does, he'll never be forgiven."

Will flinched, cringing. "That's what my mother said before she disowned me for 'killing my father,' so I could take the shop from him."

I stared at him, confused. "What?"

"I didn't. It was suicide, but I couldn't convince her of that. He had her so brainwashed. She was willing to give up her only son to believe he was innocent. When I inherited the mechanic's shop, she told me she never had a son. She was certain I'd murdered my father so I could inherit the shop and kicked me out on the streets. That's when Isaac and Matt took me in."

I recognized the genuine fear in his voice as he gazed into my eyes. I'd never seen anyone more vulnerable in my life. My heart hurt for him. I couldn't imagine going through something so horrible. Were there really people in the world that cruel?

"Will," I began hesitantly. "I'm so sorry. Thank you for being honest with me. I'll talk to my dad. Maybe he'll understand."

He squeezed his eyes shut, relief obvious in his relaxed shoulders as he let his forehead fall against mine.

"God, I love you," he sighed, slowly shaking his head. His hair meshed with mine on my forehead, rubbing against my skin and reminding me of how close we were.

I smiled, tangling my fingers in his hair, and pulling him into another kiss. Quick and sweet.

"Don't go," he groaned, though a smile lightened his tone.

I laughed lightly, kissing him again. His hand laced through my hair and he pulled me against him. The tension from moments ago didn't seem to matter anymore as we smiled between kisses.

"That's enough, Bianca." Daddy roared.

Startled, I whirled around to him leaning against the car with folded arms, a disapproving grimace on his face. I rolled my eyes and groaned inwardly as my happiness diminished some. I'd forgotten about Daddy.

"Duty calls," I said, stepping out of Will's embrace. Panic glinted in his eyes.

"When can I see you again?" he asked, his voice heavy with dread.

"Soon," I responded, winking at him. His fingers clung to mine as long as they could before I got too far away from walking toward Daddy who opened my car door for me.

Will stood with his hands in his pockets, uncertainty and obvious worry in his expression.

Daddy followed me home since I'd driven to the temple myself.

Finally, when we stepped on the driveway after parking, he sighed loudly, letting his hands drop to his lap with a loud clap against his leg. I watched him carefully, not sure what to expect, but prepared for the worst.

"Why, Bea?" he asked unexpectedly. "Why did you choose him?"

I hesitated, trying not to get too defensive. "Because I didn't want to judge him for an appearance. And he's wonderful if you get to know him."

"How long have you been seeing him behind my back?"

I refrained from rolling my eyes at his wording of the question. "About two months. And I didn't mean to lie to you about it or go behind your back. He's the best guy I've ever met and he cares about me more than anyone ever has before."

"What about Jace?" he asked, disappointment and hurt in his tone as he looked at me with saddened eyes.

The mention of my ex's name sent shivers through me and I instinctively watched my back. I hadn't spoken to Jace for almost a year, though his presence still haunted me with the awful things he'd always said about me. I'd almost gotten a restraining order after he followed me around for months after we broke up, begging me to take him back. I shuddered. If it hadn't been for Isaac's threats toward him, I would've. He certainly had Daddy wrapped around his little finger though. They still talked every once in a while, from what I'd heard.

"Daddy," I began, choosing words carefully. "Jace wasn't as nice as he seemed. He may have been a returned missionary and good guy on the outside, but he was manipulative and didn't know how to treat me right when you weren't around. Will, on the other hand, respected me and loved me even before he knew you. Jace never did that. He was more worried about impressing you than me."

Hearing myself admit that brought a smile to my face I couldn't avoid. The kisses Will and I shared tonight flashed across my memory, their excitement still hot in my system. I bit my tongue in an effort to stop the girly giggle wanting to arise in my throat.

"What if he reverts to his father's old habits? More often than not, Honey Bea, people who've been abused don't face it and therefore tend to relive their experiences through their own actions. I doubt he's worked through it properly."

"And you have the right to assume that?" I spat defensively.

"No," he muttered, his voice surprisingly calm. "But I'm telling you my concerns. Frankly, I have a lot of them. If he wasn't Bill Markus' son, I'd probably feel differently. But out of all the city, you chose *him*. How am I supposed to feel about that, Honey Bea? I panicked."

I paused, letting his words settle in my thoughts for a moment. I understood him. He really did just want to protect me. He wasn't there to intervene, but he was trying to save me from what *he* thought would turn out to be an abusive relationship. I smiled slowly as this sunk in. For the first time, I saw Daddy as a man doing his best to protect me. He was human too and, as such, he was prone to fear just as much as I was.

"But you won't stop me from seeing him?" I asked, afraid for the response.

He hesitated, his focus wandering. "I don't like it. But . . . your mom thought I should be more understanding and trust you more. She thinks he seems like a nice boy, though I don't. So," he said, swallowing nervously and avoiding eye contact. "As much as I hate it and think it's unwise, your mom thinks it's time for you to have that extra half hour of curfew."

My heart lifted into my throat. I'd been trying to convince him to let me stay out later since I was eighteen.

The reluctance in his voice visibly weighed on his shoulders as he continued. "And I also recognize that I have the potential of pushing you away if I don't let you date this Markus kid. So, if it really means that much to you . . ."

All at once, I threw my arms around his neck, thanking him before running inside.

TWENTY-EIGHT
William Markus

I sat back as another bailiff stood me up, unlocking my handcuffs. I looked at him, confused and dazed. He pursed his lips tightly, an apologetic look in his eyes. He said nothing, walking away without really acknowledging me.

I stared blankly ahead as the chatter from the courtroom blended into the back of my head, clouding my thoughts with an ambiguous sense of loss.

What just happened?

One minute, I was bound and held together by metal handcuffs. The next, I was . . .

"Free," Smitty exclaimed, throwing his arms in the air and wrapping them around my shoulders for an embrace. He squeezed tightly, lifting my feet off the ground with startling strength. I grunted, my heart leaping from surprise and shock as I gasped. My chest felt tight and I stumbled backward against the gates between the stands and congregation. I lifted a hand to my chest, staring at it, perplexed at its freedom to move. I'd been in handcuffs for so long, being out of them left me unsettled.

"We did it, Willy." Smitty's grin split his face in two as he embraced me. I fell limply into him, not sure how to move without the restraints on me. "You're free."

Those words made no sense to me. No matter how much I tried to understand what he'd said, I couldn't.

"I'm. . ." I muttered, still trying to piece the words together in a sensical way.

"Yes," he cried enthusiastically.

My breath fogged my thoughts like a clouded window. *Free. . . I'm free.*

"How?" I asked dumbly.

"I looked into Isaac's backstory after you mentioned him to Detective Cole and found out a lot of interesting stuff about him. He was interrogated as a possible suspect and I talked to the detective afterward. She mentioned there seemed to be something off about him. But I said, 'There's something a little off about everybody, isn't there?'"

I narrowed my eyes at him, wishing he'd stop rambling and get to the point. "What did you find? I thought I knew everything about him."

Smitty patted me on the back. "His father has been hiding in a trailer park called *Lucky Lane,* only coming out for gambling nights every so often. He's hardly come out of hiding since kicking Isaac and his mother out of the trailer over two years ago, I'm sure you already knew about that one."

I nodded. Smitty continued.

"Turns out, he was diagnosed with a pretty severe form of paranoid schizophrenia over twenty years ago and never went back to the physicians to get his meds refilled. When Isaac was confronted about his father's mental state, he mentioned the fact that he never saw his father take medication. Therefore, there's no evidence showing he was ever really treated, which can severely hinder someone's quality of life. Sometimes, they become incredibly dangerous, as you've seen today. Geez, after that I'm a little scared to sleep tonight. I'll have to start keeping a nightlight."

"I lived with Isaac though, Smitty. He wasn't like his dad," I said, still trying to process.

Smitty raised an eyebrow at me, folding his bulky arms across his chest. "Willy, how many times did he talk to himself or things that weren't there? Think hard now."

I hesitated, wracking my brain to think of instances where that'd happened. All at once, it hit me. He was constantly talking to himself, sometimes derogatory, sometimes not. Constantly muttering under his breath. All those times he spoke to inanimate objects like eggs and his socks as if they were alive. How many times he'd be in the middle of speaking then stare off into oblivion with the same terror in his eyes as he exhibited on the witness stand, only to act normal again a few seconds later. How jittery he always was, flinching at every little sound.

"So . . . this whole time," I mumbled, still not wanting to believe it.

Smitty nodded, his eyes sympathetic. "The mental illness of schizophrenia, from what I've researched, is hereditary in some cases. I did a little digging into his history and, sure enough, he was diagnosed six years ago. The same situation. He never refilled medication and, after you told me about his odd behavior, it wasn't hard to connect the dots."

I frowned, staring blankly toward the ground. "How could I have not known any of this?" I asked myself aloud. The weight of his words pulled on my shoulders like I still held shackles. "He was my best friend."

Smitty wrapped his arm around my shoulders and shook me firmly. "Hey, but you're free."

I shot a glare at him. Should I have been happy? My best friend killed the most precious part of my life because some ambiguous voice in his head told him to, then twisted it to look like it was me.

What would my life be like from now on? I couldn't go back to normal. Not after this.

I'd as good as lost my shop. I didn't have a home. I doubted anyone wanted me as part of their lives after this. People already had a tendency to treat me like a criminal. Now, I had more on my record than a stupid DUI.

"You okay, champ?" Smitty asked.

I meandered with him out to the courthouse lobby.

"No," I mumbled half-heartedly.

How could he think I'd be okay? I may have been set free in the eyes of the law, but I still felt trapped in a torrent of betrayal and fury. Part of me wanted to finally leave it all behind me in a shadow. The other wasn't ready to let go.

"Hey." Smitty caught my arm before I could get too far, his eyes kind. "You have a place to stay tonight?"

I didn't look back at him and sighed, realizing that the apartment I used to occupy was probably already taken over and my former roommate was now incarcerated. I didn't have anywhere to stay. No one to turn to. But I didn't want his pity. Though it had been a few days since I'd showered.

"I'm fine, Smitty," I grumbled, lost in a haze of exhaustion.

He turned me toward him, both hands firmly grasping my drooping shoulders. "Will, do you have a place to stay?"

I hesitated, trying to think of where my car was. Groaning, I realized they probably confiscated it after she was killed.

"No. I don't even have a car." I felt homeless. I *was* homeless. This time, I didn't have Isaac to help me out. And I wouldn't ask the Wixoms to help me.

"Why don't you stay with me and my wife for a little while until we can get you back on your feet? Clara's an amazing cook,"

Smitty offered, licking his lips and groaning. "You're gonna love it."

He'd never mentioned a wife before. "Someone married *you?*" I said, a heavy smile making its way across my face. It was hard to imagine.

He shook my shoulder slightly. "She was desperate when she married me. And she's lucky to have me."

"I'm sure for laughs, mostly," I teased, feeling a little better. Somehow, knowing I'd be taken care of for the night put my mind at ease . . . at least a little.

He smiled, patting me on the back again as he led me out of the courtroom. Before we closed the doors, however, I looked back. I wasn't ready to put it behind me yet. It'd ended too soon. I'd just gotten used to the idea that I was sentenced to life in prison. Now, I had to re-evaluate what my life course would end up being.

Thinking of never entering that room or a jail cell again meant I needed to let it go. I'd have to let go of the differing visions I'd had of my life leading up to this point.

I'd have to let *her* go.

I wasn't ready yet. And if looking back at that courtroom one last time meant I could hold onto that last chapter of my life just a little while longer, I'd do it. If it meant I could relish in her memory for one more moment.

TWENTY-NINE
Bianca Wixom

The church's halls were nearly vacant.
Sardines was a game frequently played in our
Young Adult group. The person we were
supposed to find and hide with was Lucas, a
short guy with glasses. He hid somewhere in
the darkened rooms of the church and
somehow, I always ended up being one of the
last ones to find him. People slowly
disappeared from the halls as the game went
on, probably hiding with Lucas in some
random room that I couldn't find.

I rounded the corner of a small
classroom, chairs stacked in the corner by a
table. Someone moved. My heart jumped and
I rushed to his side, flopping recklessly on the
floor beside him.

"Hey," Will laughed when I tumbled
across his lap.

"Will, what're you—"

"Shh," he whispered, cupping his hand
over my mouth.

I used to hate it when Mitchel would do
that to me. Mischief sparked inside me and I
licked his hand.

"*Gah,*" he muttered, yanking his hand away and shaking it off. I laughed, cuddling against him with my arms wrapped securely around his torso.

"That's what you get for putting your hand over my mouth, mister."

"Lesson learned," he said, hoisting me onto his lap.

I gasped, laughing before his lips shut me up. He was dangerous the way he kissed me, teasing me with his tongue and reeling me in with the intoxicating smell of his cologne. I smiled, encircling his face in my hands and letting my fingers comb through his thick hair. I really did love him.

My heart raced as his fingers curled around my neck and tilted my head. Before I knew it, his lips had left mine, making their way across my cheek, by my ear, and onto my neck. I gasped from the flood of warnings and adrenaline that tingled across my spine and rose to the surface of my skin, ridged with goosebumps. My breath was heavy and thoughts of home flashed into my conscious. I saw my family, my little brothers, and sisters. My mom . . . My dad. What would they think of me if they saw this?

I decided a long time ago that I'd save whatever I had for the man I married someday. Nothing would keep me from the goal.

"Will," I said, surprised at hearing myself speak as I pushed him from me. "No."

Breathless, he pulled back, concern in his expression. His hair hung forward recklessly and I blushed. I'd done that with my fingers without even realizing it.

"What's wrong?"

I frowned. I ran my fingers through my hair, unable to look at him through the shame I felt. I almost let myself go too far. What was it about him that made me want to break all the rules I'd had set in my mind since I was a little girl? I felt dirty, useless, and forgotten by God. Disconnected and hurt. This wasn't me. This wasn't what I wanted for myself. I never realized how easy it was to get caught up in a moment. Subtly, I slipped off his lap and settled in beside him, avoiding eye contact.

"You okay?" He brushed my hair away from my face and turned my head toward him.

With a deep sigh, I reluctantly looked him in the eyes. "I don't want you kissing me like that again," I said firmly, but slightly afraid of what he'd think.

Will hesitated, clearly bewildered, before his expression softened. His eyes sparkled in the light from the hall and he nodded once.

"Okay," he answered simply.

That surprised me. "Okay?"

He shrugged nonchalantly. "Yeah. Okay. I'm not about to force you to do anything you don't want to."

I stared at him, dumbfounded. The sincerity in his expression showed no sign of remorse or resentment. No anger or shattered ego. Instead, he smiled back at me then slipped his hand in mine, leaning against the wall behind us with a sigh, still a bit winded.

"Really? You're not going to fight me?"

He knit his eyebrows together. "Bea, I watched my parents fight about their sex life for eighteen years. I heard and saw things that no five-year-old should ever have to. I heard all about my parent's time in the bedroom . . . or lack thereof. Most of the time, it was about how he'd hurt her somehow and he refused to apologize for it. He'd belittle her and tell her that, 'as a man, he needed it,' or something stupid like that. He never respected my mother's boundaries so she stopped setting them. Eventually, she became so withered that she almost turned into dust.

Sometimes, I worried the breeze would take her away, she was so fragile. She drowned herself in alcohol because she thought it would either change her circumstances or make them better, but it only made it worse."

He paused, his expression falling. I listened intently, my heart sinking into my stomach with empathy. In an effort to comfort him, I lay my head on his chest, wrapping my arms around his torso and holding him tightly. His arm wrapped securely around my shoulders and he squeezed me gently, holding me closer to his heart as it jumped through his shirt.

"I never want to do that to you," he concluded, pressing a kiss to my forehead. I nuzzled into him. After a minute, he chuckled.

I pulled back to look at him. "What?"

"I did like having you on my lap though," he muttered, his eyes saddened, but his smile lighthearted.

I grinned, climbing on his lap again with my legs tucked into my chest, out of view of the door. He wrapped both arms around my torso and legs, holding me against him with contentment on his face as he rested his head on my knee. He gazed at me, his expression thoughtful.

"You didn't feel pressured into that, did you?" he asked, narrowing his eyes slightly.

I shook my head. "It's fun."

He turned serious again. "I never want to disrespect your boundaries. They're just as precious to me as you are."

"This looks like a cozy party," Isaac retorted in a hushed whisper as he plopped himself onto my knees. Will grunted under the extra weight, his eyes bulging out.

"Get off, get off," he groaned. Isaac wrapped his arms around my neck and pressed his cheek against mine.

"Why would I do that when there's so much love going around?" he teased, puckering his lips. I laughed, shoving Isaac off my lap and onto the floor. "Hey," he chuckled as he toppled onto his back.

I wrapped my arms around Will's neck and held him close. "This seat is taken, Isaac, find your own."

He puffed out his lower lip and curled into a fetal position, pretending to cry as he playfully sucked his thumb. "But I don't have one," he whined. "I thought what we had was special. What happened to my Bea?"

I scoffed, rolled my eyes, and held tighter to Will. Matt walked in, diving for the floor in an array of lanky legs as he tumbled over Isaac.

Will and I snorted, covering our mouths as if that would hold back the sound.

"What the heck, man?" Matt yelped. Isaac grabbed Matt's face in an effort to shut him up before Natalie came in and switched on the lights.

"What the *heck,* man?" Matt cried again, throwing his arms in the air, exasperated. "Don't any of y'all know how to play this game? Will and Bianca are over there makin' out while Isaac's huddled on the floor doin' I dunno what, probably watchin' 'em like a creep, then you come in and—"

"The game got over like, ten minutes ago. You guys found the wrong people to huddle with. Everyone else is already eating pizza," Natalie said.

"What kind?" Will asked.

"Pepperoni," she answered, flipping her silvery blonde hair. "Now c'mon, let's go." She waved us out of the cramped classroom filled with chairs and tables used as barriers to hide behind.

Will moaned and I slid off his lap. "You okay?" I asked as he sat up straighter and rubbed his back.

He nodded, giving me a knowing look before standing up with a loud and overdramatic grunt. Reaching out for me, he helped me stand, letting our hands naturally intertwine. I loved how easy it was holding his hand.

"What were you guys doing in here if you weren't the ones we were supposed to find?" Isaac asked, twitching his head and blinking rapidly. He stretched, cracking his neck to blend the quirk with something a little more natural.

I blushed. "Nothing you need to know about."

Matt grinned slowly, nodding with a mischievous smile directed at Will who shifted awkwardly beside me, hiding his free hand in his jeans pocket.

Isaac's expression darkened. "Oh, I see," he said. "I see how it is. Choosing the love bird over me, I get it."

I pursed my lips and jokingly shoved a hand against his chest. "Shut up."

He held his hands up in surrender as he twitched again. "I'm just saying. Butterflies of love in the air, dark room, you two . . . Alone. Just be careful, WilliBea."

Will and I looked quizzically at each other.

"WilliBea?" we asked in unison.

"Yeah." Isaac walked backward down the hall, hands in his black jacket pockets after he tossed on its hood. "It's a shortcut. WilliBea. Will and Bea."

I laughed, shaking my head at him. "You're weird, Isaac."

"That's why you love me," he said, twirling on the balls of his feet as he sprinted toward the gym where the pizza was.

Will shook his head, watching our feet. "Sometimes I don't understand him. He acts so cocky, but he's just a bundle of fluff underneath it."

I laughed at that description. It was accurate.

"You guys never dated, right?" Will asked, insecurity seeping through.

I shook my head. "Maybe one date. We went bowling, but it was so unbelievably awkward I'd never do it again. That was the night I decided he was more like a brother to me."

"What about you and Matt?"

I laughed at that. "He and Mitchel are practically the same as far as I'm concerned. He was the one to comfort me after Mitch left on his mission, so he's kind of replaced him."

Will didn't respond once we entered the gym. My taste buds watered at the scent of pizza and I realized I hadn't eaten dinner before the activity. Grabbing a few slices, we went to stand by Natalie, Isaac, and Matt congregated by the edge of the stage.

THIRTY
<u>William Markus</u>

I didn't know what freedom meant anymore. I'd been in jail for months. I felt like anywhere I stepped, flowers died. I wasn't right with the world anymore. I wondered if I ever had been.

Smitty kept me talking the whole way back to his house. He lived by Scheels in Sparks, the next city over. I was grateful for the distraction, though I found myself staring blankly out the window on occasion to watch the city drift past in a sparkling array of flashing lights and casinos. I hadn't truly been out in the world for so long, it seemed completely new to me.

"This is such a surreal feeling, Smitty," I mused thoughtfully. "Things I took for granted before seem like the most beautiful things in the world to me now. Like the fact that I don't have to wear those handcuffs anymore. Or that I can breathe fresh air or have a phone on me."

From my peripheral, I noticed Smitty nod. "It's amazing the things people take for granted around these parts."

His voice changed. Startled, I turned to him. He chuckled, one hand resting on the steering wheel of his flat-bed truck the color of a beet and a grin on his face.

"You have an accent," I observed. *Have I just not noticed before?* It was subtle enough that I could see how I overlooked it. Maybe I'd been too distracted by his quirks to really notice the light accent emphasizing certain sounds more than others.

"I grew up in Elko. Moved to Reno to attend the University of Nevada, where I met Clara. We got married before moving to California for law school. She became a lawyer before I did since the woman's a workhorse. I'm so stinkin' proud of her. Moved back here when I got my degree. Been living in Sparks ever since," Smitty explained.

"Why have I never noticed your accent before?" I asked, bewildered.

He shrugged. "How should I know, Willy? I'm not in your head. Maybe just try paying attention more. I do tend to hide it more when I'm in court, so that's probably why. You're seeing the *real* Gingerhead Man now. It's an honor if you think about it."

Gradually, I let my focus wander back to the window, smiling slightly at the nickname.

"You know, the last thing she was doing before she died was admiring the city."

Smitty firmly patted my shoulder. "Why would she be doing that? It's all just a bunch of flashy lights and weirdos if you ask me. I'd much rather admire the stars."

I hesitated. "She always saw the good in everything . . . Even me."

"Willy Will, you're a good person. Stop beating yourself up over this. We've already established it's not your fault, so stop blaming yourself. You can start over now—"

I shook my head. "No. I don't want to. I don't want to let go. I know it sounds dumb, but I'm not ready to let go of her yet." My voice caught.

Smitty pulled up to a house beside the bay, literally a house sitting *on* the water, and stopped the engine. "Will, I'm gonna give you some tough love right now. Ya ready?" He glanced at me, wiping a sausage finger across his large nose with a sniff.

I frowned. "No."

He hesitated. "I'm giving it to ya anyway. Don't let yourself get dragged down any more by this. Find a new life and don't dwell on mourning the last one for too long. I've seen it tons of times now with several clients. I try to keep in contact with a lot of them, especially if they're in a bad position. I've seen lives thrive and I've seen lives crumble before my eyes after my clients have been either released from prison on probation or found not guilty of their respective crimes. I care about you, Willy. Please don't let this drag you down any more than it already has."

I stared at him, my eyebrows knit together sadly. "Have you ever come close to losing Clara?"

He paused and turned his entire body to face me, his knee sprawled across his seat. "I get what you're saying. I'll never truly understand what you're going through. It's okay to mourn. In fact, please do." He gripped his heart, squeezing the shoulder of his blazer as the passion in his voice escalated. "Feel *every* second of the mourning process and don't suppress anything. Not a single thing." He stopped for a minute, pausing for emphasis as his blue eyes dug into my soul and set on fire. "But let it pass and don't loiter there. Remember, loitering's illegal too."

I spat an emotionless laugh as I pulled on the door handle, pushing the door to his truck open and stepping out.

"It's not really that simple, Smitty," I said once I heard his door shut as well.

He shrugged off his brown blazer, exposing a matching set of recklessly decorated men's accessories. Green suspenders with purple pinstripes and a bowtie of the same design. At least they matched. Slinging the blazer over his forearm, he led me into the garage with an arm around my shoulder as he tugged on his collar.

"Clara," he shouted as he entered.

As soon as the door opened, a thick scent of barbeque chicken wafted into the air, hitting my empty stomach with a lust for its flavor. I hadn't eaten a decent, home-cooked meal in so long, I almost forgot what it felt like. My taste buds thirsted for a bite of juicy, grilled chicken the second I breathed it in and I almost collapsed from the impact. To say it smelled Heavenly would've been a disgraceful understatement.

A woman's voice came from the kitchen. "Hi, honey—"

Smitty ran in, swopped her up in his arms, and spun her around the kitchen. They laughed and kissed as a small chicken leg fell from her tongs and onto the floor. An impulse made me want to dive for it before anyone else could. I stopped myself, though I ached to taste it.

Have I really sunk so low that I'd eat a chicken leg off the floor of a stranger's home?

I frowned, watching Smitty hold his wife and tell her about me. I saw only the back of her head of thick, brown hair as she nodded. She turned to me leaning against the doorway, my knees weak with hunger. Her eyes were large and brown, glowing with the same kindness I recognized in Smitty's. I was stunned. She was . . . *pretty.*

How had Smitty gotten *her?*

My eyes flashed to the way Smitty held her around the waist and couldn't think of anything except what I'd lost. And how deeply I missed her.

"So, you're William Markus?" Clara asked, her voice high and pleasant.

"You know me?" I asked. I'd heard vaguely what Smitty said to her and hadn't heard my name once.

She nodded, stepping out of his arms to tend to the chicken on the stovetop. Smitty sat on a stool beside an island counter separating the kitchen from the dining room.

"Come on in, Willy, don't be shy. You're our honored guest," he exclaimed, throwing his arm in a gesture intended to invite me in. Cautiously, I entered the house, basking in the aroma of real food again.

"We always talk about our cases at the end of the day, so I've heard all about you. I've been following the trial myself. I'm so sorry to hear about your girlfriend," she said, chopping veggies.

"Fiancée," I corrected.

"That must've been awful for you, poor guy. Want a sample?" She held out a piece of celery.

Though I usually hated celery, I grabbed it and thoughtlessly chowed down like my life depended on it.

She laughed, an incredibly calming sound that filled my senses with serenity just hearing it.

Just like hers, I thought, still not ready to think of her name again. Too painful. Embarrassed, I bowed my head, my shoulder-length hair dangling forward.

"Will doesn't have a place to stay, Clara," Smitty said, turning his attention toward her. "Spare bedroom?"

I glanced up, fear striking me as it sunk in that I might still be left homeless for the night.

"He wasn't guilty after all, right?" she asked.

"Never was," Smitty answered confidently, nibbling on a stolen piece of celery.

"Then sure," she said before she directed her attention back to me. "It's not the first time someone has come to stay with us, it's no trouble."

"If you need a car too, we've been trying to sell an old Toyota. You can just take it," he offered, waving a hand at me and screwing up his face with pursed lips and scrunched nose.

I stared at them, amazed by their generosity. "Why are you doing this for me, Smitty?" I breathed.

He smiled and shrugged. "You're my client. And more importantly, I've come to see you as my friend . . . *Wayne*."

THIRTY-ONE
<u>Bianca Wixom</u>

"When is the ski trip again?" Natalie asked as we sat in front of the fireplace at Bishop Gordon's house.

We wrapped ourselves in a blanket together while Isaac, Matt, and Will talked in the other room. I didn't know what they talked about, but by the way, they kept their voices low, glancing my direction every once in a while, I wondered if it had to do with me.

"Tuesday, I thought. I hope so, I asked my aunt for the day off at the gallery for it," I said, cuddling the hot cocoa against my fingers to keep me warm.

"It's Christmas Break, she doesn't give the time off?" Natalie asked.

I laughed at the prospect. "Christmas Break is probably the biggest time of the year for people sight-seeing."

Will looked at me, a mischievous grin sparkling in his eyes. I returned it, lifting my eyebrow flirtatiously. Isaac spoke to him, though he didn't seem to be listening. Rolling his eyes, Isaac grabbed Will's cheeks between his fingers and forced him to focus. Matt laughed, grabbing a muffin from the counter as the bishop approached them with a pat on Will's back.

I smiled. I liked how welcoming he was toward Will. I wanted him to have good impressions of our religion outside of Daddy's attitude. If someone had an impression of the entire Latter-Day Saint religion based solely off of him, we'd never convert anyone. He'd gotten better toward Will, as far as I could tell, though Will swore otherwise.

"Hello," Natalie interrupted my thought process by waving a hand in front of my face. "Earth to Bea."

"Isaac said the ski trip is gonna be up at Lake Tahoe this year," I blurted, turning my attention back to her like I'd been listening the whole time. "Have you noticed anything different about him lately?"

Natalie's pencil eyebrows pulled together and I sipped my cocoa. "No, why?"

I glanced at the Christmas tree, glittering with life, warmth, and color. I loved seeing all the different ways people decorated for Christmas. Bishop Gordon's home had an old-fashioned kind of feel that gave just the right amount of coziness to the environment.

"Will said he's been acting snippy and more reclusive the past couple of days."

"Speaking of Will," she said, nudging me with a sly smile. "I heard you guys are planning on tying the knot soon."

A nervous and giddy sound like a laugh erupted from me with starting volume. "Natalie, where'd you hear something like that?"

Will and I had talked about the prospect, even though we'd been together only six months. It scared me a bit because it'd grown increasingly hard to hold back sometimes. I loved him so much, but I didn't want to get married just because of that. When I asked what he felt on the subject, he seemed open to it. *I* was the one who was terrified. He told me he couldn't do better and was ready. That surprised me, but I liked it about him. He was open to new ideas and willing to take chances like that.

I loved him tremendously, but something inside me still felt unsettled by the idea of getting married . . . especially not in the temple. It was something I'd dreamed about since I was a little girl. The idea of giving that up still felt so final. I mean, I guess there was still time for Will to come around with his investigation into the Church, but it seemed unlikely. He only seemed interested in the idea of an afterlife of Heaven and Hell with different levels of glory. But that wasn't enough for him to join and be ready for temple marriage anytime soon.

And last time I thought I was getting married, I was wrong. I didn't want to be wrong again.

"Have you guys talked about it at least?" Natalie asked.

I shrugged nonchalantly.

"Perhaps," I teased, smiling smugly. "I may have caught him checking out my grandmother's ring with my mom last week."

Natalie squealed, making people look at us quizzically. I grabbed her mouth to clamp it shut.

"You can't tell anyone," I snapped, realizing who I talked to as soon as I said it. "Oh, who am I kidding, the whole ward will know by tomorrow, won't they?"

She giggled, nodding. "Not the *whole* ward. Just a few friends . . . and their friends . . . and their dogs."

I scoffed, shaking my head. "I don't anticipate a proposal anytime soon though. There still seems to be the hurdle of my dad he hasn't quite jumped through. And no way Daddy will let him marry me without his permission. And he won't give it if he doesn't feel like he deserves it. Especially this soon."

"And apparently Isaac," she mumbled.

I questioned her with my eyes before someone grabbed my shoulders. Screeching, I jumped, whirling around to find Will behind me, laughing before he kissed me.

"Hi, beautiful," he greeted, his entire countenance glowing.

"You're lucky I just finished my cocoa or I would've splashed it in your face for scaring me like that," I bellowed, playfully slapping his arm and kissing him again.

He chuckled, wrapping his arms around my shoulders from behind and holding me securely against him. "I love you, Bea," he said, his tone lighthearted.

"I love you too, butthead," I grumbled, stroking his wrist tattoo with my thumb. "Sometimes I wonder why though."

Isaac clamped my temples between his finger, honking like a penguin before sitting cross-legged beside me on the ground.

"BB, you hitting the slopes with us Saturday?" he asked, his voice sounding a bit drained as he munched on cashews. I nodded, pushing on his shoulder a little to lighten his somehow dreary mood.

"Heck yeah, I'll kick your butt at it too."

Will was right. He seemed different somehow.

✳✳✳✳

I sucked at skiing. It was proven as I stumbled recklessly over the slopes while everyone else at least got the hang of it. I didn't. I fell every five minutes. I got even more discouraged when it was nearly dusk and Christmas light were coming on at the lodge.

If Will hadn't been there when I crashed, I probably would've just been abandoned in the mountains by myself. Matt, Isaac, and Natalie already made their ways up the ski-lift ten times before I could make it down the hill once.

"I should've just stayed at the lodge," I said sarcastically after tumbling again.

Will laughed, pulling me to my feet again. "You can do it, just try again."

"No, Will. My bottom has taken a beating today. It feels like my tailbone is bruised from falling so much," I said, rubbing my backside.

With a teasing glint in his eyes, he glanced downward.

"What are you looking at?" I asked.

"I could help with that, you know," he said, his voice twinkling with mischief.

Playfully, I glared at him. I could see now how much he entertained the idea of my bottom and covered it.

"Don't even think about it, Mister," I warned, unbuckling the skis from the terribly uncomfortable boots and heading toward the lodge. "Marry me, then maybe we'll talk."

Laughing, he followed me up the hill until we reached the lodge. As soon as I found a bench, I yanked off those horrible boots and wiggled my toes inside my wool socks. Letting out a deep sigh, I rested my head against the wall behind me. Will smiled at me, removing his boots too and replacing them with his favorite pair of combat boots.

The lights dimmed with the glow of a sunset. His face lit up with the beauty of a Christmas. When I got my winter boots back on, Will took my hand and pulled me to my feet. Holding me around the waist, he clung to me when we watched the lodge now alight with the beauty of the season. "What if I asked you to marry me right now?"

I paused, a feeling I didn't recognize sweeping over me.

"You're not really . . ."

"What if I am?"

"No," I snapped before I could think twice. Cringing, I backpedaled. It wasn't what I meant. "If you asked me like that, I'd say no."

He hesitated. "Hmm . . . What if I did this?"

He took my hand, spinning me into a slow dance. His eyes glittered in the colored lights adorning every corner of the lodge as we danced in the profound silence of the growing snowstorm. The light of a black lamppost warmed the atmosphere with a feeling of peace as he pressed his forehead against mine. His hand on my waist caressed slowly as he swayed us back and forth. The piney, cinnamon smells of Christmas wafted in the air around us, enveloping me in the beauty around me.

"I love you, Bianca," he whispered, his voice low and intimate. I smiled and sighed the sentiment back to him. Somehow, he always managed to give me a weakness in my knees I couldn't control. I wanted to collapse into him when he pronounced my full name. I basked in it for a minute before he spoke again.

"Will you marry me?"

We stopped dancing. It took my brain a minute to process . . . I pulled back, stunned as I searched his expression. Flushed, loving, and frightened all at once. He appeared completely calm, yet flustered beyond belief as he awaited my response.

Did he just propose?

Is there supposed to be a ring?

Where is it, if there is?

I swallowed as he dug briefly in his coat pocket and pulled out a small, velvet box. My heart leaped and I clasped my hands over my mouth, trying to contain the unpredictable emotions that thudded against my ribs.

"Bea . . . Will you marry me?" he asked again, his tone growing concerned.

I'm supposed to answer. What am I supposed to say again?

My mind drew a blank. All I could think to do was nod so hard my neck almost hurt as a giggle choked in my throat. His expression lightened until his eyes glistened with joy. He laughed with obvious relief, wrapping his arms around my waist and spinning me in the air, his face buried in the curve of my neck. When he set me down again, I held my hand out and he slipped on the wedding ring that was my great grandmother's heirloom. Its ruby center glittered brilliantly in the lights.

I kissed him. I kissed him everywhere from his face, to his lips, to his neck. I loved him *so much*.

"Let's go," Will said, taking my hand and towing me toward the parking lot.

"Where?"

"Where I was supposed to do that in the first place."

THIRTY-TWO
<u>William Markus</u>

I drove to the Wixom's a few days later in that old Toyota the Edwards gave me. It ran like the rust bucket it looked like, but it ran. I spent the better part of the next couple of days trying to fix it, but Smitty hardly knew anything about mechanics and didn't have a lot of tools necessary. I thought about taking it into my shop but didn't dare set foot in there after everything that'd happened. All things considered, driving that truck was better than using my legs. So I was grateful.

Tom would probably kill me on sight, but at that point, he'd be doing me a favor.

I rang the doorbell, ready to beg on my knees for forgiveness. Two minutes after the fancy doorbell I knew so well finished tolling, Emily answered. I winced. It was the first time I'd faced her since admitting false guilt. Her beauty resembled that of her daughter's, though her hair had lost quite a bit of luster, a few grays streaking her once warm hair. Bags darkened her eyes and she looked more haggard from stress. My heart sank. Part of me wished Tom would've answered so I'd get what was coming to me.

I smiled at her as sincerely as I could, which wasn't much.

"Will?" she asked, breathless as she pressed a startled hand to her chest.

Cringing, I hung my head. "I'll understand if you slam that door and bolt it shut."

She looked stunned, eyes wide, as Julia rushed to her side, hiding behind her mother's leg as she looked up at me with a shy smile.

"Good heavens, Will," she breathed. "Where have you been? You look like you haven't slept in months."

I scoffed. "I haven't."

Tears formed in her eyes as she pressed her fingers gently to her lips, shaking her head. "Oh, Will."

Before I knew it, she held me. So tightly I gasped for air. I felt her body tremble as she hiccupped through tears.

"You're always welcome here," she whispered. "We'll always love you."

With that, I grabbed her as tightly as she had me, my fingers prodding the back of her blouse as if it would release some of the pain stabbing my gut. "*Why?*"

With a sniff, Emily pulled away. "Come inside, it's cold tonight." She wiped at tears as she grabbed my arm to bring me into her home again.

"No, Emily," I ordered, halting before she could take me past the threshold. "Why do you still care about me? After all the pain I've put you and your family through . . . Why do you still treat me kindly?"

Her blue eyes softened and she rubbed my shoulders, making me look at her directly.

"I know you, Will. I knew you would've never done that to our Bea. You loved her too much."

"But you seemed so heartbroken when you heard my confession."

She pursed her lips and nodded. "I was. But not because I thought you did it. Because I was mourning my daughter and hearing them try convicting you was as painful as watching it happen to my own son." She paused, smiling at me sadly. "Now, if I have anything to say about it, you'll sleep here and get the best night of rest you've ever had."

"What about—"

Tom rounded the corner, his eyes dark when he saw me. "Get out of my house," he barked, the tendons in his neck tightening, nostrils flaring. Emily stood between us, pressing a hand against his chest.

"Tom, please—"

"Get *out* of my house," he bellowed, thrusting a finger at the door. "I knew from the very beginning you were dangerous for our daughter to be around. Now she's *dead* because of you."

I didn't have the strength to do anything to defend myself physically. His bellowing voice caused jolts of anxiety to rise into my throat. But I'd cowered from him too often. I was done with being afraid of that man.

"I am *innocent*," I growled, slowly pronouncing every syllable carefully through gritted teeth in an effort to hold it together.

"You know you're not, kid. The bullet wasn't yours, but you still killed her. If it weren't for you, she wouldn't have been there. She would still be alive if it weren't for you. I knew from the very beginning I'd regret letting you into our home and I didn't listen to those warnings given to me by the Spirit because I wanted to believe in my daughter. But you lived up to every expectation I had for you and now I have to pay the price for it. You defiled my home and my family the moment you snuck in that door—"

"Tom, stop it," Emily interjected. "You're not helping."

"I did *nothing* wrong and your daughter said so herself in her dying breath, so don't throw that stupid crap at me," I yelped through my cracking voice.

My jaw set and I glowered at him through my quivering body. All the anger I'd felt toward Tom heated in the pit of my stomach, boiling into my throat in the form of words I'd longed to spit in his face since we met.

"I am *not* a murderer and if I have to spend the rest of my time on this earth proving that, I will. And you'll be the first to believe me. Now shut up and listen."

Tom stared at me, surprise striking his features before anger overpowered it. "How dare you speak to me like that in my own home. I said it before and I'll say it again. Get out of my—"

"*No.* Your wife invited me in and this is just as much her house as it is yours. Now *I* said it before and I'll say it again. Shut up and listen to me."

He opened his mouth to protest before Emily stopped him.

"Please, Tom . . . Listen to him," Emily pleaded.

Folding his beefy arms across his broad chest, he stood taller, looking down on me with anger in his eyes. He reminded me of a volcano about to erupt. Part of me wanted to cower. Instead, I straightened my own posture.

"They should've kept you there 'til you rotted," he grumbled.

I swallowed, trying my best not to let that comment sink in as I breathed slower, my heart racing and thrashing against my chest. For the first time, I held Tom Wixom's attention.

"I loved your daughter, sir. I loved her so much that I was willing to deal with the nightmare that was sure to follow me after we got married because I wanted to be with her that badly. I knew she was worth every bit of hardship that might follow us every day of our lives. She was worth every bit of it. And if you don't believe me, then you must be more blind than I ever thought you were. I loved her. I had nothing to do with it. And you know it."

Tom stood in silence. I could hear his breathing from where I stood across the room, slow and intense.

Taking his silence as a cue to keep speaking, I continued. "If you'd taken the time to know me rather than sulk about your daughter's choices in life then you'd know that I would've never hurt her. I'm not going to stand here again and be degraded by you anymore. I'm done with that. You claim to be a Christian, sir, but you are so far from it. You've treated me like dirt since the second you saw me. Believe me when I say that I have repeated to myself every word you've ever spoken to me thousands of times in that cell you cursed me to the night we met. I didn't kill her, Tom."

"Then who did?" Emily asked, genuinely puzzled.

I hesitated, surprised she didn't already know. Glancing at Tom whose spine stiffened uncomfortably, I realized he hadn't said anything to her about the verdict. *Too much of a blow to that inflated ego?* How could he have not told her?

"You don't . . ." I muttered.

She turned to Tom who watched me darkly. "Tom, who did it?" she asked, folding her arms as anger flared in her eyes. "Who killed my baby?"

I guess it didn't surprise me that she hadn't followed the trial after what they'd already been through. She had a tender heart.

I'd noticed her leaving after I'd admitted false guilt, but I figured Tom would've kept her updated. Guess not.

"Isaac Petersen did it, Emily," I said reluctantly when I saw he would've remained silent.

Both Emily and Tom's eyes widened. His expression was more like a poisoned dart thrown at my forehead.

"What?" Emily breathed, stumbling against Tom as her complexion paled.

"You just *love* causing trouble around here, don't you?" Tom hissed.

I frowned, ignoring him. "Isaac's been put into a mental institution for six months before being taken to prison for the same sentence they would've given me. Twenty-five years to life in prison," I explained as calmly as I could manage through the pain those words brought me. "He's apparently dealt with severe schizophrenia under everyone's noses for years. It's been passed down through his bloodline for generations. He had an episode in the courtroom and nearly attacked my public defender while threatening me with the same fate as her. They had to drag him out, kicking and screaming."

The devastation in Emily's expression was almost too much for me to handle. I wanted to comfort her somehow, but couldn't think of anything to do.

"You should've left when you had the chance, Will," Tom warned. "But I just can't seem to protect my family from you."

I sighed. Conviction drained from my system. I couldn't fight anymore. Everything was too exhausting. "I'm sorry. I'm sorry any of this happened. I never meant to destroy your family. I can get out of your lives for good now."

I began toward the front door before Emily caught me again. "I said you were sleeping here and I meant it. You're not going anywhere."

"Emily—" Tom objected before she shot him the nastiest glare I'd ever seen on that face before.

"He's *staying*, Tom," she snapped through gritted teeth. "*You*, on the other hand, can spend the night in a hotel for not telling me they came to a verdict already. I'll deal with you later."

I hesitated, startled by the fire in her tone. Tom opened his mouth to say something more but clamped it shut soon after.   Part of me wanted to grin at his astonishment as pride swelled inside me.

"Actually," I began. "If you could just tell me where she's buried, that'd be all I need. I never got to say goodbye."

Emily frowned, turning back to me with concern. "Will, you don't have to—"

"Please," I said.

She sighed, her shoulders slumping. "She's buried in Mountain View Cemetery downtown in a lot on the hill. We go there every Sunday with the whole family."

I nodded, tossing open the door and pausing to look back at them. I wanted to paste them into my memory forever.

"Thank you," I said quietly. "You've shown me more kindness than I ever thought I deserved. Even through all this, you two were more family to me than my parents ever were. I love you. I hope you know how much she loved you too."

Giving them a swift, half-hearted smile, I headed back to my car. I slammed the door shut, grabbing a bottle of liquor in the passenger seat and guzzling it. It seared my throat as it went down. Its foul taste drowned out my dark thoughts enough for me to focus elsewhere. I wouldn't drink again until I got there. Then, I'd drown myself in it.

THIRTY-THREE
<u>Bianca Wixom</u>

I swallowed my strawberry lemonade, and then pulled my hand away to look at the stunning, ruby engagement ring I'd admired for years from Mom's credenza. She'd let me look at it several times, but never for more than a few minutes. It must've been her idea to let Will give it to me. She knew more than Daddy how much I wanted it when I found the guy I wanted to marry.

I looked at Will whose insecurities shone through like the sun. He was thinking about Daddy again. He probably hadn't gotten a blessing to marry me. Knowing Will, he didn't really ask my parent's permission. He probably just *told* them what he planned on doing.

Nervously, I swallowed. I could only imagine how that conversation went. Daddy was stubborn and hard-headed and still didn't like Will very much. At all.

I smiled reassuringly at him. "And I love you, with or without a missionary badge."

He looked back at me, his countenance beaming with joy I'd never seen so brightly before. Then he kissed me again. In front of everyone in the buffet.

I giggled under his lips, raising my hand to tangle my fingers in the back of his hair. My heart leaped into my throat with a jolt of excitement through my bloodstream. I pressed his lips tighter against mine, caressing his cheek with my thumb. I loved when he was spontaneous like that. My heart thumped rapidly against my ribcage, threatening to burst through if I wasn't careful. Finally, I parted us, breathless.

"Are you done?" I asked.

"No." He kissed me again, briefly, before standing from the booth. "Let's go."

I narrowed my eyes at him. *That was a quick transition.* Sometimes, I didn't trust him when it came to his affection. He wanted a lot of it. I did too, but he had a different idea of romance than I did a lot of the time. I never knew where he'd want to take it.

"You're not going to try anything, are you?" I asked, seriousness tinting my tone as I grabbed my purse and tossed a tip on the table.

Tilting his head, he watched me with raised eyebrows, the innocent expression on his face too adorable for anyone to stay mad at. He rocked back and forth on his heels, hands in his pockets.

"I just want to kiss my fiancée without an audience, that's all." He wrapped an arm securely around my waist, pulling me close. I loved when he held me that way and I rested my hand on his chest.

Fiancée . . . I like the sound of that.

"Besides, I wouldn't dream of trying anything," he continued. "Your dad would shoot me in the head then bury my remains somewhere in the Nevada wilderness if I ever did."

I laughed heartily, my head falling back. His irrational fear of being killed and dumped in the wilderness was a frequent subject shift that I'd grown to expect from him. I never knew where it came from, but it made me smile every time.

"What? He would," Will laughed.

No matter how much reassurance I gave for how much Daddy didn't hate Will, he never believed me.

Will led me through the casino, the heavy haze of cigarette smoke fogging the air as we passed endless rows of slot machines. A plump man with a beer in hand dangled over the side of one of the slot machines, his eyes dazed as he stared up at it. A cocktail waitress walked by and the man drug himself up like a limp puppet dragged by the shoulders, whistling at her as she passed. She ignored him and he turned back to his gambling.

Poor man, I thought. It was nine o'clock at night. Where was his family? Did he have one? Maybe he didn't. He probably spent most nights getting drunk and gambling.

My heart ached for him. I wanted to help but knew that if I even walked past him, I'd be resigned to the same fate as the cocktail waitress. Catcalling and whistles.

I rolled my eyes at that thought, holding tightly to my fiancé's arm for protection. Will grinned, squeezing my hand. He made me feel so secure in that place. I never would've gone into those casinos without him. Too risky.

I was grateful for other entrances into the magnificent buildings known as casinos in Reno. We just happened to park in the lot in front of the casino area of the building.

I looked back at him as we exited the Grand Sierra Resort and he kissed my forehead, his expression suddenly sullen. His dark eyebrows knit together seriously. Something was wrong. I could sense it.

But then again, it was the GSR parking lot. That place could be scary at night. Entire sections of the lot didn't have lights and it was almost as massive as the building itself. I glanced up at the skyscraper-like casino in time to see the tall, lighted Christmas tree in front shift colors. The diamonds on the other side of the building led to the *GSR* glowing atop the highest, rectangular tower.

Will inconspicuously slipped his hand into mine, holding tightly as he pressed another kiss to the side of my head. I smiled in contentment, nuzzling into his shoulder with a sigh.

The fur around my coat's collar tickled as I bunched it over my mouth to warm my nose and cheeks. Winters in Reno could be unpredictable, as far as the weather was concerned. Wet snowflakes danced in the air, even though I knew they wouldn't stick to the ground for long.

"You know," I began thoughtfully. Will leaned closer. I loved when he did that. It made me feel intimately heard like he wanted to memorize everything I said. "I've lived in Reno for six years now and I don't think I've really taken the time to enjoy the beauty this place has to offer. I mean, look at those lights." I gestured to the layered diamonds as they changed colors.

After a minute, Will's hand landed on the small of my back, his smile wary as he said, "Let's go, Bea."

"Wait," I said, turning toward the Sierra Bay. It glittered in the light of a full moon, twinkling and swaying as its water crackled in the silence of the night. A breeze brushed through my hair, bringing with it a whisper.

Get in the car.

I knew that feeling, an almost urgent need to act. I didn't want to though. I was at peace and didn't want to ruin it with some unrealistic panic. Nothing was going to happen. "I want to enjoy this," I said aloud in response to the Spirit's whisper.

I opened my eyes. Someone was behind the small trees surrounding the parking lot. Squinting, I tried to make sure I hadn't imagined it. It moved. It was definitely a man. We made eye contact. I knew the slender shape of that silhouette.

"Bianca, please," Will said.

Isaac?

"Get in the car—"

All at once, the earth-shattering, shrill sound of a gunshot echoed in the darkness.

And pain. So much pain in my chest. As a reflex, my hand pressed against it. My fingers met a strange, wet feeling over my clothing. I breathed, but no matter how hard I tried, the oxygen seemed impossible to acquire, cutting short before my lungs could feel satisfied. I pulled my fingers back to see my bloodied hand. My vision faded into a haze. When I opened my eyes again, I felt as though I'd just woken up from an incredibly deep sleep. It hurt to move. It especially hurt to breathe.

Will called my name, telling me I'd be okay. Confusion overpowered me.

"This is my fault," he mumbled, his voice muffled by my hair.

A light appeared in the distance, cutting through the darkness surrounding us.

"W—Will," I managed to choke through the blood pooling on my tongue. Vaguely, I noticed the metallic taste before coughing it out.

The light came quicker.

Wait. No. I'm not ready to go.

"Bea, I'm . . . Protect you. . . Go. . ." Will's voice faded quickly. My consciousness could only pick up so much.

"Will—It . . ." I coughed, stabbing pain in my rib catching my voice. My mouth felt wet and the blood had lost its taste. I couldn't hear much aside from Will's voice still pleading with me to hold on. I didn't want to fight it anymore though. I still had more to say to him. "It's not your f—fault . . ."

I knew he'd blame himself. And I would die. I could feel it. The light came again, beckoning me away from the excruciating pain that seared my bloodstream like poison. I heard another voice. One called me to a Home I'd always dreamed of but had long forgotten.

No, I'm still not ready. Don't take me yet.

"Bea . . . Okay." Will's voice still came to me through fits of light and darkness.

All at once, the darkness left and the pain ended. My consciousness left my body. I saw Will shouting my name, cradling my body against him. I could hear him clearly now. The pain subsided significantly, to the point I couldn't feel any of it.

Sadness overwhelmed me watching the man I loved so dearly suffer so much. I knelt beside him as he cried, placing my hand on his shoulder and rubbing his back. I knew he wouldn't feel me there, but it gave me some comfort and I hoped it could help him eventually.

He looked up, eyes wild with danger and fear. He looked after Isaac who stared at him, the same amount of fear in his eyes.

"Help me, please," Will cried as he stood, my body dangling in his arms.

Isaac dropped the gun and *ran*. I didn't know he could run so fast. Will chased after him after placing me on the pavement. He grabbed the handgun from a puddle.

"Coward," he shouted, aiming the gun in the air. "I'll kill you myself if I have to."

A hand landed on my shoulder and I stood, blinded at first by the radiant luster of His countenance. The man standing beside me wore a robe as bright and white as a blanket of fresh snow.

With a heavy burden, I turned to see that my surroundings had changed. I stood in a grove of wildflowers and luscious trees. Facing the man again, I finally recognized Him and fell at His feet.

"Savior."

THIRTY-FOUR
William Markus

I stumbled out of my car, head pounding and the bottle of liquor barely holding onto my fingers. I didn't want to think about what I was there to do. I just wanted to do it. My hair dangled over my eyes as I pressed the bottle to my lips and drank the deliciously foul liquid again. It stung as it drifted to my stomach, burning my insides. Numbing my pain.

I winced, coughing from the alcohol infecting my bloodstream with its intoxicating magic. Every headstone looked different. Emily texted me her grave's location, but it was hard to read through watery eyes.

When I finally found it, I stopped, standing at her graveside with a deep frown on my face. Rose petals scattered across her headstone, a picture of a rose above her name.

Bianca Marie Wixom
Beloved Daughter and Sister

And fiancée. Interesting they left that out.

I gulped more alcohol.

* * *
348

I hadn't really gotten drunk since before I met her. But right then, I wanted nothing more.

A picture of her sat on an easel above her headstone, flowers strewn across the base as a symbol of her death. They mocked my dull existence without her with their bright and vibrant colors. Her eyes shone brightly with hope in the future she'd never live to see because I hadn't protected her.

I glanced at the mound of dirt they'd buried her under. I'd missed her funeral by months. I knelt on the ground beside her grave, placing my hand where I knew her beautiful face would be inside the earth.

"Bea . . ." I whispered. It was the first time I'd dared say her name since being released. Its bittersweet sound tickled my tongue and ears with exhilaration and loneliness. "I never thought I'd be here. At least, not until we were much older. Guess that didn't work out." My voice squeaked, shaky and unrecognizable to me. A breeze tickled my cheek with my scraggly hair. I flipped it away, biting my lips in a pathetic attempt to hold myself together. "They found him, baby. He's been put into a mental hospital for killing you. Then they're taking him to prison where he'll serve my sentence. We always knew he was crazy, but never knew how messed up he really was."

My voice shook harder. The dark world shivered with sadness as I stroked the small blades of grass between my fingers like it was her face.

"Remember our vision, Bea? We were gonna live downtown in a crappy apartment and not care if it was perfect. We were gonna have a family. Buy a house . . . And this—" Words failed me and cut me off. A flare of anger burned my chest as I clenched my fist, dirt gathering between my fingers as I gritted my teeth. "Was *never* our plan. I'm not ready to let that go yet. And I don't know if I'll ever be able to. I need you, Bianca. Why'd you leave me like this? I wasn't ready. I still need your influence in my life. I still need you."

I lost it. For the first time since the night it happened, I cried. Finally, I *really* cried. I let it all out, draping myself prostrate across her grave as if it were the only way I could hold onto her.

"Take me with you, Bea," I pleaded, my voice muffled by my bicep. "I miss you so much, baby."

Something vibrated in my pocket. I exhaled in a gust and sat up, blinking through my blurry vision. I yanked my phone from my back pocket, sitting on my heels. It was weird having stuff like that on my person again. I hadn't realized the luxury of having a phone until I didn't have one.

Guzzling more liquor, I squinted against the bright screen. It took me a solid two minutes to focus enough to read the name flashing across my phone's screen. Pressing what I thought was the button to answer the call, I held the phone to my ear.

"What?" I growled, my voice gruff and unfamiliar.

"Will? Where are you?" Smitty's voice cried from the other side, genuine worry in his tone.

I groaned, rubbing my arm across my forehead. "Mountain View . . . C—cemetery. Why do you care?"

"Gosh darn it, Will, I told you no loitering," he snapped. "You've been drinking, haven't you?" he asked, his voice waning in and out of my consciousness. "For Heaven's sake, Will, the last thing you need is a DUI on top of everything else. I'm coming to get you.

Stay put. And Willy . . . don't do anything stupid."

I hung up with a drawn-out sigh. "Why does he still care about me?" I asked the universe, squeezing the phone between my fingers.

Before I realized it, tears streamed from my eyes again. I gasped, desperate for relief of the Hell I lived every second since she was taken from me.

"Why don't you care about me, God?" I bellowed, letting my head fall toward Heaven. My voice slurred with slower speech. I curled into myself, hugging my abdomen tightly. Her name repeated itself in my thoughts in loud shouts of agony. "Why'd you do this to her if you loved her? Why, God? Why?"

I crumbled into a heap on the ground, finally able to fully mourn her loss as Smitty had told me to. I hadn't been given an opportunity to really understand what happened to her for being asked about it. My head throbbed with my fingers as I dug them into the ground, drawing blood as they scraped across her headstone.

Through my pain, the familiar click of a gun vaguely caught my attention. I looked up, noticing the silhouette of a round man I recognized as Jack Daniels, Isaac's psychotic dad. A gun positioned at my head.

I grunted, pulling myself onto all fours and letting my head dangle forward. Throwing my head of stringy, dark hair back, I sat back on my heels again.

"Go ahead, shoot," I dared, my speech slurred. "Put me out of my misery, *please.*"

My mouth hung open as breath huffed into the night's chilly air. A cigarette lit at the corner of Jack's mouth, his hand trembling over the trigger.

"They said you'd be here, William. You're a bad man, They say," he muttered, his voice shaky as his body.

Scoffing, I rolled my eyes. "Here we go again. I've heard it before. 'Beware the smoking gun,' right?"

"You know too much, William. They've sent me to get you. They can't trust you."

Smoke puffed from between his lips like a breath in winter, thick and nasty as it drifted into the air.

"Just like everyone else in this God-forsaken city," I grumbled. "Ya know what, I don't even care anymore." Desperate, I looked up the barrel of his pistol. "Please, just kill me. I'm begging you. Make the pain go away."

His beer belly hid some of his face from my view. Rain pattered onto my forehead, sudden and quickening at an ever-increasing pace as I gazed up at him. I yearned for it to soak me up. I just wanted it to end.

"You're an evil man. My son is incarcerated because of you. You took my son away from me. They know that. My boy was supposed to end up with that pretty girl of yours. Destined from birth. Didn't ya know that?"

A flare of anger burst through and I stood up, shoving my forearms into his fat, grungy chest.

"Yeah, I'm sure those stupid little voices in your head have told you a lot of things just like that good-for-nothing son of yours. You're just as much of a psychotic bastard as he was. He's just as dead to me as she is now. What're you afraid of, ya old psycho? Huh? Have I gotten you angry enough?" I shoved him again, an impressive amount of strength in my slurring speech. "Or do you need me to keep going?" I jabbed my finger into the center of his chest and let my head fall to one side.

Jack's entire body trembled with the fear evident in his dilated eyes. I felt the gun's barrel pressed against my ribcage. I didn't look down at it but held his gaze. I didn't want to see it happen.

"Your son ruined my life, Jack. And for what? Some stupid, schoolboy crush he had on *my* fiancée and those demons in his head. It's over for me here anyway. So, what're you waiting for? Shoot me. I dare you—"

The earth-shattering sound of the gunshot brought me back to that night. I didn't have time to feel the pain before blood splattered from my mouth and I fell to my knees. My fingers gripped my upper abdomen, wet with my own blood.

A memory of her blood on my hands flashed behind my eyelids. I saw myself catching her after she'd been shot as I fell to the ground beside her grave, my vision hazing out.

Through the blackness surrounding me, a light cracked the abyss.

"Will. . ."

I knew that voice as clear and beautiful to me as fresh air.

"B—Bea," I coughed, blood spurting from my lips with a vague, metallic taste. My consciousness of mortal surroundings faded as I lay beside her grave. A subtle sensation of my body convulsing entered my awareness as I coughed, quickly fading with me. "S—stay with me . . ."

"Will . . ." she said again, her voice echoing through the narrow tunnel, growing louder and more dominant.

Without effort, my consciousness drew me closer to the light as my body relaxed. My mind and body seemed to be completely separate entities now.

"Bianca," I whispered when I finally reached for her voice. Everything was blinding only for a moment as I broke through a veil of light to see her.

For the first time since she died, she stood before me. I saw her smile at me again, reassuring and beautiful as I remembered, as she reached for me.

"Come with me, Will," she said. "I'm here to bring you Home."

Her angelic voice glided with sweet tones that calmed me like nothing else ever could. It sounded like nothing short of Heaven to me.

THIRTY-FIVE
<u>Smith Edwards</u>

I drove to the cemetery as fast as I could, but traffic through Sparks was horrible. Like there wasn't a way to the next city without the freeway. Those crazy late-night travelers drove me nuts. *Psh, gosh.*

Somehow, I knew something was wrong. Will seemed abnormally angry over the phone. He wasn't exactly the most chipper egg in the carton, but he was clearly drunk. Anyone with that amount of slurring in their voice wasn't in their right mind. And if he was drunk and driving? No. I wouldn't let him do that. Especially in that Toyota.

He clearly hadn't heeded my advice and loitered in a deep state of mourning for longer than he should've. It'd only been three days, but mourning the loss of someone you care about doesn't ever justify driving under the influence. He wasn't doing himself any favors with that one, especially if he got caught. Or killed himself. Or someone else.

I glanced at my phone on the passenger seat, fingers coiling around the steering wheel with nerves. Clara still slept soundly at home, though I couldn't have even dreamed of getting a good night's rest until I knew Will was alright.

I wondered if he wasn't.

Maybe I was already too late.

What if he'd already tried driving home?

I could feel the tension in the air around me as I resisted the urge to blare my truck's horn at the slowpokes in front of me. Beads of sweat formed on my eyebrow and I wiped it off with a quick swipe of my arm.

I glanced at my phone again. Nothing heard back from him yet. Maybe he'd listened to me and stayed put. Or maybe he hadn't.

Finally, I grabbed the phone and dialed Will's number. The phone rang, but no one answered.

"Flippin'—" I cursed. Traffic moved forward. *Finally!*

My favorite, lucky socks stuck to my toes as I curled them anxiously inside my shoes. "C'mon boys," I said, referring to my socks. "Don't you lemme down now."

I headed straight for the Mountain View Cemetery, the same place my brother was buried. A memory of him playing in the yard caught my attention. Instantly, I tried shoving it away, though it persisted.

Now isn't the time to reminisce.

He tossed a ball in the air, catching it over and over again. He asked me if I'd play with him.

Unexpected emotion caught in my throat and I pressed my lips together against the regret.

"Find someone else. I'm busy."

I never knew such words spoken by my own mouth would haunt me so deeply for so long.

I shook my head, forcing myself back into the present as I parked, scraped at the tears forming and flew from my truck in one slick movement.

"Smooth, Ace," I said to myself. "You're a ninja."

My eyes scanned the cemetery as I hastened up the walkway, calling his name against the sound of rain.

"Will," I bellowed, cupping my hands around my mouth to amplify the sound. I listened. Nothing but rain as it patted my fabulous head of fiery curls. "W—"

My foot caught on something and I stumbled. After regaining my balance, I turned around to see a man sprawled across a grave, curled almost in a fetal position on his side and dark hair hung across his face.

Curiously, I stood over the sleeping man until the foul odor of gore rotted my nose when I inhaled.

"*Gah,*" I cried, plugging my nose and waving a hand in the air. That was when I noticed the pool of blood in front of the young man's stomach.

My heart sank.

"Will," I breathed, recognizing him through his grown-out hair. "Willy, who did this to you?"

Biting my knuckle, I approached him slowly, my arm outstretched. I dreaded the test I had to do but pressed two fingers to his neck.

"Mighty Lord above, please," I prayed, hoping for any sign of a pulse.

Nothing. Silent and still.

I cringed, fearing the worst. My fingers shook, though this wasn't the first scene of death I'd witnessed. As a lawyer, I'd investigated a few murder scenes before in hopes of gathering evidence.

"You didn't . . ." I muttered, stepping away from him and petting my chin. It helped me think better.

I glanced at the bullet hole in his clothes, drenched in blood. I almost hurled, my head spinning. It did seem to be a close-range shot. Where would he have gotten a gun though, if he shot himself? And, if he didn't, who would have the motive to. . .

A memory from my conversation with Detective Cole stood out in my mind. She told me of Isaac's father. How he wanted Isaac to marry Miss Bianca so they could get a good fortune. When Will asked Miss Bianca to marry him, he must've gone *really* insane. Then his son was incarcerated because of Will and me . . . he would've had a motive to kill for revenge.

With a reluctant sigh, I grabbed my phone to call the police, taking pictures at a few different angles before dialing 911. Couldn't hurt to have a little evidence for myself.

"911, what's your emergency?" the woman on the other side asked.

"This is Smith Edwards, the public defender for the Grand Sierra Homicide. I have reason to believe that my client, William Markus, was shot and killed tonight by the father of the young man who was incarcerated in that case."

The woman hesitated, telling me to remain calm and that they'd be there shortly.

I looked down at Will. Kneeling beside him, I gently moved his hair off his face. To my surprise, his expression seemed completely at peace, a small smile relaxing his pale features.

My throat tightened and my chin quivered. "You're with her now, aren't ya, buddy?" I asked, knowing he was. "Rest in peace, Willy. I'll take it from here."

THIRTY-SIX

Isaac Petersen

They were everywhere. If I could've made them stop, I would've. Their demonic voices constantly chattered in my mind at high speeds. Throwing me from one side to another. They were *always* talking. Telling me things. Telling me to do things I didn't want to.

Like shoot people.

I didn't want to kill her. I didn't want to hurt my friends like that.

They were never your friends, Isaac. We are. We're the only people you need to rely on. Follow Us . . . Trussst Us.

They tickled my skin and ratted my hair. They controlled my movements. They made me yank my hair. They rocked me to sleep. They calmed me. They frightened me.

I shrieked, struggling against the cords and straightjacket the people locked me in. It wouldn't stop. Not until the doctors came. The doctors would come in soon. The doctors would help.

They hated the doctors. The doctors silenced Them with injections.

They'd kill those ones too. They'd kill everyone. No one was safe. It was only a matter of time before the entire city was consumed by Their black parasites. And *I'd* be at the head of the army. Just like They said I'd be.

Little noises scattered across my brain like little mouse feet, tickling my ears and scraping at my jaw. I twitched, trying to scratch at them without the use of my arms. My shoulder would've done if I could've moved more than a few inches.

My room was padded, white, and cramped. Too close. Everything was too close. I couldn't stand it.

We hate you, Isaac! The world knows what you've done. You despicable scum. You're scum. You're worthless.

I screamed, throwing my head around to shake free. "Get out, get out, get out."

Before I knew it, I was on the ground of my padded room, kicking at the bugs coming at me. They were sending Their bugs now. Not the bugs. I hated the bugs. There were millions of them. They were everywhere. They did this to me as punishment.

Colors flashed in my vision and I sat up, gasping as my eyes flitted across the room as the bugs crawled in from the corners.

"No, stop," I screeched. They came faster. "Help, help me."

We know what you've done.

The voices screamed at me. Millions of them. All at once. They spoke in such perfect unison.

They were back. They never left. They were always there. I didn't want Them there anymore. They were there to hurt me. The more people tried telling me They weren't there, the more hateful They became. I just wanted peace. They'd never give it to me.

There, there, We're here for you.

I hate you! I wish you'd just die!

It's alright . . . We're here.

"What do you want from me?" I cried, cowering from the bugs and voices as I rocked myself back and forth . . . Back and forth.

We're here for you.

We're here to kill you.

The doors to my room opened. I screamed, tumbling backward as the bugs crawled on the doctors who injected me. Slowly, the injection they stabbed me with surged through my bloodstream. I breathed a sigh of relief as the bugs eventually slithered away, exposing the medic's pleasant face.

I knew They'd be back though. The meds would wear off and They'd be back. It never truly got better. The medics said little. Asked me how I felt, took vitals, maybe adding a, "see you later," and I was alone again.

Solitude was empty as I sat on the floor. Part of me wished for the numbing sensations through my body to go away so I could hear the voices again. They gave me someone to talk to. But I had to admit, it was nice to get a moment of peace for once.

I leaned back against the wall with a heavy sigh. Everything was calmer. My brain slowed down enough to form at least comprehensible thoughts again. But it wouldn't last.

They'd be back again. I wondered if it would ever truly go away.

I closed my eyes, relaxing for the first time in hours. My body felt heavier.

I missed Bea. She would know how to get Them to go away. She knew everything. Why'd she have to die? Why did They do that to her? It wasn't *me*. They made me do it . . . And Dad too. They made me do it. But, because I listened to Them, she was dead with her blood on my hands. They made me frame Will too. They made me do it all. It wasn't my fault.

I looked up. "I'm sorry. I'm sorry, Bianca," I wailed, overcome by the guilt shrouding my heart in darkness. "I'm so sorry."

Will didn't deserve the blame either. It was an accident, after all. No one was to blame. Except Them.

"I'm sorry, Will. You needed a better friend than me." I stared at the ceiling of my padded room, eyes and cheeks wet with tears. "I'm sorry, Papa. I failed you. I'm sorry, God. I should've known better. I'm too far gone for the forgiveness I've heard about. I know I don't deserve Your kindness. Please . . . I don't want this anymore." Sobs heaved out of me with the agonizing weight of what I'd done. "Please forgive me, Jesus! Save me from thy evil brother."

Someone drifted in the air in front of me, smoke cascading from their translucent feet. My eyes slowly scanned up their appearances until I reached their faces. I gasped.

Will and Bianca smiled down at me, their bodies completely translucent with smoke dancing around their figures.

"WilliBea," I muttered, a very welcomed feeling of warmth swelling into my body. For the first time in months, a smile lifted my countenance with the joy of seeing my two best friends again.

My heart sank, however, as I realized what this meant.

"Will, you're . . . Dead?"

Will's eyebrows pulled together sympathetically before he turned to Bea who slid her hand into his. I'd seen that so often, it felt as real as it had been when they were still alive.

Bea blew me a kiss with her free hand, Will gazing at her as he always did. He always did adore her. Their apparitions disappeared in a cloud of smoke, almost as quickly as they'd appeared.

I sat back again. I'd seen dead people before, but the warm feeling that accompanied that visitation was no demon.

Will and Bianca didn't need to speak to me in order for me to understand them. They were okay. Even better, they were together again forever.

Convicted: 25 to Life

End

Convicted: 25 to Life

Chandler R. Williamson

The Story Behind
Convicted: 25 to Life

I began writing this book after listening to the song, *Kiss it Better* by the band, He Is We, about five years ago. For some reason, this song spoke to me in a way I couldn't explain. This story came to me so clearly while listening to that song, I just had to do something about it. It was something so vastly different from anything I'd *ever* tried before, so I didn't think anything would come of it. Then I told my best friend, Jessica, about it and she begged me to write it. She's been bugging me about it for five years straight now.

So, here ya go, Jess. I hope it lives up to your expectations.

Everyone I've shared this book with has told me basically the same thing, which is kind of surprising to me.

I decided to set this book in Reno, Nevada because I lived there for three months and completely fell in love with it. The setting fit the story so perfectly. I loved being able to set it in a place I grew to know and love. Most of the places in this story are real, with the exception of the art gallery Bea volunteers at and Will's mechanic's shop. I made those up since they were small enough that I could get away with sneaking them into the city without being too obvious. The mention of a shooting in Scheel's a few years before the story takes place isn't a real event either.

This book is, by far, the riskiest book I've ever written. These characters truly have minds of their own and have created the story on their own pretty much from the beginning. So, I don't consider myself accountable for anything they say or do.

This is the first book I've ever considered incorporating my own religious beliefs from different points of view into characters and into a story, but I kept feeling like it was right. My purpose in incorporating my religion in this book is to demonstrate different points of view of people I've known as well as my own. *The Church of Jesus Christ of Latter-Day Saints* is not affiliated with this novel, though the beliefs and general ideas expressed such as 'families are forever,' is. Like Bea, religion has always been a massive part of my life, but I never considered putting it into a story, especially one with a character like Will in it who likes to run his mild sailor mouth and drinks alcohol so openly.

Will is especially a rebellious character as far as having a mind of his own is concerned. A lot of times, he'd do something, I'd keep writing, and he would've said or done something I totally didn't want him to. I could almost hear him laughing in the background, the sneaky, little troll. His character came from a dark place in my life. Many times, I had to channel that part of me while creating him in order to really get the feelings he displays during this book, particularly in the end. He's so vastly different from the way I am otherwise, so writing from his perspective proved difficult at a lot of points. I was so intimidated to write from his perspective, so I procrastinated writing this story for nearly six years. He surprised me much more than any other character I've created . . . except maybe Gingerhead Man.

Bianca is a very precious character to me who got a lot of her qualities from what I was like as a young single adult. Her perspective is very similar to the way I've felt in my life on many occasions, so she's very special to me.

Smitty . . . I have *no idea* where he came from. Five years ago, I was writing the second scene I ever wrote in this novel, the scene where Will meets him the first time. I knew he was going to be a strange one when he made Will's name into a pun and called himself the Gingerhead Man because of his fiery, red hair. He started out as a joke character. Seriously. He was never supposed to be a big part of the story. But I just totally fell in love with this ridiculously weird character and I couldn't stop bringing him in.

His name, Smith Nathaniel Edwards is actually an accidental reference to the store for farming supplies in Willard, Utah, called *Smith and Edward's*. It was a total accident, but it suited him perfectly and people loved it, so I kept it. Smitty is, by far, the most beloved character I've ever created by everyone who knows him. I'm not sure whether that's a good thing or not since he's so bizarre. His big heart has warmed mine on several occasions and I've been advised by him many times in my low moments just like he did for Will.

Isaac was always the crazy one who 'done it,' but it wasn't until later that I found out what a big-hearted sweetheart he is. It makes his fate so much sadder when I think of how much he really did love WilliBea. I hope you can forgive him and love him like I do.

I did a *ton* of research in this book, including research on schizophrenia. Isaac and Jack have several different problems aside from that, but it is the main inspiration for how I created their characters. I'm sure I'm not going to be perfectly accurate as far as that, the legal stuff, and technicalities of arrest, life in a jail cell, and things like that. But my intent is to entertain my readers with characters who bring the story to life in ways I never could've if I was completely, 100% accurate.

I knew people who suffered from some of the situations depicted in this story and they gave me their personal accounts and I based some details off of what I've been told. I apologize if it's not completely accurate. I did my best.

I hope you enjoyed reading Convicted: 25 to Life. I loved writing this book and getting to know all the wonderful characters that blessed me with their influences in my life. I hope they touch your life as much as they did mine.

Love,
Chandler R. Williamson

57251402R00210